Kayleigh,
Enjoy
xo
J.C. Hannigan

A WELDER ROMANCE
COALESCENCE
J.C. HANNIGAN

Coalescence
Copyright © 2018 by J.C. Hannigan
All rights reserved.

jchannigan.com

No part of this book may be reproduced or transmitted in any form or by any means, electronic or mechanical, including photocopying, recording, or by any information storage and retrieval system without the written permission of the author, except for the use of brief quotations in a book review.

This book is a work of fiction. Names, characters, places, and incidents either are products of the author's imagination or are used fictitiously. Any resemblance to actual persons, living or dead, events, or locales is entirely coincidental.

More or less...

Whether you function as welders or inspectors, the laws of physics are implacable lie-detectors. You may fool men. You will never fool the metal.

Lois McMaster Bujold

CHAPTER ONE

PATHETIC

May 2017
Gwen

I scarfed pad Thai siew while I scrolled through Netflix, searching for something to watch. Reading wasn't taking my mind off my grousing thoughts like it normally did. All those super-swanky book boyfriends that occupied my shelf were not making it easier to fill the hole he left in my heart. I needed to mindlessly indulge in something, anything to divert my attention from *him*.

At the mere thought of him, my eyes darted to my phone on my lap, where his Facebook page was still open, taunting me via happy photos of his fabulous life with his new girlfriend. Frustrated with myself, I flipped my phone over and stabbed at the noodles with the plastic fork, imagining Erik's face. It brought me a smidgen of comfort.

My gray tabby cat, Dahmer, jumped onto the sofa beside me, stalking over to sniff at the carton in my hand. He liked Thai food almost as much as I did.

"Back off," I grumbled, pulling the carton away from his searching nose. He began to purr loudly, pushing his head against my arm, gently nipping at me. Sighing, I relented, picking up a tiny piece of beef and offering it to him. He snatched it from between my fingers and looked at me expectantly, as if waiting for more.

Dahmer was named after the Milwaukee Cannibal. I was a little angry when I'd chosen that moniker. Angry at men, specifically Erik, and angry at myself. My mother had been horrified to find out that I'd named my cat after a serial killer, but honestly, the cat needed a name as crazy as he was, and I wanted a name that didn't reflect my new cat lady spinster status.

Ever since the day I brought him home from the pound seven months ago, he'd kept me on my toes. Dahmer gave affection when it suited him, for as long as it suited him. He also punished me as he saw fit—ignoring me, attacking my legs when I came home from work a little late. Sometimes, he left me dead things. Usually just bugs, but one time he managed to catch a mouse, and he deposited that prize on my pillow.

Neurotic cat-like behaviour aside, he was surprisingly good at sensing my moods and drawing me out of them, and he made me feel a little less alone.

Before Dahmer, the silence of my apartment was too much, even for me, and I was a girl who liked her solitude. I needed it after working in an office all day at a job I couldn't stand.

Administration. I'd picked the most basic, brainless program to take in college. I was shoved from the unforgiving, angst-filled halls of my former high school and pressed with the task of deciding my entire future in what felt like a single moment. It was overwhelming, and instead of selecting the program I'd *wanted* to—which was creative writing—I'd chosen one in which I could find steady work and that my parents would approve. For stability.

All my choices had been for stability. Take Erik, for example. He was safe, and he was supposed to be my forever. But he'd cheated on me, and when I found out, I tossed all his things onto the tiny patch of yellowed grass in front of the apartment.

If only it were as easy to toss away the influence of his destruction, but I was still working on it.

I realized a few things after the breakup. The most obvious being that I was no longer content with ignoring my dreams. Ever since I was a little kid, I'd dreamed of becoming a published author. I'd always loved writing, always kept notebooks around, and amongst the collection of dresses in my closet were stacks of binders full of short stories, poems, and outlines for romance novels.

Ironic, I know, especially given my current state of hating everything to do with men—which is why I hadn't bothered to open a notebook in months. Having my heart broken had hindered my ability to put pen to page and let the words flow through me. I'd grown desolate from the blank pages.

Severe writer's block aside, a couple more things were holding me back from pursuing this dream of mine.

For one, my blue-collared, straight-out-of-a-nineties-sitcom family. My parents didn't believe writing books was a sustainable career for a young woman, especially a young single woman. In our family, my dad had always been the sole provider. He owned his own welding fabrication shop, had about twenty-six employees working under him, and had contracts all over Southern and Central Ontario.

Since my parents were self-made, teaching my sister and me the importance of having a stable career was high on my father's list of priorities. According to my dad, writing was a hobby, so, I'd hopped into the corporate world of business administration.

Once I graduated, I encountered an unforeseen problem. For every administrative job post that I found, there were at least thirty other interviewees, and over half of them were more qualified than me. This lack of available employment was how I ended up as my father's administrative assistant at the shop—just like he'd hoped.

I'd worked there for the last three years, and every day was the same. It was slowly killing me, but I hid it well, knowing my dad would be hurt to discover how miserable I was at my job. It wasn't the job, per se. It just wasn't what I wanted to be doing with my time. Office work was boring, and sitting alone in the office all day long was torturous.

To make matters worse, I no longer had a boyfriend at home. My heart twisted with the betrayal at the mere thought of him.

I'd been so blindsided by his deception, but the worst part was that when he left, he took my dignity and my mojo. Which is why I found myself sitting on my sofa on a Friday night with a carton of my ultimate comfort food and my cat for company, letting the memories wash over me like acid, knowing that I was intentionally picking at the scab.

I met Erik six years ago on my first day of college in the student ID cards line. I'd been there for an hour already, and it felt like the line wasn't moving. He looked more approachable than the crew-cut guy in front of me, and he was holding a book. My kind of people held books.

He was lean, fit, and dressed in dark blue slim jeans with a white button-up shirt and a maroon V-neck sweater. He had dark wavy hair that was cut shorter on the sides, longer on the top, and a little unruly, like he'd spent the day raking his hands through it.

I felt an overwhelming urge to talk to him, so I struck up a conversation by asking what he was reading. It was *The Pragmatic Programmer* by Andy Hunt, and he happily explained a little about it. Computer Science wasn't really my forte—I was more into romance, the classics, sci-fi, some horror, and maybe even a little mystery—but I let him tell me about it. Cute guys digging books were my kryptonite, and Erik was a cute guy.

The conversation only flowed from there. To my astonishment, we hit it off, and he seemed to like me. He was attractive, easy to talk to, and we enjoyed a lot of the same things like videogames, paintballing, and Comic-Con—what my older sister would call "nerdy things." When I finally made it to the front of the line an hour later, I left with his number programmed into my phone and plans to meet for coffee. It was the start of our very safe, very comfortable relationship.

Or at least, it *had* been safe and comfortable. I didn't see the many holes in our relationship until long after he'd left. We were constantly doing things together—checking out the art scene and museums, craft breweries, and other neat little tucked-away adventures—but I guess they weren't enough to keep Erik interested in me for the long term. One day, Erik pulled the rug out from under me and confessed that he'd cheated on me with a girl he met at work.

To say I never saw it coming would be an understatement. Erik was *supposed* to be the trustworthy good guy. He didn't fit the stereotypical mold of a cheating bastard. It had been a sucker-punch straight to my sensitive heart.

Being replaced by the one you thought was your forever—it left a bitter aftertaste.

To amplify matters, in two months, I'd be twenty-five years old. As my mother reminded me *every* opportunity she got, she'd been married for five years *and* had two kids by twenty-five.

Interrupting my internal lament, three loud bangs resounded throughout my apartment, and I scowled at the door. Thirty seconds later, I was still debating answering it when I heard the muffled voice of my older sister, Kelsey.

"Gwen, answer the door. I know you're in there. I can smell the Thai." She let out a heavy sigh at the end, and I wrinkled my nose. Betrayed by the comfort food.

She always seemed to pop up when I least wanted company.

Huffing with aggravation, I stood, abandoning my Thai food on the coffee table. I padded over to the door, opening it reluctantly.

Kelsey took in the baggy t-shirt and boxers look I was rocking. "Really, Gwen?" she said dryly, rolling her cornflower blue eyes.

"Oh, please, throw your opinion upon me," I deadpanned, standing aside to let her walk in.

Kelsey was my Irish twin, born eleven months before me. She was a lot like our mother—very big on rules and appearances—and right now, my appearance wasn't working for her.

My sister had always been the popular one, the pretty one. Being so close in age was brutal, especially in high school. I was that kid—braces, glasses, pimples. No boobs. At least, not until the twelfth grade.

I was a late bloomer. But thankfully, my tits eventually came in, and my skin stopped breaking out, and I ditched the horrible red tortoise glasses I'd worn since the ninth grade for a more flattering pair—my beloved black and blue Tiffany specs.

I started watching makeup tutorial videos and practiced all the time, perfecting my application skills, playing up my eyes and my lips. I also developed a better fashion sense, which I'm sure helped. Now, my closet was stocked with outfits that were fashionable and fit me properly, not the black cargo pants of my past.

But presently, all bets were off. My hair was piled on top of my head in a messy bun, and I was shamefully wearing an old band t-shirt from my high school days.

She tapped her perfectly manicured finger against her lips, her critical eyes on me like I was a problem for her to solve. Her focus shifted to the chestnut nest atop my head. "It's Friday night."

"I'm aware." I gritted my teeth, adjusting my glasses. It was one of my many nervous ticks. Charming.

"I'm worried about you, Gwenny," Kelsey sighed. I could hear the judgment and concern in her voice.

"Don't be." I waved away her remarks, laughing a little. It sounded fake to me, too.

"You always do this." She frowned, crossing her arms. "You sink into yourself and hide. And I'm not going to let you do that anymore. Get ready. We're going out."

"I really don't feel like going anywhere," I told her. "I just wanted a chill night."

"You can have your chill night tomorrow," she said decisively. She grabbed my hand and started dragging me toward the bedroom. Releasing her hold on me, she stomped to my closet. "Go shower. I'll handle the wardrobe."

"Kelsey, *really*—"

"Don't." She spun around, raising her finger at me threateningly—the same thing our mother did when she was lecturing one of us. "You've been moping over Erik for *eight months*, Gwen. It's time to move on. I want my sister back."

I gaped at her, wanting to argue, to dispute her claim. But she wasn't wrong—I was wallowing. It was easier than putting myself out there or enduring the disappointment of being let down, having your hopes and dreams for the future crushed.

But I wasn't any happier, and I knew Kelsey wouldn't give up until I'd let her think she'd won. I threw my hands up in exasperation. "Fine, I'll go!" Turning on my heel, I stomped to the bathroom.

"Remember when we were still in high school, and we'd sneak out to watch the battle of the bands?" Kelsey asked as I applied a coat of my favourite red lipstick—*Outlaw* by Kat Von D.

Setting the tube of lipstick down on the counter, I put my glasses back on and assessed myself, making sure I didn't have lipstick on my teeth and that my winged eyeliner was even. Turning around, I leaned against the counter and folded my arms across my chest. "Yes…"

Kelsey stood in the doorway with her phone in-hand. "There's a band playing at the Watering Hole tonight, and the reviews of their music are pretty positive. We should check it out."

"All right." I nodded, the nervousness I felt in the pit of my stomach easing some. Kelsey preferred clubbing to live music, and I'd been busy expecting the worst from tonight, so I figured that's where she'd drag me. I could get behind a live band at the Watering Hole.

I grabbed my black clutch from my closet and stuffed my keys, debit card, and phone into it before following her to her newer-model, white SUV parked in front of my beat-up Mazda on the street.

Truthfully, I was a little envious of her. There wasn't even a full year between the two of us, and she was already ahead of me in the success department. She worked full-time at a job she seemed to love, and she'd recently gotten engaged—to a good guy, too. Like, it was almost impossible to find fault with Elliott, and it was difficult to begrudge her happiness. They were sickeningly cute together, and I was ecstatic for my sister.

But...Kelsey was exactly where I *hoped* to be when I was younger and looking to the future. They'd already purchased their first home together, a tiny two-bedroom bungalow near Port Hope's downtown district. They were happy, in love.

They had what I *thought* I had with Erik before I was blindsided by his betrayal; before I realized we never even had it, because if we did? He wouldn't have dipped his wick elsewhere.

Now I was single, living on the second floor of a three-storey apartment building near the highway. We had chosen this apartment because of its proximity to the highway and my job at the shop. The rent was cheap and all-inclusive, so I stayed even after Erik left, but things were tight. I was used to splitting half the cost of everything, and now I covered it all. After paying rent, my car insurance, my cell phone and Internet bill, and buying groceries, I was pretty much broke. I'd called in for Thai food using my credit card, *knowing* that I shouldn't but needing the food hug after I tortured myself by looking through Erik's Facebook page.

The kicker was that he looked *so happy*, way happier than he ever seemed with me.

But I would take being broke over the alternative any day. The only thing worse than having my heart smashed was having to return home to my parents' house with my tail tucked between my legs, clutching said broken heart. It was bad enough I had to go to my father to get a job; I couldn't tolerate living there, too. Surely, what was left of my pride and dignity would evaporate in my mother's company.

"Tonight's objective—secure a rebound," Kelsey said, speaking like a spy and waggling her eyebrows at me before turning the key in the ignition.

"You're ridiculous. I don't need a rebound," I scoffed, rolling my eyes.

"Actually, you do. You know I'm not for whoring it up, but I do believe you need to pound out the cobwebs if you know what I mean." She snorted.

"Nope, I'm good," I said, going for the door. If tonight's purpose was to force me at some sad bloke, I didn't want to take part.

"Wait," she laughed. "Look, just flirt with someone—a little, okay? It'll make you feel good."

"How do you know that?" I asked, pausing long enough for her to throw it in drive and go.

"Trust me, okay? I know these things. You know I know these things," she reminded me, looking at me to drill her all-knowing gaze into me.

The bar was crowded, and we had to squeeze our way inside. The Watering Hole was one of the more popular bars in town.

Erik and I used to come here a lot.

I'd left this minuscule detail out because if Kelsey knew, she would steer the night in the direction of club hopping, and I really didn't have it in me. I was in a brooding mood, and it was tough to mope with house music.

We pushed through the bodies gathering near the door, and that's when I saw him. All six foot something, rippling muscles, thick, dirty blond beard and flowing hair. He would have made a better Thor than Chris Hemsworth. His eyes were just as powerful; a piercing blue. They pinned me from across the room, and I halted abruptly.

"Umpfh." Kelsey walked into me from behind. "Move it, sloth," she grumbled, irritated. But his eyes held me in place, and the corner of his lip tugged up in a smile that ripped through me like thunder. Kelsey shoved me, steering me in the direction of the bar, her eyes on the only two empty stools in the entire place.

I craned my neck, trying to keep my eyes on Thor—which is what I'd taken to calling the unbelievable god of thunder in my head. The nickname suited him.

"I think I just got pregnant," I exclaimed, falling heavily onto the stool. It wobbled, and I grabbed hold of the sticky bar to catch myself from toppling over.

"What?"

"Do you see Thor? By the stage?" I told her, gesturing with my thumb behind me. She looked over my shoulder, her jaw widening with surprise before she clamped it shut and nodded. "I want that for my rebound."

"Oh, now you want a rebound?" She frowned, sulking at me.

"Um, HELLO! Wouldn't you?" I whisper-shouted, waving my hands dramatically. "He looks like Thor!"

Kelsey looked again, tilting her head thoughtfully. "Actually, now that you mention it, he does. And he's staring at you, too…"

"Oh, God," I murmured, whipping my head around to look at her. "What do I do?"

"Play it cool," she said calmly. I had a tendency of *not* playing it cool. In the past, it had worked in my favour. I was the quirky one, but as I stole a glance over my shoulder, I couldn't help but worry that quirky shit wouldn't fly with *him*. He was a whole lot of man and was probably used to commanding women like Kelsey—self-assured, confident, articulate.

"Can I get an Alice in Wonderland shot?" I shouted to the bartender. "Maybe three?"

"Too cool." Kelsey clicked her tongue in warning.

"One of those is for you," I frowned. The bartender pushed three shots toward us, and I tossed down a twenty, my hands shaking a little.

I felt jolted awake, and for the first time in eight months, I wasn't thinking about Erik or the breakup. I wasn't thinking about how stuck I felt.

Nah, I was thinking about how incredible it would feel to touch that fine specimen. Just his arm or his chest…just to see if he was carved from stone. If it weren't for Kelsey seeing him too, I would have thought he was a figment of my writer's imagination. He was too perfect not to be.

I took the first shot, a tasty combo of Grand Marnier, tequila, and Tia Maria. For the last six years, it'd been my go-to shot. Risking another glance, I turned my head slightly, trying to be discreet.

Our eyes collided, and I smiled just a little. His responding grin sent tingles down my spine. Kelsey was on to something—flirting with an attractive stranger could very well make me feel good.

"Should I go talk to him?" I asked her, taking the second shot while I waited for her answer.

"Not yet," she responded. "Keep doing the glancing-flirty thing."

So I did. We stayed on our stools, listening to the band play, and I traded flirty glances with Thor while I sipped a beer and let my imagination run wild.

There was no harm in a little fantasizing, and I couldn't help but wonder how the perfect stranger across the bar was in bed. I was barely able to handle the intensity behind his gaze without melting off my stool, and if he kissed as well as he stared—there was no way I'd be able to resist bringing him home if I got the chance. I'd be certifiable not to.

He was ideal—totally different from Erik in every single way, which would have been enough. But it was the confidence he exuded that caught my attention. He knew he had me.

"I read somewhere that beards are dirtier than toilet seats," Kelsey remarked thoughtfully. I swiveled to scowl at her.

"Ew, that's so not true. And I don't care if it is. I'd lick every toilet seat in this bar for a chance with him."

"Okay, *that* was disgusting." She laughed. "Sometimes, I can't believe we're related."

"You and me both, sister," I murmured, rolling my eyes a little. Kelsey was tall and slender, with dark blonde hair and blue eyes. I was shorter and curvier and darker, and in a lot of ways, her polar opposite. But despite our differences, she'd been there for me through thick and thin.

Regardless of her tactics.

"Oh, look, he's leaving," Kelsey said, and I turned in time to see Thor's glorious back disappearing out the patio door. Noting the disappointment on my face, my sister jumped up. "Come on."

"What are you doing?" I hissed, having no choice but to follow her as she headed for the patio after him.

CHAPTER TWO

CLICHÉ

Alaric

I've seen this cliché somewhere before.

Pretty girl walks into a bar. Guy notices pretty girl, pretty girl notices guy. They take turns staring at one another, sometimes catching each other's eyes. He thinks about spreading her out on his mattress and lapping her up like ice cream, she's probably thinking something similar.

But I've seen how it ends, too.

A positive sign on a pregnancy test, two years of trying to make it work, and then she leaves anyway—taking the kid, too. Visits every other weekend and one week in December, limited bursts of time that I had to fight for. The knowledge that some other man is there to tuck my daughter in at night, while I lay in my empty house feeling helpless.

When Cheryl decided to move in with her boyfriend a year after we separated, I didn't get a say in the matter, even though it meant she would be taking our daughter three hours south to Cobourg to live with him.

I tried for a year, but I hated being so far away from Sawyer. I didn't like spending half of our limited time together driving from her mom's place to mine and back again. So, I sold my business, sold my house, and left everything behind, thinking that maybe Cheryl would let me see her more. I had this naïve notion that despite the way things ended between us, we could set it aside to raise Sawyer.

I got the keys to my new place two weeks ago, and so far, Cheryl hadn't budged on allowing me more time with my kid.

Bringing my almost-empty beer to my lips, I took a sip, letting my gaze drift back to the woman across the bar. Even if this bar setup was a tired cliché, I saw the beauty in that instantaneous mutual attraction, the draw two people inheritably felt for one another. Sometimes, it lasted just a minute, a night. Other times, it led to more. I was only interested in one night, and this girl—this stunning girl with piercing eyes the colour of polished shards of metal, a killer rack, and a blinding smile—she rattled me enough to shake me from my ruminating.

Pulling my gaze away from her, I turned my head to the stage, watching Jamie Wilkinson crooning into the microphone. Jamie had been the real estate agent that I'd reached out to when I was looking for a home in Northumberland County. He was a Port Hope native and knew the area well. He found a gem of a house in the country, eighteen minutes away from downtown —close enough that the highway was a hop, skip, and a jump away, but far away enough from people that it appealed to my need of avoiding them.

In addition to being one of the best real estate agents in the area, Jamie was the lead singer and guitarist in a country folk band, and he invited me to his show. I didn't have anything better to do on my Sawyer-free weekend, and I didn't mind Jamie's company, so I agreed to go.

Worst-case scenario—I'd get a change of scenery. Best-case scenario—I'd burn off some steam before I started my new job on Monday.

When Friday night arrived, my desire to leave the house diminished, and I nearly canceled. I had my keys in my hand and almost dropped them. But something drove me out. And right now, I couldn't shake the feeling that the *something* was looking straight at me with fuck-me eyes and lips so red and full, it was easy to imagine them wrapped around my cock.

When Jamie's set was halfway over, I headed to the patio for a smoke. I kept telling myself I'd quit, but I didn't have any reason. I ran my fingers through my hair, debating whether I should bolt or not. I felt a tug, a yearning to go back in there and buy her a drink.

Before I could finish the thought, the patio door opened, and two women stepped out—the girl from the bar and her friend.

The friend marched over, and she followed almost timidly behind, her gray eyes full of apology. "Hey, could I bum a smoke?" the blonde asked, blue eyes watching hopefully, the way a lioness watches its prey.

My eyes darted to the woman behind her, lust awakening in my loins as I took in the curve of her jaw and her red-as-sin lips. "Yeah, sure," I said, fishing my pack from my back pocket. I held it for the blonde without looking at her, and she took one. I heard the click of a lighter and the intake of breath as she inhaled, but my focus was on the dark-haired one. She was biting on her bottom lip, her gaze shifting from me to her friend.

"Gwen, hold this," her friend said, shoving the cigarette at her. "I have to pee!"

"Kelsey!" the brunette, Gwen, called, but the girl—Kelsey—carried on like she hadn't heard her. The patio door opened, and the sounds of the crowded bar and the band spilled out until they were silenced the moment the door clanged shut behind her.

I chuckled, rubbing at my beard. Subtle.

Gwen flushed and drew in a deep breath. "So…" she said, peering down at the cigarette and watching it burn for a moment.

"Gwen, is it?" I asked, feeling amused.

"Yes, Gwen." She nodded. "And you are, Thor?"

"What?"

She blushed. "I mean, what's your name?"

I laughed. She was like a breath of fresh air, and she blew through me with the warmth of sunshine. "Alaric."

"Huh," she said thoughtfully. "Well, Alaric. It's nice to meet you, and I apologize for Kelsey." She held the smoke out to me. "Neither one of us smokes, so…"

Laughing again, I took it from her, our fingers brushing ever so slightly. I put it out against the railing and let it drop into an ashtray, my gaze never leaving her. A moment of silence stretched between us as we eyed each other with curiosity and fascination.

"So…do you come here often?" she drawled, her lips curving in a smile that smashed into me like a tidal wave.

I laughed at her cheesy line. "Not usually, no. A friend of mine is playing tonight and told me about it. Figured I'd come to see him play."

"You're missing the show," she pointed out, arching a delicate brow at me.

"I wouldn't say that," I replied, leaning against the railing and tossing her a smile that I knew charmed her when her eyes took on a dream-like quality.

She blinked a few times, her thick lashes brushing against the lenses of her glasses. She cleared her throat, beaming. Her white teeth offered a sharp contrast to her red lips. My cock stirred with desire.

"So, if you don't come *here* often, where do you usually go on a Friday night?" she asked, her dimpled smile stoking my attraction to her. She was charming, cute. Engaging.

"Well, I'm new to the area. So, I don't really do much, yet," I explained, unable to keep my lips from curving. Smiles hadn't come easily for me over the last few years, and yet here a perfect stranger was, coaxing them from me effortlessly like she'd done it a hundred times before.

"Oh! Well, I'd be happy to give you a tour if you'd like. I've lived here my whole life," she said, her eyes shining. "Let's start with my favourite bar." She leaned forward enough to reveal some of her ample cleavage and gestured grandly toward the Watering Hole, waving her hands dramatically. "Tada!"

"This is your favourite bar?" I grinned.

"There're not many in town, unfortunately." She laughed, straightening and tucking a strand of hair behind her ear. She had a cute laugh—the lilt of it, joyful and free, was the kind that made you want to hear it repeatedly.

"Well, so far, I'm impressed. It's a nice bar."

"You should try the Shiny Bootleg Pale Ale. It's so good! They make it at a nearby microbrewery."

"You're a beer girl?" I arched a brow, mesmerized.

"I enjoy a good ale every now and then, but you won't catch me drinking a Coors." She shivered with disgust, and I chuckled lightly.

"So, any other recommendations?"

"There's a burger joint you should check out and a pizzeria. What we lack in bars, we make up for with great food. Which is my secondary love, after craft beer."

Our connection was broken by tires squealing against the pavement. We both turned to look, watching a white SUV cruise by.

"God damn it, Kelsey!" Gwen swore, turning beet red as she watched her friend drive away. Spinning around, she headed for the exit to the street while she wrestled her phone from her clutch. She paused abruptly, reading something on her phone, her wild hair falling like a curtain, veiling the expression on her face.

"Hey, if you want, I could give you a lift," I told her, the words escaping before I could call them back. She turned slowly to look at me, her phone still in her hand.

"You could be a rapist slash murderer," she pointed out, arching a brow. "A very attractive one, and an honourable way to die, but I digress." She placed a hand on her hip, jutting it out.

I grinned, my eyes crinkling as I laughed lowly. "You could be a rapist slash murderer, too." I took a step toward her. She watched me, her eyes darkening with need.

Shaking her head, another smile graced her red lips. The small silver hoop in her left nostril glinted beneath the streetlights, and she exhaled. "All right, I accept your offer for a ride home. But know that I have a vicious attack dog."

"Noted." With a nod, I led the way to my 1989 Heritage Softail Classic. I bought it when I was nineteen and worked on it with my dad, restoring it to its original glory, and continued improving it every year since then. I'd almost had to sell it a handful of times, but I somehow always managed to hang on to it. Next to my daughter, it was my pride and joy. I loved the open road, the wind in my hair.

"Are you fucking kidding me?" she said, her mouth agape. "A motorcycle?"

"You okay with that?" Most women melted for motorcycles, but there was the odd one who was terrified of them.

"Oh, absolutely." She nodded decisively, her eyes sparkling as I pulled out the spare matte half helmet from my saddlebag and stepped toward her. Clearly, she fell into the first category. I helped her put it on, adjusting the straps and brushing her hair from her face. I felt her intake of breath and stepped away, grabbing my regular helmet from the other bag.

I mounted, holding the bike upright. "Climb on." Tentatively, Gwen swung her leg over and gripped my shoulders for balance while she settled behind me. The warmth of her body was a tangible promise that I wanted to keep, at least for tonight.

"Wait!" she said when I went to turn the key. "How am I supposed to give you directions?"

"Shout out the address, and I'll put it in the GPS," I replied, turning my chin to look at her over my shoulder. The tops of her cheeks flushed with embarrassment.

"Right," she said woodenly, clearing her throat before adding, "Wellington Street."

I typed it in, then turned the key, the bike roaring and rumbling to life beneath me.

Gwen frantically gripped the arms of my jacket. I took her hands in mine, pulling them so that they rested on my stomach.

"Hold on," I told her, pushing the kickstand up with my work boot and walking the bike forward a little, checking behind us to make sure it was clear. It was late, and there were hardly any cars, but I still used extra caution as I pulled onto the road.

We took off, the powerful machine vibrating between both our thighs. I leaned with the bike, bending into the turn, and Gwen's hands tightened against my torso, sending a jolt straight to my cock. Gritting my teeth, I did my best to ignore the way it felt to have her against me.

It wasn't a far drive, and within six minutes, I was stopping outside of her apartment building. Gwen slid off, unbuckling the helmet. She held it in her hands for a moment, looking at it. I kicked the stand down with my toe and lifted my leg over.

Taking the helmet from her, I put it back in the saddlebag and looked around. Her complex seemed a little dodgy at night, and I didn't like the idea of her walking alone.

"Mind if I walk you up?" I asked, deciding to base my chivalrousness on her comfort level. If she still thought I could be a rapist slash murderer, she'd take her chances walking through the parking lot alone.

"Sure," she said, smiling, leading the way to the heavy glass door. We walked up one flight of stairs before she paused at the first door on the right side of the old, beige hallway. "Thanks for the ride home."

"My pleasure," I replied, giving her a crooked smile.

Pulling the keys from her clutch, Gwen opened her door and paused in the doorway, her eyes drinking me in. She bit her lip, considering me. "This is going to sound crazy, and I really hope you don't judge me but…did you want to come in, maybe?"

"I'm not sure, Gwen." I raked my fingers through my hair and inhaled slowly, trying to ignore the ache deep within my balls that her invitation had evoked. "I want to—don't get me wrong, you're gorgeous, and I haven't been able to stop looking at you all night—but I'm not in a good place for a relationship right now."

Her expression softened, and she smiled. "I'll let you in on a little secret," she said, stepping toward me. "I'm not in a good place for a relationship, either. I'm sort of on an *I hate all men* kick."

"Why is that?" I laughed, wondering how a girl like her got to a place like that, relating to her a little, too. Only, in my case, I didn't hate women. I just wasn't sure if I'd ever trust one again. Better to keep them at a distance.

"The story is long and boring and probably doesn't make me look very desirable, so I think I'll keep it to myself." She adjusted her glasses as she spoke.

"Now I really want to hear it." I grinned, intrigued.

"Would you now?" she teased, arching a brow. She was close enough to touch—we were separated by just a hair's breadth. "I can think of a better way to occupy our time."

I knew what she was insinuating, and my cock jumped eagerly at the sultry way she looked at me. Weighing the pros and cons of this decision was easy.

Pro—she was hot, in that *really* sexy, dirty librarian way. Something about her piqued my interest, and she'd said she wasn't in a place for a relationship either. The expectations were laid out before me: one night of allowing myself to escape in her.

But there were plenty of cons, too. While she might *say* that she wasn't looking for a relationship, she could change her mind—or maybe, she didn't know it herself. Women were fickle creatures—they often did the opposite of what they said, or at least the women in my experience had.

Then her eyes dropped to my mouth, and she slowly licked the seam of her luscious red lips, the sinful action overriding every reasonable thought in my head. Instead, all I could concentrate on was how badly I wanted her.

I stepped toward her and kissed her without thinking, the same way one pulls oxygen into their lungs. You need oxygen to breathe, and at that moment, I needed to taste her lips.

She responded in kind, her tongue dancing with mine, a moan resounding deep in her throat. Her hands fisted my shirt, dragging me against her. I backed her into the doorway, my hand tangling in her hair. Everything ignited within me, and I felt more alive than I had in years. She tasted like tequila and apples—her lips needy and tongue searching. Her hand rubbed against my straining erection, and I released a low growl.

"Take that peep show inside!" An old woman's irritated voice snapped. We both looked over, seeing the door on the other side of the hall wide open. An elderly, angry-looking woman with long silver hair pulled back in a loose braid glowered at us from the doorway of her apartment.

"Sorry Mrs. Hewitt!" Gwen apologized, her cheeks burning. The woman let out an irritated grumble before she slammed her door, leaving us alone once more. "The joys of apartment life." She rolled her eyes.

My cock rubbed the zipper of my jeans, and I couldn't help but push against her a little. My efforts earned me a wicked grin, and she bit her lip. Her hand dropped to my chest, her fingers gripping the material of my shirt as she turned, dragging me the rest of the way into her apartment.

She closed the door with her back, pulling me toward her. Our lips met, and our tongues tangled for dominance. As shy as she'd seemed at first, Gwen wasn't holding back. She matched me, kiss for frantic kiss and touch for desperate touch.

"Where's your bedroom?" I growled.

"Down the hall," she managed, tugging my buckle free and popping the button on my jeans in the same breath. Somehow, we got there, taking lots of breaks along the way to peel off clothing and slam each other against the walls in the hallway. By the time we made it to her bedroom, Gwen had lost her shirt, and I'd lost mine.

My pants were unbuckled, and they'd loosened with every move we'd made. I kicked them off and stood before her in my black boxer briefs, my hand pressing down on my straining erection as I watched her step from her jeans.

Gwen revealed a red lace thong that matched her bra. The contrast of red against her creamy skin was mesmerizing. She stood slowly, and I swallowed hard, my attention lost to her. Underneath her layers, she was even hotter, and I was surprised to see she had a few tattoos of her own.

They'd been covered by her clothes, but now that she stood before me in only lacy lingerie, I had ample view of them. A blood-red long-stemmed rose sat just above her left hip on the flat planes of her smooth, pale stomach, a jackalope in a bed of spring flowers and greenery was inked on her right thigh, and she had a sparrow sketched just below her right collarbone.

While I drank her in, she was busy reciprocating. Her dark gray eyes blazed across my chest, and her tongue darted to lick her lips. "Wow. Okay, so wow."

"What?" I asked, looking down. I'd always been in shape, but after Cheryl left, I started working out more regularly, just to occupy my mind and body, and to burn off some of the anger I felt about the way things had turned out.

Gwen's eyes blazed with appreciation as they raked across the designs of the full sleeve tattoos on my arms. She stepped toward me, spreading her palms against my chest, her skin hot against mine.

The soft pads of her fingers traced the bio-mech gear and piston design on the left side of my neck before slowly exploring all the other random pieces I'd gotten over the years. As her hands glided over my skin, her touch awakened every nerve ending in my body.

She bit her lip, grinning up at me. "You should model if you don't already. You'd look great on a book cover," she said before pressing her lips to mine. She kissed me once, then nipped playfully at my lips.

My cock jumped against her abdomen, and I dropped my hands to grip her hips, dragging her against me, pulling my mouth away to look down at her incredible body.

"Well, you'd look great spread out on a mattress," I retorted, smirking.

She laughed richly, her cheeks dimpling, and stood on her tip-toes to press her lips to mine. Our lips fusing and moving together with a sense of familiarity should have had me putting the brakes on the whole thing. But then, Gwen's hands slid around the nape of my neck, and her breasts rubbed against my chest. I could feel her hardened nipples through the lace, and it drove me past reason.

I wanted her. Badly.

Lifting her, I cupped her ass with my hands and carried her the rest of the way to her room. I broke our kiss to deposit her onto the mattress. She bounced back against it, her tits swaying, but before I could climb on top of her, she was sitting up and grabbing the waistband of my boxer briefs, tugging them down over my hips. My cock sprang up, almost smacking her in the face.

I chuckled lowly when her eyes widened with surprise. "You're fucking massive, too," she exclaimed in disbelief. She paused, staring at my dick.

"Everything all right down there?"

"Oh, yeah, it's grand. Massive. Erm," she cleared her throat and looked up at me. "Alaric? Before we do this, I need to know—you're not crawling with STIs, right? Because that's a hard no for me, even if you look like a Nordic god."

"No," I said, guffawing.

"What?" she asked, her lips twitching.

"Nothing. I've just never been asked so bluntly before," I explained, unable to keep the grin from my face.

She bit her lip and shrugged. "You can never be too careful. And just so you know, I'm clean too."

Before I could respond, her hand gripped my hard length and pumped slowly. I dropped my head back when she took me into her mouth and let out a low moan as her tongue swirled around my crown.

"Fuck," I hissed, opening my eyes to watch her take as much of me as she could. My tip hit the back of her throat, and she gagged a little, her eyes watering. She drew her head back and worked her hands in sync with her mouth.

I didn't think I'd make it to the grand event if I let her continue the way she was, so I pulled out of her mouth and leaned down to kiss her before I dropped to my knees in front of the mattress. Sliding my hands down her thighs, I spread her legs.

I peeled her red lace panties off, baring her to me. She bit her lip, watching me as I settled between her legs, kissing the sensitive flesh on her inner thigh.

CHAPTER THREE

EAT ME

Gwen

Alaric pressed heated kisses to the inside of my thighs, his breath fanning out, hot against my core. His hands slid beneath my ass, and he pulled, placing my thighs over his shoulders and tugging me to the edge of the mattress.

The playful grin he gave me made butterflies take flight in my stomach. I lived for butterflies—I loved the weightless feeling that lust and attraction brought forth.

Usually, I preferred a committed relationship to a one-night stand, but like Kelsey had pointed out, I needed to force myself to move forward, and a rebound one-night stand was the perfect solution. Especially with a Thor lookalike. It was my nerdy, Marvel-obsessed, dirty-girl daydream, and it was happening. Only, it was even better than I'd ever imagined.

His muscular arms were tattooed—I hadn't time to fully explore all the intricate designs, but they definitely added to his hotness scale, making it impossible to really be all that mad at Kelsey for ditching me. In fact, I should send her a gift basket to thank her for this opportunity. My head fell back, and I let out a little gasp.

Alaric was assertive, the ultimate alpha, and I had no idea what to do with him now that I'd gotten him into my room, but I was up for the challenge. His muscles were coiled and taut, and his blue eyes raked across my body with hunger that made it impossible to feel insecure.

His kissable lips covered my centre, his tongue stroking against me. I closed my eyes to keep them from rolling into the back of my head—or at least, to keep Alaric from witnessing it. I'm sure looking up and seeing the whites of my eyes would have been a mood killer for him, but I couldn't help it.

Alaric's mouth was magic, his tongue, too. My orgasm hit at breakneck speed, and I came undone when his thick index finger slid in. I tried to arch off the mattress, but his heavy, tattooed arm kept me pinned, while he slipped a second finger inside, working them in and out.

It was single-handedly the hottest thing to have ever happened to me.

I shattered, my walls clenching around his fingers as I came. The whole time, he didn't stop licking me, lapping up every bit of wetness that seeped out, his eyes hungry.

It was wild, feral, and I fucking *loved* it.

"Oh my God," I gasped, lifting my head to look at him with astonishment.

This wasn't my first rodeo—I'd slept with three other guys in my life. Sure, it wasn't an extensive list, but I'd say I was experienced enough to know what I liked and didn't. I thought I didn't like oral—my past experiences with it had been awkward and a little disappointing—but this, *this* rewrote oral for me. I felt like I should give him some sort of reward for his brilliant efforts. He deserved it.

"You good?" he asked, smirking as he reached for his jeans and pulled out a condom from his wallet. I was thankful that he'd brought his own; I was almost certain that the ones I had left over wouldn't fit *that* beast of a phallus.

"I'm great," I said breathlessly, sitting up and reaching around my back to unhook my bra. I tossed it to the ground and removed my glasses, setting them on the table by my bed. Then I leaned forward, licking the pre-cum off the tip of Alaric's cock.

He jerked in my mouth a little, an involuntary thrust of his hips. I bobbed a few more times before I pulled back, watching with hooded eyes as he slid the condom on his hard length. Then he crawled on top of me, making me fall back against the mattress before he settled between my legs. He looked down at me, his eyes boring into mine, searching, I assumed, for any sign of hesitation.

I slid my hand around the back of his neck, tangling my fingers in his silky hair, and pulled him to me, kissing him, our tongues rolling and lips moving erotically. He was still kissing me when his hips jerked, and he slipped into me, his thickness an adjustment that my body happily made. My legs fell open wider as he pushed deeper, filling me more than I'd ever experienced before.

"Fuck," I hissed, the twinge of pain quickly swallowed by my body's reaction to him. The pleasure was blinding.

"Are you okay?" he asked, his concern making him pause, though I felt his cock pulse within me.

"Yes," I purred, running my hands along his back. I gripped his ass, wriggling beneath him. "Don't stop." He pulled out slowly and thrust hard, burying himself in me as far as he could go, swallowing my gasps and moans with his lips.

He slowed his movements, leaning on his right arm and looking down between us. He used his free arm to hook my leg up, allowing him to drive deeper into me. My tits bounced with each thrust, and he hungrily watched them, his eyes on fire.

I came again, exploding around his cock on a moan. Watching his pupils dilate, I knew he felt it. He moved harder against me, pumping his hips with powerful drives that extended my orgasm and made it feel endless.

Alaric

Gwen's hands pushed against my chest, and I followed her lead, laying down with my back to her mattress. In one fluid movement, she was sinking down onto me. My hands gripped her hips, and I held her while she moved against me.

She rolled her hips, riding me slowly, and tilted her head back, her hands on my chest. Each time she sank down on me, she got wetter. It was erotic, and I didn't want it to end. I was fighting off my own orgasm as long as I could.

The pure ecstasy on Gwen's face was almost too much to take. It mirrored the intoxicating feelings I was trying to contend with.

It's just really great sex, I told myself as she bore down, falling against my chest, still rolling her hips.

She was sensuous to watch, and I took pleasure in it that I couldn't recall before. Her breasts pressed against my chest as I pushed down on her ass, grinding up into her like it was my mission to drown in her. And right then, it was.

I felt a tightening in my balls, and at the same time, she let out a little moan. "I'm going to come again!" she breathed into the shell of my ear, her dirty words achingly seductive.

I drove up at the same time as I put more pressure on her hips, and she came around me with a moan. I thrust into her again, my orgasm ripping through me as I looked up at her.

Gwen rolled off me, panting a little. She looked over at me

with an expression of disbelief. "That was *incredible*. Don't take this the wrong way, but you've exceeded my expectations."

I chuckled, still a little out of breath. It really was unbelievable; a mind-blowing, euphoric explosion. I shifted so that I was facing her, let my eyes drink in the sight of her. The apples of her cheeks were flushed, and her dimples fully present as she grinned at me. Her intensely pretty eyes shone in the pale light that streamed through her blinds from the lamppost outside her building.

I brought my finger up, brushing her stained lips with my thumb. I'd kissed—and fucked—away the colour, but it held up better than most.

Gazing into her pewter eyes, I decided then to give myself tonight. The night was young, and Gwen was the perfect liberation from realism. "Want to go again?" I asked, offering her a crooked smile.

"I do, actually. But there are a few things I require first."

"Oh?"

"Food, fluids, and a shower. You may join me for all three if you'd like. But I'm starving and dehydrated, and I probably look like a racoon."

"You don't look like a racoon, but I can get behind those three things," I replied, grinning as I watched her stand. This woman soaking wet in a shower was probably a sight to behold.

She tossed a grin at me and pulled a Batman t-shirt over her head, tugging her long dark hair free of the collar, and left her glasses on her nightstand.

"You coming?" she asked, tilting her head at me before trekking across the hallway to the bathroom.

I exhaled, swinging my legs off the mattress. My feet hit the floor, and I bent over to grab my boxer briefs. When I sat up again, my eyes were drawn to a furry pile of gray in the doorway of her bedroom.

I slid into my boxers, my gaze on the cat. Its pale green eyes watched me, its tail flicking with irritation as it sat, seeming to judge me.

Making my way to the door, I tried to step around it, but it attacked my foot, pawing at it with sharp claws and hissing. Its sharp little teeth dug into the side of my foot.

"Dahmer! Knock it off!" Gwen's voice rang out. She'd opened the bathroom door and caught the little devil in action. Miraculously, the cat stopped attacking and took off into the bedroom, hiding under the bed. "Sorry about that. He's a dick."

"Is that your attack dog?" She'd washed away her makeup and was every bit as pretty without it, her lashes naturally thick and long, her plump lips begging to be kissed again.

"Basically." She grinned. "Although, it could be argued that my neighbour across the hall is more of a threat than the cat."

"I believe it," I sniggered.

Gwen's smile spread, the whites of her pretty teeth on display. Turning, she stepped back into the bathroom, leaving the door open. She tugged her t-shirt off, and my eyes went to the curve of her back as she bent to turn on the shower.

I walked the rest of the way into the room, and she looked at me over her shoulder, smiling seductively before disappearing around the curtain.

When I joined her, she was standing beneath the hot stream, her hair spilling down her back like a black waterfall, working the soapy loofa over her skin.

I stood behind her, my hands reaching to stroke her lower Venusian dimples. She inhaled softly as my fingers slipped to her hips. Pulling her back against me, I moved her hair over her right shoulder, pausing to kiss the crescent moon tattoo on the nape of her neck. Gwen leaned into my embrace, letting out a sigh of contentment. She turned her head and looked at me.

"I was kind of hoping we could pull off shower sex, but now that I have you in here, I can see that might be a little challenging," she commented, hanging her loofa and turning her body so that she was facing me.

"I wouldn't say it was impossible," I replied, arching a brow. She smiled, her dimples flashing, and dropped to her knees, taking me into her mouth. I let out an inaudible groan as I tangled my fingers in her wet hair, holding it away from her face.

She bobbed, taking as much of me as she could. Her hot tongue swirled around the tip of my cock with torturous precision. Her hands moved with her mouth, working me until my balls tightened.

"Gwen," I warned her, trying to pull out of her mouth before I came, but she held tight, moving with me, and looking up at me with lust-filled eyes.

Her fingers brushed against the underside of my balls, and I exploded, my cum shooting down the back of her throat. She swallowed it greedily, sucking every last drop from me.

I pulled out of her mouth, helping her stand. Slipping my index and middle fingers into her sex, I stroked her slick, velvety lips.

It was my turn to sink to my knees, and I did so, looping her right leg over my shoulder. I licked her, my tongue tracing patterns against her core that made her legs tremble. Working her with my fingers, I drew another orgasm from her, tasting her pleasure.

I wanted to pick her up, to hold her up against the tiled wall while I drove into her wet pussy over and over again, but like an idiot, I hadn't brought a condom into the bathroom, and I'd long since learned my lesson about protection.

But fuck, I wanted to. Gwen seemed to sense my hesitation, and she leaned around me to turn off the shower. "Let's call this an intermission," she said breathlessly, handing me a towel before grabbing one for herself.

I chuckled, shaking my head a little as I stepped from the tub. Drying off, I watched while she pulled on her t-shirt and started walking down the hall. I yanked my boxer briefs back on and followed her.

"Now, I've got frozen pizza or Thai food leftover from earlier today. Since you've spent a greater part of this evening munching on my honeypot, I figured you wouldn't care if I'd previously attacked it with a fork."

"Yeah, I can't say I'm a germaphobe." I cocked a brow. She laughed, turning around and disappearing into her little kitchen. I peeked in, leaning against the doorway, watching while she stood on her tip-toes to put a cardboard carton in the microwave above her stove.

Her shirt rode up, revealing her round ass, and my cock swelled at the sight of it. She dropped back down on her heels and raked a hand through her hair, pulling it all over one shoulder. She bit her lip as she turned her head to look at me.

The microwave dinged, and she reached to grab the food, taking her time. Knowing I was watching, Gwen stretched a little further, allowing her shirt to ride up a little more.

Now I was uncomfortably hard, ready for more—again. It'd been a long time since I'd allowed myself an escape, one where I didn't immediately run for the door. Of course, none of the other one-night stands had left me feeling like this.

A lot of it had to do with her personality. She was casual, friendly, with a sultry side that made me want to stay. It was hard to walk away from a woman wearing nothing but a snug-fitting t-shirt.

Best of all, she wasn't asking questions, and that made me want to stay for a little while longer before I returned to the mundane.

Gwen grabbed two forks and sauntered over, her hips swaying subtly enough for me to know it wasn't a show, she just moved in a way that was both exquisite and understated.

I pushed down on my cock, trying to adjust it. Her eyes followed my hand, and there was no way to hide the effect she had on me. She smirked, her dimples flashing and her eyes sparkling.

"Want some?" she offered, holding the container out to me. The tips of my fingers brushed against hers. I took a bite, chewing slowly, watching her while she watched me with a private, knowing smile on her face. She stabbed at the noodles, drawing it into her mouth, her lips fitting around the fork erotically.

Dahmer, the cat, ran from the room like a bat out of hell, slapping twice at my bare leg with his lightning-fast paws before he raced and hid under the couch. She clamped a hand over her mouth to silence her laughter.

"You think that's funny, huh?"

"I'm sorry." She giggled, trying to regain her composure. "I really am. Maybe he's just not used to males. You're the first one he's met."

"Really?" I said with my brow lifted in mild surprise.

"Sort of crossing into personal territory there," she warned with a wry grin, pointing her fork at me for a moment before she attacked the noodles. "But really. Usually, I don't bring home strange guys from the bar."

"Is that so?"

"Don't look so horrified, I'm not attempting to rope you

into a relationship. I am, however, planning on using your body a few more times before you go, if you're cool with that."

"Oh, I'm cool with that," I said thickly.

"Great, because I've had a hell of a dry spell, and you're just what I need right now." She grinned, clearly pleased with the arrangement. I let out a chuckle, low and rumbling, more than willing to help break her dry spell.

Gwen was nestled against my chest, her head on my shoulder and her leg over both of mine. Every time she breathed in her sleep, her heavy breasts would push against the side of my ribs.

I should have already left, but something was holding me here. God knows I had enough on my plate—I was starting a new job, adjusting to life in a new town, and trying to get through to my ex without involving the courts. I didn't have time for a relationship, and I didn't want one.

But sex with Gwen was out of this world. The entire time we'd hung out, she'd kept it light and relaxed. She didn't ask me personal questions, didn't share personal things with me, either, and didn't try to make it more than it needed to be. She was using me, too, and I was all right with that.

With her soft, curvy body pressed against me, I hated to move. I wanted to wake her up with my lips on her pussy—and that meant I *really* needed to leave.

Moving slowly, I detangled Gwen's limbs from mine. She murmured in her sleep, but didn't wake when I slipped from her bed. With the light of the lamppost outside to guide me, I found my clothes, dressing silently.

I walked lightly down the hall, pulled my boots on, and glanced back toward her bedroom before turning to the door. I opened it, locking it from the inside before I walked through it, closing it softly behind me.

Jogging down the stairwell, I left her building. Digging in my pocket for my key, I walked to my bike. I shoved my helmet on and climbed on. Turning the key, I glanced up at her apartment building once more before pulling onto the road, I headed north on Highway 28.

The ride home was quiet; nobody was out at this hour. Twenty minutes later, I pulled into my driveway, my eyes on my new house. The dark gray siding and red doors had first appealed to me, but when I'd walked through it, I fell in love with it. I'd purchased it outright, using the money I made off selling my business and last house.

Jumping off long enough to open the garage door, I drove the bike inside and locked up, exhaustion bludgeoning me. Walking in through the front door, I pulled it shut behind me, locking it. I set my helmet on the bench beside the door. The sound echoed with every movement I made.

The house was too silent without her here, and I hated it.

The hardest thing about the breakup hadn't been losing Cheryl, it had been losing the ability to see my daughter every single day, to tuck her in at night and make her breakfast on weekend mornings while her mom slept in.

My relationship with Cheryl had never been perfect—we were poorly-matched from the start. We conceived Sawyer the first time we hooked up, and we were parents before we found out just how badly we meshed.

But still, despite our rocky relationship, I'd been faithful to her. I tried with everything I had to make it work between us, for Sawyer's sake. Cheryl had sucked me dry, emotionally and mentally, and then she'd left.

She'd been pissed that I'd moved closer, thinking I was trying to intrude on her new life. It always had to be about Cheryl—it couldn't possibly be because I'd hoped I could occasionally pick Sawyer up from school, which, so far, hadn't happened.

Every other weekend was too long to go without seeing your child, and I wished she would understand that. Even though I was less than half an hour away from them, Cheryl still insisted on sticking to our every other weekend arrangement.

I walked through the kitchen and climbed the stairs to my bedroom, falling onto the mattress, my body exhausted, spent from the rigorous, six-hour work out I'd just put it through.

Usually, it took me hours to fall asleep—it didn't seem to matter how hard I worked out before bed, the moment my head hit the pillow, my mind wouldn't shut off. Tonight, though, I quickly fell into a heavy slumber.

Gwen

"So, how was your night?" Kelsey asked, a smirk on her face as she turned her head to watch me.

"Amazing," I purred with contentment, leaning my head back against the pedicure chair, enjoying the attention the nail technician was giving my poor, neglected feet. "I feel so relaxed. Which is shocking, because I've never had a dick that big before."

"Oh my God, Gwen." Kelsey laughed, shaking her head apologetically at the two women who were privy to our conversation. "I'm sorry about my sister, she's insane."

"Not clinically," I argued, rolling my eyes. "And hey, you asked."

"Yeah, I can't say I'll make that mistake again." She snorted, stretching her toes out so her technician could apply the hot pink polish. "So, I guess this means you aren't mad at me for purposely ditching you?"

I let out a contented hum, resting my head against the back of the chair again. I felt like a new person. Sleeping with Alaric had been the best decision of my life—it'd chased all thoughts of Erik clean from my head, or at least the ones where I pined for what I thought we'd had.

I wasn't pinning anymore. Somewhere between the first orgasm and the fifth, I'd realized that what Erik and I had wasn't all that great, to begin with. Sure, we got along well enough, we'd enjoyed a lot of the same things, and we had fun when we were together—but Erik had never been able to make me come multiple times.

In fact, the only way I'd been able to get off is when I climbed on top of Erik and rode him. I had to do the work to achieve the goal, and I hadn't realized how...boring that was.

Last night, Alaric had me in so many different positions, my body was still aching in the best way possible, and I'd orgasmed so much I was certain I'd wake up looking like a prune. Thankfully, I hadn't.

"He's the Holy Grail of sexual escapades," I remarked, sighing dreamily.

"Did you get his number?" Kelsey asked, sipping at the cappuccino the salon provided.

"No," I said, somewhat regretfully. He'd snuck out after I'd fallen asleep. I'd woken up a little bummed about it, and I'd spent the night dreaming of morning sex, but I understood. Was it even a one-night stand if someone wasn't sneaking out before dawn? "That felt like it'd be crossing a boundary, especially since he didn't offer or ask for mine."

"What a dick." My sister frowned, displeased.

"Yes, *what* a dick," I repeated, only whimsically. I harboured no ill feelings toward the incredibly sexy man who'd made me come repeatedly. In fact, I hoped I would run into him again.

"Jesus Gwen, we're in public!" She slapped my shoulder, gesturing to the technicians at our feet, who were both laughing a little.

"Oh, it's all right. This is tame compared to some of the stuff we overhear," my nail girl said, grinning.

"See, she loves it. Every girl loves a good dick story," I remarked airily. "And besides, he's not a dick for not giving me his number or asking for mine. He told me straight up he wasn't looking for a relationship, and as much as I'd like to lock down that cock, I'm not looking for one either."

"You shouldn't let Erik ruin men for you." Kelsey frowned.

"I'm not. I'm just not interested in signing up for heartbreak right now. I'll sign up for multiple orgasms, but I'll pass on the whole fusing-my-life-with-someone-else thing. That only leads to disappointment. I've decided I like my life."

"*Must* have been a magic cock," Kelsey muttered to her nail girl. "She's been sulking about her breakup for eight months now."

"Hey!" I protested, glaring at her. "It was kind of a shocker, don't you think?"

"Not really, no." She shook her head. Apparently, everyone saw Erik's betrayal coming but me. Lovely. Another reason why I needed to stay away from relationships. It seemed that I didn't know how to tell if I was in a decent one or not.

"Anyway," I sighed dramatically, an attempt at steering the conversation back into my court. "Last night's escapades inspired an idea for a novel."

"Another one?" Kelsey arched her brow, turning her head to stare at me.

"Yup, and this time, I'm actually going to finish it. I've decided that I can't be in a relationship until I'm happy in every aspect of my life, and that won't happen until I start following my own dreams. Putting myself first, you know?"

"How will you find time for that?" she asked, not unkindly, just curiously. Kelsey operated similarly to our mother. She thought my writing was a cute hobby but an impractical career choice. She was likely worried that I'd up and quit my job at the shop and leave Dad hanging.

I shrugged, unconcerned. "What else do I have to do with my spare time?"

"Well, I'm happy for you," Kelsey declared, sending me a relieved grin. "Now can we talk about the bachelorette party?"

"Yes." I grinned. "Absolutely. I'll need you to email me a guest list, and I'll get everything sorted. I know your tastes, so don't worry—I won't hire any strippers."

"Why don't I believe you?" she asked dryly.

I smirked, tapping the side of my nose with my finger, and winked. "Because you know me."

"Ugh, please don't spend my money on strippers," she pleaded.

"Fine, I won't use your money on strippers," I replied.

"Or your money." Kelsey frowned.

"What about Montreal?" I suggested, arching a brow.

"Oh, I hear Montreal is *the* place to go for bachelorette weekends!" my nail girl piped up.

"See? We'll do Montreal. It'll be fun," I remarked, trying to not think about how much a weekend in Montreal and a stripper would cost me. But your sister only gets married once —hopefully, anyway—and I still had a few months to save.

CHAPTER FOUR

JUST MY LUCK

Gwen

"Morning, Gwen, how was your weekend?" Dad asked, pausing by my desk. He smiled affectionately at me, and I almost winced.

"It was good," I responded, turning my attention to my computer screen to mask my discomfort and awkwardness. The last thing I needed to do was to think about my one night stand with the magical cock, especially with my father standing there watching me, but that's where my thoughts kept going. Over and over again.

"That's good. We've got a new employee coming in today. He'll have to fill out the paperwork before he can get started. You'll help him if he needs it?" he asked, business as usual as he set a stack of paper down on my desk.

I resisted the urge to roll my eyes, wondering if reading wasn't a prerequisite to welding. It seemed that the majority of welders my dad hired could scarcely read a form.

"Yes, I'll assist if need be," I replied, using my best

professional tone. The last guy I had to help fill out paperwork had been dumber than a stump, and he hadn't lasted very long at Williams' Tech.

"Good," Dad said. He was interrupted by the chiming of the bell over the office door. He turned and smiled. "There he is now!"

I lifted my head, my eyes landing on the sexy owner of said magical cock I was trying so hard not to think about.

Alaric froze, his eyes on me too. It was evident by the expression on his face that he hadn't counted on running into me again, lest of all at his new place of work.

Crap.

"Alaric! This is my daughter, Gwen. She's also the office manager, and she'll help you get started on the paperwork. Come find me when you're done. I'll be in the shop."

"Sounds good," Alaric said somewhat stiffly, and Dad nodded with satisfaction, his hands slapping against my desk lightly before turning and walking down the hall that led to the massive steel shop.

When the door shut behind him, I took a deep breath and stood, collecting the pile of paperwork my father had left on my desk. I cleared my throat, pushing my glasses up the bridge of my nose, stalling for time.

My heart was pounding frantically in my chest, and I had to focus on not trembling while I recalled exactly how remarkable this man had made me feel Friday night—and well into Saturday morning.

The holy grail of penises, the one that was forever supposed to top my list but definitely *never* supposed to walk into my place of work as a new employee of my father.

I cleared my throat, looking up, and nearly jumped backwards at Alaric's sudden proximity. "If you'll follow me," I managed, pasting on what I hoped was a professional smile but was probably more of a nervous grimace.

The heat and questions in Alaric's gaze were unnerving, and I inhaled sharply when I moved past him, drawing in the intoxicating scent of him to my starving lungs.

Walking through the main part of the office, I led him to the meeting room in the back. It was where my dad met with his engineers to go over blueprints and where we had new employees fill out the massive stack of paperwork.

I left the door open as I walked into the room and set the papers on the round table, turning to look at him again, finding him less than two feet away, his unwavering gaze on me.

The silence stretched between us, and I swallowed hard.

"So, this is unexpected. And a little awkward," I blanched, unable to stop the nervous blurting of things I should keep to myself. I guess that's what happens when you don't ask your one-night stand what they do for a living. A smile ghosted his lips, and I licked mine, remembering how those lips had felt on various body parts. "All right, I'll leave you to it. Let me know if you have any questions."

"I have questions."

I hesitated just in front of the door, turning slowly to face him, arching my brows and cracking a sideways smile. "Yes?"

"Your father is my boss."

I whipped my head around, making sure the office was still empty. The office rarely ever saw action, save meetings with engineers, but sometimes the shop manager would wander in to look for blueprints.

Luckily, the office was presently vacant, but I still closed the door more before turning back to him. "Yes, and I'm sorry. I had no idea you were starting here on Monday."

"You're the office manager," he pointed out, his brow rising as he eyed me, and I winced.

"I didn't say I was a *good* office manager," I responded. "I knew some guy was starting today, but I didn't read your folder." I shrugged helplessly, hoping he'd believe me. It was true, after all. My dad went through a lot of hires, not because he was a bad boss, but because he expected a lot from his employees. If they didn't deliver, he didn't hang onto them.

Alaric let out a low chuckle, shaking his head. "All right. Well, what now?"

"Now, you fill out your paperwork," I said, gesturing to the table, heart pounding. I needed to get out of this room. Every time I breathed, I could smell him—it made me want to rip off my blouse and pull up my skirt, and that was bad.

I turned around, opening the door and slipping through it, closing it behind me to keep the scent of his alluring pheromones locked away from my sensitive nostrils, and walked back to my desk.

Already, this situation was horrific. My intended one night stand was my dad's new employee. I'd done the naked dance with someone I would have to see every day. And worse still, I'd have to fight this overwhelming attraction to him and his magical cock.

It was like resisting a huge brick of chocolate in front of you. Diet be damned, if it's sitting in front of you, you're gonna sneak a piece. If he wasn't in front of my face every day, I could let myself indulge in the fantasy of him, bask in it, really. However, with him being *here*, I had to stop that.

Sulking a little, I pulled my cell phone from my purse, bringing up my messages and clicking my sister's name. My fingers flew across my iPhone screen as I threatened to skin her alive if she repeated a word of what I was about to tell her to anyone, especially Dad or Mom.

Kelsey: *OMG. You're dramatic. Just tell me what's going on.*

Me: *Dad hired Thor.*

Kelsey: *WHAT!*

Me: *Yup. Thor's a welder at the shop now.*

Kelsey: *...I can't tell if this is good or bad?*

Me: *It's TERRIBLE Kelsey. He said he wasn't in a place for a relationship, and neither am I, but I want him again, and he's now an employee, and it's all awkward and terrible.*

Kelsey: *Hmm. Still not seeing a problem. Wanting someone doesn't need to mean a relationship. Ever heard of fuck buddies? ;)*

I stared at my phone, my nose wrinkling slightly as I considered it. Casual sex friends could be fun—it was something I'd never experienced before, and the idea intrigued me. But the problem was, I didn't know how I could be around him every day, sleep with him, and *not* develop feelings—or at least an acute addiction to him. I was already jonesing pretty bad.

Plus, that would probably be way outside his comfort level. The way he'd pointed out I was the boss's daughter suggested he had a problem with that, and maybe there *was* a problem with that. I had no idea what the policy was on employee relationships.

I really *was* bad at my job.

Exhaling, I dropped my phone back into my purse, my eyes darting to the meeting room door. I wondered how Alaric was making out or if I should go in and ask him if he needed any help. He was one welder I wouldn't mind helping line by line.

Thinking the better of it, I shook my head and grabbed my computer mouse, moving it to wake up the monitor.

Alaric

I stared at the endless stack of papers in front of me unable to concentrate on the black and white words on the pages.

This was the last place I'd expected to ever run into Gwen again. It was a small town—I realized that—but I figured we'd cross paths at the grocery store or the gas station, not at my new job.

And she was the boss' daughter, too.

She was responsible for filing employee paperwork, and it was only a matter of time before she learned more about me than I'd ever intended her to know.

But I needed this job. Full-time hours, benefits—both drug and dental, and life insurance. The pay was thirty-two dollars an hour, too.

I'd be one of the head welders, as I knew how to do both TIG and MIG welding, and I had more experience than any of the other applicants. It was still a step back from owning my own shop, but it stung less than the other job offers, and travel wouldn't cut into my time with Sawyer.

This job was perfect, but if I took it, it meant I'd be putting myself in Gwen's proximity every day. It was hard to look at her and not picture the expression on her face as she came on my cock.

But it was only supposed to be one night, and now, I'd have to face her every day and not remember how she tasted.

It made me want her again. Especially when she'd been in this tiny little room with me. Four walls, her pencil skirt and white blouse, her dark hair twisted in a bun. Those glasses, her painted lips, her rapid breaths and wide gray eyes.

It was a dangerous fantasy I hadn't known I even wanted until the moment her perfume coiled around my senses. The scent of her alone made keeping my distance a challenge, but I was used to fighting my basic instincts, and I'd managed to resist. Barely.

I exhaled, running my hand over my beard. Picking up the pen, I started filling out the forms, my need to secure employment greater than my need to avoid complication. There were child support payments and bills to consider. And maybe down the line, a lawyer to try and get more time with my daughter if Cheryl didn't come around on her own.

Besides, Gwen worked in the office. The chances of running into her were slim.

Within half an hour, I had the paperwork completed. I stood, collecting the pile and leaving the meeting room.

Gwen sat at her desk, typing on the keyboard. She glanced up when the door opened and drew in her bottom lip, dropping her gaze as I approached like she was ashamed to look me in the eyes.

"All finished?" she asked, her voice an octave higher than its usual lilt.

I nodded, and she took the stack from me, placing it in the folder on her desk. She kept her eyes downcast, and that was a crime. I didn't want her to hide from me or for things to be awkward.

"Gwen," I said, my voice commanding her attention. She lifted her chin, her eyes locking with mine. I choked on my words. I didn't know what to say to make the situation less than…what it was.

"It's okay," she said, giving me a small smile. She tapped the side of her nose just above the sterling hoop and winked. "Let's just forget about Friday night and start over."

"Sounds good," I responded, the words feeling wrong.

"Enjoy your first day," she said, her smile a little pinched like she was just as eager to escape the discomfort as I was.

"Thanks," I said, nodding at her. I went to my truck to get my welding helmet, gloves, and toolbox. When I returned to the office, my new boss was waiting for me.

"Gwen says you're done with the paperwork." Russell Williams grinned. "Ready to start welding?"

"Absolutely," I said, smiling and doing my best to ignore the heavy knowledge that my boss was Gwen's father. He'd likely fire my ass if he knew what I'd done to her over the weekend.

I followed Russell down the hall to the metal door that opened into the large shop.

"Since you're an ironworker, I won't waste your time or mine having you paint the first week. I'm going to throw you straight into it. Cut, assemble, and weld the handrails. You'll find the blueprints are already at your station," Russell said after giving me a quick tour and introducing me to the other welders working in the shop.

Once he left me to it, I got to work, losing myself in the task.

At the end of the day, I had all my pieces cut and laid out. More than half the rails were already tacked together. Russell looked on, inspecting my welds, his brow rising. "Great job, son. Welcome to the team," he said, shaking my hand.

Satisfied that I'd managed to impress the boss on my first day, I grabbed my gear and headed out through the metal door at the side of the shop. My head turned as I passed the two glass doors that led to the office.

I could see Gwen through the panes, standing at her desk, looking at something on her computer screen. She glanced up when I walked by, and our eyes locked.

She smiled tentatively, and I smiled back. I didn't want her thinking I was pissed at her—I wasn't. A little thrown, maybe, but it wasn't her fault. Neither one of us had really talked about what we did for a living.

That was the problem with small town hookups. I should have known better. But Gwen had given me a pass, and I was going to have to put that night behind me.

I tossed my gear in the bed of my truck and climbed behind the steering wheel, closing the door. The engine rumbled to life as the glass doors to the office opened, and Gwen stepped outside. She locked it behind her, adjusted her purse strap on her shoulder, and turned, walking to a red Mazda, pausing to open the door. She looked up, catching me watching her, and gave me a coy smile before climbing into her vehicle.

Shaking my head, I backed from my spot and headed home, driving up 28 with the windows down. I pulled into my gravel driveway, parking in front of the double-vehicle garage.

I sat in the silence of the cab for a few moments, looking at the house. I'd bought it because I could picture myself living there with my daughter. The house was perfect for us. It was a restored and renovated five-bedroom, two bath farmhouse that sat on twenty-six acres of land.

The previous owners had kept the traditional features and added modern amenities. They'd put a lot of work into the house to sell it, decorating it in warm contemporary tones, which wasn't my first pick, but Sawyer loved it. I'd adjusted comfortably enough to it.

It was bigger than I'd planned on purchasing, but the price was right. I could weld in my garage, and with a functional barn to the north of the house, I could get some farm animals for Sawyer.

There was plenty of space for her, too. But when my daughter wasn't around, the house was way too big. The silence echoed, and it made me feel displaced. I'd spent a lot of my time in the garage, tinkering on projects to keep busy.

Four more days, I told myself, moving out of the cab. I grabbed my work gear, bringing it into the garage and setting it down on my workbench. Pulling my phone from my pocket, I checked for messages. I'd missed a call from my mother, and guilt churned in my stomach.

I needed to decompress before I faced that particular storm. Shoving my phone into my back pocket, I left the garage and walked into the house. The connecting door opened to a small room off the foyer with a sink, counter, storage, and rods to hang coats.

On the other side of the foyer was the great room. My last house hadn't had quite so many rooms, and I was at a loss for what to do with it. The entire back wall was brick, with a brick enclave for firewood.

A hallway led from the great room to the eat-in kitchen. It was a little clinical for me, with its shaker cabinets, white quartz counter, and classic subway tile backsplash, but I could always change that.

The dining room on the west side of the house had a huge bay window. Between the dining room and the mudroom was an old wood-stove, which helped heat the main floor during the winter months.

One of the five bedrooms backed off the dining room. It was the smallest of the bedrooms, and it was currently filled with boxes and other random things I hadn't gotten a chance to unpack.

The living room sat off to the left of the kitchen. At the back of the house were the laundry room and mudroom, with a door leading to the back porch. Directly across from the mudroom was the wooden staircase that led to the second floor.

Moving through the kitchen, I emptied my pockets, setting the contents on the counter as I walked into the laundry room.

I tugged my work clothes off and tossed them into the stackable washing machine before jogging upstairs to the bathroom.

Turning the taps on, I let the water heat while I stripped out of my boxers. I stepped under the stream, letting the hot water pound against my aching muscles, and allowed my thoughts to drift to the day I'd had. It was satisfying to get back to welding in an actual shop. The smell of metal, the heat of the welding gun—it allowed me an escape, a distraction.

Welding had been my first love. My old man was an ironworker who had opened his own shop when I was five. I spent a lot of time there with him, wearing one of his old helmets and listening while he talked about what he was doing.

I knew how to weld better than most of my instructors had in college, and when I graduated with the licences and tickets, I'd gone to work at my dad's shop. He made me a co-owner—I was the son of Petersen and Son. When Dad died of a heart attack a few years back, he'd left the entire business to me.

The last thing I wanted to do was sell my father's legacy, but Cheryl had left me no choice. I needed to be closer to Sawyer, and it was the only way I could be near my daughter.

Mom understood—she said it was the exact same thing that my father would have done had he been in my shoes. But I still felt guilty every single time I talked to her. Guilty for selling what he worked so hard to build, guilty for moving three hours away from her, leaving her alone in Ottawa. She had lived there all her life, and she had plenty of friends, but still.

Now both Sawyer and I were gone.

I exhaled deeply, turning to face the tile wall. Running my hands through my wet hair, I lathered the shampoo, washing away the metal, grime, and regret.

Once I'd finished showering, I turned off the water and

reached for the towel on the rack, my eyes going to the neat little row of my daughter's bath things.

I sighed, pushing open the curtain and stepping onto the mat. Tucking the towel around my waist, I walked down the hall, avoiding looking in Sawyer's bedroom. I knew the bed would be made, her stuffed animals arranged carefully. Her bed, empty.

I constantly thought about begging Cheryl for more time, but I knew my ex-girlfriend, and she wouldn't give in easily to my request.

The courts had awarded Cheryl with full-custody since she'd always been a stay-at-home parent while I worked. I got visitation rights, and if I wanted more time, I'd have to rely on the goodness of Cheryl's heart—which had hardened to me years ago—or go the lawyer route.

Cheryl didn't want me around when it wasn't my days to have Sawyer, and she made that perfectly clear all the time. She'd conveniently forget to tell me about school plays or dance recitals, and she didn't want me sitting in student-teacher meetings. I think that was why she'd put the distance between us and was so pissed that I'd sold everything to move twenty-five minutes away.

Jogging down the stairs, I stopped in the mudroom to grab my phone, bringing it into the kitchen and plugging it in to charge. I heated up some of the leftover steak and potatoes from the night before and ate standing up, leaning against the counter and looking out the dining room window, my thoughts drifting to my daughter.

I finished eating and cleaned up the minuscule mess before taking out the trash. I opened the garage doors and flicked on the light. Standing in the driveway, I stared at my bike, my hands twitching at my sides. Closing my eyes, I concentrated on breathing, trying to squelch the desire to hop on it and go for a ride. The last time I'd taken it had been Friday night to the Watering Hole…and to Gwen's apartment.

Thoughts of her assaulted my conscious mind, and I allowed myself to indulge in the memory of her body pressed against mine. All of Saturday and Sunday, I thought about running into her a hundred times, about going back for more, breaking my own most crucial rule.

Seeing her in the office, finding out who her father was—it hadn't doused the desire the way it should have.

I entertained the thought of a different morning than the one we'd had, one where I was fucking her in that meeting room, bending her over the table and taking her from behind.

Knowing that if I hopped on the bike, I'd end up somewhere I had no business being, I walked to my workbench. I pulled my hair back from my face and picked up my welding mask, all the while thinking about her.

She could have provided a great distraction, and maybe if she wasn't the daughter of my new boss, I could have seen if fucking casually was something she'd be into. But this was a recipe for disaster, and I had enough of that in my life already.

Bringing up a playlist on my phone, I plugged it into the speakers and hit play, getting to work on the metal fire pit I was building for the backyard. It was a project to occupy my time while I waited for the weekends with Sawyer.

Half an hour into my project, I caught a movement in the corner of my eye and nearly jumped out of my skin when a large black shape that looked strikingly like a bear cub wandered into my garage. Realizing that it was a dog, I relaxed and set my welding gun down, powering off my machine.

"Are you lost, bud?" The dog's tail wagged tentatively as it ambled over. Its coat was matted with mud and burrs, and its brown eyes looked up at me pleadingly, begging me to save it.

When its large pink tongue lapped my hand, I let out a

heavy sigh. Clearly, the dog was tired and had gone a long time without a good brushing or a bath. It was either lost or abandoned, and I didn't feel right about sending it back into the night without at least feeding it.

I reached for my phone, cutting the music and unplugging the speaker cord. It was almost eleven, too late for any stores nearby to be open. "Guess you get what's left of my steak, bud." I exhaled, opening the door to the house. The dog stayed in the garage, watching me warily. "Come on."

The dog obeyed me, its tail wagging lowly again as it padded over to me. Once it reached the wooden steps, it looked up at me with sad eyes that broke my heart a little. "Come on," I said again, gentler this time.

It followed, lifting its front paws heavily up the stairs over the threshold. I walked to the kitchen, opened the fridge, and put what was left of the steak on a plate. Setting it down in front of the dog, I straightened.

The dog didn't move. It sat, waiting, watching me with soulful brown eyes. "Go on then," I instructed. The dog stood, digging into the steak hungrily.

I filled a bowl with water and carried it to the laundry room, setting it beside the freezer before I grabbed a towel from the dryer and spread it over the mat by the back door. It wasn't much of a bed, but it'd have to do.

The dog wandered into the laundry room and paused by the bowl, lapping up the water. Rivulets of water poured from its jowls when it looked up with its tail wagging gratefully at me.

"Come here," I said again, and the dog did I asked, laying down on the bed I'd made. I crouched, stroking its fur, rubbing its belly to relax it. It rolled onto its back, and I checked, noting that it was a boy. "Stay." I pet it once more before standing.

Sawyer would love this. She'd been asking for a puppy for years, but Cheryl claimed to be allergic and refused all pets. I'd planned on getting Sawyer a pet at some point, but not right now. I'd barely finished unpacking.

I closed the door to the mudroom and went upstairs, thinking about the dog. I wouldn't have time to take him into the shelter before work, so I'd have to call on my break.

The stores wouldn't be open when I needed to leave for work, so as I laid in bed, I Googled human foods safe for dogs. Normally, I grabbed a bagel on my way into work, but it looked like tomorrow I'd be making scrambled eggs and oatmeal.

CHAPTER FIVE

SWEET ADDICTION

Gwen

At noon on Tuesday, I glanced up when I saw movement through the office doors. Alaric stood on the sidewalk with his phone to his ear. I was just about to dive into my lunch but seeing him made me want to go get a sub just so I had an excuse to run into him.

Shoving my homemade sandwich into the bottom drawer of my desk, I picked up my purse and phone. I'd been shamelessly waiting for another opportunity to talk to him, and I wasn't about to waste this one.

Alaric had his back to the doors, and he didn't hear me as I slipped out, catching the tail end of his conversation. "Okay, I'll give that a try next. Thanks."

Sliding his phone into the back pocket of his work pants, he turned, about to head back into the shop, and caught sight of me.

I smiled, slowing my jaunt. "Oh, hi Alaric."

"Hey." His eyes seemed to be tracing the shape of my lips. He cleared his throat, looking conflicted.

"Everything all right?" I asked, tilting my head, hoping his discord had something to do with the wanton way his gaze swept over my hips. It was a beautiful May morning, and I was feeling pretty in a peppy little dress. It was black with tiny white dots, with a bow that tied the slit from my neck to my collarbone together.

"Yeah," he replied, seeming to stand taller. "I've got to get back to work though."

"Right. I need to get lunch. See you around," I said, brushing past him on my way to my car. His head turned as I moved by him.

"Gwen," he said, and I halted, pivoting to face him. "You wouldn't happen to know the name of any dog rescue groups, would you?"

"Not off hand, why?"

"A stray dog wandered into my garage last night," he said, shoving his hands in his pockets. "The shelter said they were overcrowded."

"Aww!" I squealed, unable to help myself. Although I considered myself a cat lover, I couldn't resist animals of any type. "Stray dogs tug at my heartstrings. Those Sarah McLachlan commercials kill me every time."

"Yeah, well. Do you want it?"

"No way. My landlord would kill me. He hates that I have a cat," I replied, shivering. I tried to keep my interactions with Greg limited. The man gave me the creeps. "Tell you what, I'll do some research. Come to find me at the end of the day, and I'll have a list with some numbers."

"Thanks. I appreciate it." He looked relieved.

I smiled and turned, walking toward my car. I didn't chance another look at him, but I could feel his gaze on the back of my thighs as I walked away. It was enough knowing I had his attention. Besides, I had an excuse to see him later. Unlocking the door, I climbed into my car.

When I looked up, my eyes locked on his. I smiled again, this time just a little half grin that I hoped conveyed playfulness and not a creepy-stalker vibe. It was hard to tell without a mirror to practice, but I saw his Adam's apple bob as he swallowed, so it must have worked in my favour.

I spent the rest of the afternoon researching rescues and writing down numbers. At five o'clock, I started getting ready to leave for the day, the list tucked into my skirt pocket. Yeah, the dress had pockets, which had been the only reason why I'd bought it.

Well, maybe not the *only* reason, but still. Dresses with pockets were the shit, and after the breakup, I decided to go a little online shopping happy and buy myself a new wardrobe. Not my smartest decision, but at least I had an endless supply of cute outfits.

Every so often, my eyes darted to the shop door. I worried my lip, wondering if I should slip in and hand the list to him. After all, I'd told him to come to find me, and I was supposed to be playing it cool.

The goal was to get him to chase *me*, not to follow him around like a lost puppy. Apparently, he already had one of those.

I stood, about to start shutting off lights and locking up, when Alaric walked through the metal shop door.

"Hey." He lifted his bearded chin in greeting.

"Hey. I've got the list of local rescues for you," I told him, pulling it from my pocket. Alaric's eyes tracked the movement, and his fingers brushed against mine as he took the paper from me.

"Thanks again," he said.

"Don't mention it." I waved my hand. "Although…" I bit my lip, considering.

"Although what?"

"Well, I'm not sure how quickly the rescues will be able to get to you. There's a pet store downtown that's very knowledgeable with pet care. I've gone there with questions about Dahmer before. I wrote the address down for you."

"Do they have grooming there?" he asked, his brow furrowing.

"I believe so." I nodded. "But I think it might be self-serve."

"A self-serve dog wash?" he repeated, arching his eyebrow, amused with the concept.

"Yeah. Places that'll do it for you usually make you book an appointment."

"If he's going to stay even temporarily, he needs a bath." He sighed, sounding displeased.

"Tell you what—I've got to go there for cat food. I'll head home and change, and you go get the dog. I'll help you give it a bath."

"Why would you do that?" he asked, chuckling.

"Like I said, I'm a bleeding heart. Even though I can't take him, I'll help you find him a home. Plus, I have experience with this. I did my high school volunteer hours at a dog groomer's," I added, winking.

He exhaled deeply, considering me. "All right. Give me an hour, though, I don't live in town."

"Okay." I smiled. "I need to lock up the office and change. I'll see you then."

Alaric looked a little surprised by my dismissal, but a ghost of a smile appeared on his lips, and he nodded, walking back through the shop door. I locked it and grabbed my purse, heading for the glass doors, feeling giddy with possibility.

I sped home, changing into a pair of black yoga pants and hesitated before the Batman t-shirt. Nibbling on my bottom lip, I tugged on a Wonder Woman t-shirt instead, twisted my hair up into a messy ponytail and fussed over my reflection in the mirror.

The insecure, naïve girl I used to be in high school poked her head up, muttering knock-me-down comments about how out of my league Alaric was. I shoved the bitch back in her box; I worked too hard to let her take me down again.

Before leaving, I topped off Dahmer's food bowl, purposefully not acknowledging the almost-full bag in the cupboard. So what if going for cat food had been an excuse? There was no harm in stocking up, and I wanted to help Alaric with the stray dog.

And yeah, maybe I wanted to spend a little more time with him. I'd be mad not to hope for a repeat when the night between us still lingered.

It didn't help that I constantly revisited that night in my mind, drawing inspiration for my novel from it.

I called him *dickspiration* because his dick was my inspiration. Or at least, the way his dick had made me feel that night. I wouldn't mind reliving it. For research purposes, of course.

Grabbing my bank card, wallet, and phone, I walked out to my car. It didn't take me long to drive to the pet store, and I parked against the curb out front, behind Alaric's truck.

My heart thumped with nervous anticipation as I pushed open the door and strolled inside the pet store, my eyes moving to the back of the room, where the dog wash was set up. I could see Alaric trying to coax a large black dog into the stall.

The dog must have weighed a hundred pounds, if not more, but Alaric picked it up as if it weighed nothing, lifting it into the stall. He tied the leash up to the hook and paused to stroke the animals' face. He spoke quietly to him, murmuring words I couldn't make out.

"Who'd have thunk it; you're a big old softie underneath that tough exterior," I remarked, my voice making my presence known. Alaric glanced at me as I leaned against the tile wall. I held my hand out for the dog to sniff, offering him a playful smile. "How'd you find him again?"

"I was working on a project, and he walked right into my garage." Alaric stroked the dog's face with his eyes still on me.

"Were you welding?" I teased.

"Maybe," he replied, the corner of his lip lifting up.

"Really?" I laughed. Shaking my head, I studied the dog thoughtfully. He was docile and friendly, although he appeared to be a little nervous about the bath stall. "We should probably cut the matted fur out before we try and wash him. I think it'll hurt him if we don't."

"Okay." Alaric gave me a full-blown smile, and I nearly swooned at the intensity of it. I exhaled, glancing around the shop.

"Excuse me," I said, noticing an employee stocking the aisle nearby. "Do you happen to have scissors we could borrow?"

"Absolutely. I'll grab them for you," she said, disappearing behind the cashier counter. She walked over with the scissors, handing them to me. She studied the dog with a frown, taking in his state before her gaze shifted to Alaric, her lips pursing as she assessed him too.

"He showed up at my friend's house last night. We think

he's a stray. Thought we'd clean him up a bit before posting his picture online," I explained, and her eyes softened.

"Poor thing!" she remarked. "I hope you find his home! Let me know if I can help you with anything else."

"Thank you," I said, and she walked away. Without another word, I set to work cutting out the mats with an expert hand. I wasn't joking when I'd told him I'd completed my volunteer hours at a dog groomer's.

Once I finished the fur on my side, I moved around toward Alaric's, shifting closer to him until I was standing less than an inch away. With that done, I showed Alaric where to put in coins to get the water and shampoo dispenser to work. He stood five inches behind me, looming over me. His scent overwhelming my senses in the best way.

I stepped from his space and grabbed the hose, walking around the dog, speaking gently to him as I sprayed the warm water. Handing the hose to Alaric so he could start the other side, I lathered the pup.

It was difficult not to glance up at Alaric every three seconds just to catch a glimpse of his god-like beauty. He'd pulled his blond hair back in a bun, and he was wearing a black t-shirt that did little to hide his muscular build. The muscles in his tattooed forearms worked as he lathered shampoo into the dog's head.

And it was *really* hard to not think about the last time I was with Alaric in a somewhat similar setting. Sans dog, of course.

Somehow, I managed to keep it together throughout the two baths the poor dog needed. He wasn't a fan of the hairdryer, but once the employee brought beef liver treats over, he stopped fighting it and let it happen, growing to like the warm air, so long as it wasn't blowing directly on his face.

It took almost two hours, and my shirt was soaked and clinging to my body, but by the end of it, the dog looked completely different. His fur was silky to the touch and a shiny black, and his tongue lolled from the side of his mouth. Alaric reached to unhook the leash, and the dog lapped at his face happily.

I grinned. "He probably feels a thousand times better now," I said, sighing inwardly at the beautiful sight of a handsome man loving on a dog. "I know I do when I work out the tangles in my hair."

Alaric chuckled. "Me too," he admitted, glimpsing me, still rubbing the big dog's ears. His eyes heated when they lingered on my skin-tight, wet shirt, but I pretended not to notice.

"He suits you," I commented. He glanced back down at the dog and shrugged a little. Tall Norse god of a man and massive beast of a dog. They went together like peanut butter and jelly. "You should keep him."

"We'll see. I still want to try and find his owners."

"He might be microchipped," I supplied. "If you take him to a vet, they'll be able to check."

Alaric nodded, watching me deliberately. After a moment, he cleared his throat. "Thanks for your help tonight, Gwen."

"You're welcome," I said. *Less is better, less is better*, I repeated inwardly, trying to calm my libido and think rationally. I drew in a breath, smiling again while Alaric led the dog out of the bath stall. "Do you want me to take a picture for the rescue groups before I get going?"

"Sure." He looked at the dog. "Sit," he instructed. The dog sat at Alaric's heels in front of the aisle. He pulled his phone from his pocket and passed it to me. I snapped a few pictures, getting different angles, and handed it back, resisting the urge to take a few using my own phone.

I scratched behind the dog's ears. Chewing on the inside of my cheek, I looked up at Alaric, feeling the heat behind his gaze. "If you do keep him, you should name him Tig. Since he interrupted your welding project," I added.

"Tig, huh?" he repeated, looking down at the dog.

"Or not," I shrugged, moving toward the door. "See you later."

"You forgot the cat food," he called out.

"Right." I turned, heading for the cat food aisle. I grabbed a bag from the shelf, my cheeks on fire. Alaric nodded at me when I passed, and I went to pay while he wandered to the dog food aisle.

I tried not to look back as I left, and it took all the strength I had, but I made it to the car without peeking over my shoulder.

I drove home and parked outside of my building. I'd nearly reached the door when it opened, and Greg the slumlord stepped out, shaking his head darkly.

Noticing me, his thin lips curved in a leering smile. "Gwen. Just the girl I was looking for. Do you have my rent cheque?"

"Yes," I said, thinking of the envelope on my table. It contained six months' worth of post-dated cheques. So far, Greg had never crossed a line, but his creepy watching made me uncomfortable enough to remove the requirement of dealing with him. "I'll bring it out."

Instead of waiting outside, Greg followed a little too closely behind me. The hair on the nape of my neck stood up in warning, and I could have sworn I heard *and* felt him sniffing me.

Mrs. Hewitt chose that moment to open her door. I took advantage of her sudden appearance and put as much distance as I could between myself and Greg.

"Oh good, it's about time you showed up! I've been calling you for weeks now about the leaky faucet in my bathroom!" she barked.

"I told you, Mrs. Hewitt, I've got a call into a plumber. He should be coming by tomorrow evening, between five and eight."

"You're a man, aren't you?" she snapped. "Men are supposed to know these things. Go in and look at it yourself."

I'd never been more thankful for my neighbour than I was in that moment. With Greg distracted, I was able to quickly grab the envelope off my table and thrust it at him.

"Six months of post-dated cheques," I said, sending Mrs. Hewitt a grateful smile before closing my door and locking it—the deadbolt, the chain, and the knob.

Still, I felt revolted. I shivered and walked away from the door. In instances like this, I missed having Erik around—or at least someone else, to deal with the pervy landlord so I wouldn't have to. At least I'd bought myself another six months.

Dahmer let out a pressing mewl, demanding my attention. He jumped from the sofa into my arms, and I caught him, cuddling him close to me. As he purred, I relaxed, pushing the icky feelings away, choosing to focus on the good things instead—like the fun I'd had with Alaric and the stray dog.

As if sensing my thoughts—or finally figuring out the strange scent on me was a dreaded dog—Dahmer let out an angry yowl and kicked off my chest, his claws digging in as he pushed off me.

"Don't be jealous!" I called after him, knowing he'd disappeared under my bed. He'd be mad at me until dinner.

I poured myself a glass of wine and ran a bath, dropping in a bath bomb. I set my phone on the closed toilet lid and twisted my hair up. Climbing into the tub, I let out a sigh of contentment as the hot, fizzing water eased the tension in my muscles.

My cell phone rang, and I picked it up. Kelsey's photo and

number flashed on the screen. I answered and put her on speaker. "Why are you interrupting bath time?"

"Why aren't you texting me back?" Kelsey answered my question with one of her own.

"Sorry. I didn't realize you'd messaged me. I just got home. Had to deal with the landlord."

"Gross Greg came by? Didn't he come by last month?"

"Yeah, but apparently he wants rent every month," I teased. "What did the texts say?"

"Not to make any plans next Sunday; we're going dress shopping!" Kelsey squealed with excitement.

"Oh, yay! Wait...who's we?"

"Mom, of course. And Elliott's mom..."

"Ugh." I scowled. Elliott's mom was an uptight woman, and that wasn't a snap judgment, it was the truth. She walked around with her nose in the air all the time, and I rubbed her the wrong way. "Fine," I sighed.

"Gee, don't sound so excited!" Kelsey deadpanned.

"I am ridiculously excited to watch you try on dresses," I said sincerely. "I'm less excited that Judgy Janice will be there, too. But I get it, she's going to be your mother-in-law soon. My condolences, by the way."

"She's not that bad," my sister said in her defence. I could hear the frown over the line.

"You're right, there are definitely worse in-laws out there, probably," I relented, shrugging. "Anyway, I'll be there, with bells on."

I was gathering my things after work on Friday when the

door to the shop opened, and Alaric walked in, his welding helmet tucked under his arm, and his handsome face covered in metal shards.

It was the first time I'd seen him since Tuesday night. He'd shown up before me and left after me through the shop doors. I'd never minded how little I had to interact with my father's employees until him, and now it bothered me that it was so hard to catch him alone.

"Is it too late to pick up my pay stub?" he asked, his eyes raking over my body. I was wearing a tight red skirt with an attached navy polka dot top. My hair was up in a twisted bun with some curls framing my face. I knew I looked good, but with his gaze on me, I felt sensual.

"Nope. It's in that tray on the counter." I tilted my chin in the direction of the metal tray. I looped my purse over my shoulder, worrying my lip as I watched him. I moved toward the counter. "So, how's the dog?"

"Good," Alaric replied, his eyes moving to me briefly before returning to the tray in front of him. "Still haven't been able to find his owners."

"That's too bad." I frowned, feeling sorry for the dog. "Did you reach out to the rescues?"

"I did. Somehow, I got roped into fostering him." Alaric chuckled, shaking his head. "Took him to the vet last night. No microchip either."

I let out a heavy sigh, feeling sorry for the pup. "He could have traveled for miles before finding you."

"That's what I'm thinking, too." Alaric sighed, looking conflicted as he pulled an envelope from the pile and put it in his back pocket before facing me.

My thighs quivered at the sight of all six foot two inches of him covered in grime from a long day of welding. I'd never found welders attractive before.

Granted, we'd never had a welder that looked like *him* in the shop.

I dropped my gaze to the floor before meeting his eyes again. "Well, if you feel like celebrating the end of your first week and your new status as a foster dog-parent, we could check out that Shiny Bootleg Ale at the Watering Hole."

His eyes heated, but when he blinked he'd regained his composure. "I've got somewhere I need to be tonight."

"Oh, of course," I said quickly, flustered and embarrassed. Of course he was busy. I should have never opened my mouth. "Have a good weekend." I grabbed my keys and high-tailed it out of there, mortified at the rejection.

In my bustle to leave, I almost forgot I was the one who had to lock up, which meant I had to wait for Alaric. I paused, letting him walk by.

"Maybe next week, though. I wouldn't mind sampling some of that Shiny," he said, his voice heavy with innuendo as he moved past me.

I stupidly blinked after him before regaining my senses. Flicking off the lights, I punched in the security code and opened the door, stepping through it quickly. I was overly aware of Alaric standing a foot away, a cocky smile on his sinful lips, watching me. I shoved the key in and twisted, driving the deadbolt home, and turned.

He was still grinning at me, waiting for a response.

"Maybe. I'll have to see if I'm busy," I replied airily, walking around him with my nose aloft. I had my pride to consider, and I didn't want to come across as too eager.

Although, I kind of *was* eager. The idea of being casual sex friends had grown on me, especially since Tuesday night. I was confident I could tolerate it better than being around him every day and *not* getting another round on that magical cock.

He barked out a laugh. "Have a good weekend, Gwen."

"You too." I saluted him, like an idiot, and walked to my car.

He let out another low chuckle, heading in the opposite direction to where he parked, shaking his head as he walked. I watched him climb into his blue Chevy Silverado.

I slid into my car, closing the door, and let out a sigh. Another Friday night, another boring weekend alone with my cat.

It kind of sucked that I had so few friends. Kelsey and my childhood bestie were it, really, and Renly lived in Oakville. He'd moved there for college and had never come home, preferring Oakville to Port Hope. I didn't blame him in the slightest—it certainly offered more.

After graduating from interior design, Ren secured a job working as an interior decorator on the Home Renovation Channel's *Brightwood Interior*, working with Tatum Brightwood herself as a part of her design team. His life was a thousand times more glamorous than mine.

I was a little jealous about that, and I missed my friend. I drove home, intending on calling him. But when I pulled into my parking spot, I squinted hard, spotting Ren as he leaned against the yellow brick of my building. He looked up, spotted my shitty car, and his entire face lit.

I grabbed my purse and keys, flying from the car and squealing with excitement. "Renly! What are you doing here?"

"I came to visit my girl," he said, drawing in a deep breath for dramatic pause. "Your last message didn't sound too chipper. I had the weekend off work and figured I'd make the trip!"

"That's awesome! I'm so glad you're here," I said, unable to stop a pesky tear from leaking from my eye. I really had missed him.

Aside from my sister, Renly was my only constant. We

talked daily on Facebook, Snapchat, or texting. After Erik left, Ren had really been there, and no matter what he had going on in his busy world, he made time for me.

"Well! Let's head on up," Ren said, squeezing my shoulders. "I brought stuff to make mojitos."

"Did I mention you were my favourite person?" I sighed, leaning into his embrace as we started walking.

"Not lately, but that's okay. I already know," he said affectionately, his brown eyes softening. "You look good, Gwen. Better than the last time I saw you." He bumped my hip with his.

"Ha, very funny." I rolled my eyes, remembering his last visit. He'd driven out after the Erik thing and spent three days cheering me up. We'd come up with ridiculous names for Erik. Von Dick Shit was by far my favourite.

"I'm serious though. You've got a glow to you. What secrets are you harbouring?" Ren could always sense a change in me, no matter how subtle.

"Just you wait," I told him, unlocking the door. The most security this building saw was the constantly locked door. You needed a key to get in, but some tenants would prop it open with a brick. On those nights, it was a little harder to sleep.

We walked up the flight of stairs to my apartment, and I unlocked the door. Mrs. Hewitt's door opened quickly, and I waved at her.

"Another man?" Mrs. Hewitt croaked judgmentally, like the peach she was. "Girls today are far too loose."

Ren and I looked at each other and busted out laughing. He swept at the corner of his eyes. "I missed Mrs. Hewitt. I'm glad she still lives across the hall."

"Me too," I confessed. "I feel much safer with her around." I thought of Tuesday night.

"I bet," Ren cackled, shaking his head. His dark brown hair

was impeccably styled in a side part pompadour. He'd lost some weight and looked a little older. "Now what's this about another man?" He arched a brow.

"Well, she may have caught me making out with this guy I met at a bar," I replied airily. Renly gaped at me.

"Excuse me? You brought home a guy from the bar? Tell me everything!" he said, steering me into the living room.

At the sound of our voices, Dahmer waltzed down the hall. Ren halted, spotting the cat.

"What is that?" he asked, pointed at him with a bewildered expression on his face.

"I got a cat." I shrugged.

"When?"

"The day after you left." I grinned. "It was really quiet without you, and without—"

"Thundercunt Twatwaffle," Ren supplied helpfully. "Good riddance to him. He was far too bland for you. Now dish."

"I will." I sucked in my bottom lip, clapping my hands together. "But first...I thought I heard you say something about mojitos?"

"Ah, yes. You do have wonderful hearing, although your eyesight is crap."

I smirked, enjoying his ribbing. Ren unzipped his duffle, pulling out a brown paper LCBO bag and a plastic sack. He headed to the kitchen, making himself right at home as he rooted through my cupboards for two tumblers and a plastic cutting board. He removed the lime juice from the plastic bag and set everything on the counter.

"Be a doll and get the sugar?" he asked, batting his lashes at me while he pulled open drawers and looked for a teaspoon.

He chopped the mint leaves, mushing them against the sides of the glass like his full-time job was bartending, not designing houses on a Canadian home improvement television network.

"Do people recognize you in the street yet?" I joked, removing the sugar from the cupboard and placing it beside the limes.

"Ha, sometimes," Ren admitted. "But don't change the subject. I've been patient enough. Spill."

"Kelsey dragged me out last Friday and told me I needed to find a rebound."

"I always said your sister was smart," he remarked. "Go on." He blinked impatiently at me as if I'd stopped talking on my own accord. It made me laugh.

"Well, she also happens to be an incredible wingman. I ended up hooking up with this sexy guy. I'm talking tattooed Thor, with long flowing locks and a beard and everything."

"Sounds delightfully barbaric," Ren commented, shivering. He grabbed the ice tray from the freezer and filled each glass two-thirds of the way with cracked ice.

"Right? And he was huge, too. Like, six-foot-two *and* packing a long schlong. I almost didn't know how to handle it."

Ren laughed loudly, nearly spilling the rum he was pouring into each glass when his arm jerked. "I hope you figured it out."

"I did," I said proudly. "It was awesome. But it was only a one-time thing. He made it perfectly clear that he wasn't looking for a relationship, and I'm not either, so…"

"So…" Ren shook his head, waiting for me to continue. "What's the problem, exactly?"

"One—I can't stop thinking about him. And two, that Monday…he started working at my dad's shop."

"No!" Ren gasped, his hand covering his heart.

"Yep," I said, popping the 'p.'

"Wait...he had no idea you worked there, and you had no idea he was starting?"

"None. I might have known if I did my job better, but I don't," I replied, shrugging like it couldn't be helped. "We didn't actually ask each other for our last names, and we were mostly focused on exchanging bodily fluids."

"Awkward." He winced, sipping at his drink.

"Very. And as if all that wasn't enough, I had to be an idiot and ask him for drinks tonight." I rolled my eyes, still frustrated with myself.

"What'd he say?"

"That he had somewhere he had to be," I repeated, sighing with defeat. "Maybe he's just not that into me."

"He'd have to be brainless to not be into you. You're a catch! I'm gay, and even I can see that." Ren said, and I grinned at him, thankful. "Maybe he really did have somewhere he had to be. Stranger things have happened. Did he say anything after?"

"Well, yeah...he said maybe next week, but I'm trying not to get my hopes up. I mean, he looks at me like he's picturing me naked a lot. And I know I look at him like that too, because I do, picture him naked, I mean. And I'd love another go at him. But he hasn't made a move, not even when we hung out on Tuesday night."

"Wait, you hung out on Tuesday night?" Renly interrupted.

"Yeah, he found a stray dog, and I helped him bathe it at the pet store."

"That's promising," he remarked thoughtfully.

"Yeah, and it was fun but..." I trailed off, worrying my lip.

In a lot of ways, I still channeled that nerdy outcast I was in high school. Boys didn't talk to me. They went after my older sister. His brush-off had hit my self-esteem and made me feel like I was sixteen again, getting laughed at when I asked Mike Wilson to the winter semi-formal.

"You're adorable. You've got it bad," Ren gushed, gently shoving at my shoulder.

"But I don't. I just really liked the dick, you know?" I said, lying through my teeth.

I *did* really like his dick, but it was more than that, or at least…it felt like it could be more than that. Maybe. I didn't know. Dropping my head in my hands, I exhaled heavily.

"Hmmhmm," he said, pursing his lips thoughtfully. "So go for drinks with him next week and see what happens."

"It's so simple when you put it that way, but you haven't met him. He's intimidating, like, I honestly don't even know how I got him into my bed in the first place. I don't think I can do it again."

"Stop with the self-deprecating talk right now," Ren ordered sternly. "I didn't come here to listen to that."

"I know. I'm sorry." I pouted. "But anyway, workplace romances are never a good idea."

"That's what makes it so fun," he pointed out, tilting his head and waggling his eyebrows. I shrugged, taking another sip of my drink and walking to the living room. I sat on the couch cross-legged, facing Ren. "I think you should go for it. Be boning buddies! What did you say his last name was?" He pulled his cell phone from his back pocket and sat opposite of me.

"I didn't."

"Really, Gwen?" He arched a brow at me.

"Alaric. Petersen, I think, spelt with an 'e' not an 'o.'"

"You think," he scoffed, typing it in. "Lucky for you, Alaric seems to be an uncommon name as far as Facebook profiles go. Is this him?" he held out his phone to me, open to a photo of Tattooed Thor himself.

"Yes, that's him," I said, my fingers itching to snatch Ren's phone from his hands and creep through his profile, but I promised myself I wouldn't resort to Facebook stalking.

"His profile is on lockdown." Ren frowned. "But you're right; he is very hot. Good job." He held up his hand, and I high fived him before I took another sip of the mojito. It slid down almost too easily.

"Right?" I giggled. "God, it's good to see you. Did you really come all the way here because I sounded off in my last message?" I couldn't even remember what the last thing I'd texted him was.

"Well...I wanted to see you, of course. But Nan's in the hospital."

"Oh no. What happened?" I exclaimed, feeling concerned about Ren's grandmother. She'd always been nice to me when we were in high school, and she made the best peanut butter cookies.

"Slipped and fell off her deck, broke her hip." He sighed, his brow furrowing with worry. "I just spent the day with her at the hospital. She insisted I leave her alone, so I'm giving her the evening free of my overzealous company."

"How kind of you," I said, bemused.

"I know. I'm very thoughtful." Ren grinned. "So what are we doing tonight?"

"We could go to the Watering Hole?" I suggested, a part of me hoping we'd run into Alaric there. Wishful thinking, I knew.

"Ugh, please." He rolled his eyes. "I'd rather stay home and pet your kitty cat."

"He's deadly," I warned, remembering how Dahmer had reacted to Alaric. It had been strangely adorable to watch him try and gently shake my asshole cat off his foot. Then watching him with the stray dog, well...that had been torture.

"Exactly," Ren deadpanned.

"I'm in the mood for carbs, anyway. You know how I get in times of stress," I said, my stomach grumbling. "Let's get pizza, then we'll come back and have more mojitos."

"Deal."

CHAPTER SIX

DOG GONE MAD

Alaric

I rushed home and showered quickly, changing at breakneck speed. When I came downstairs, the dog followed me to the front door, his tail wagging hopefully.

I had sent his pictures to local lost and found groups, but so far, nobody had stepped forward to claim him. I even took him to a local veterinary for an appointment. He didn't have a microchip, and the veterinary hadn't heard of anyone missing a one-year-old Newfoundland. Dr. Han gave him a clean bill of health after a set of boosters, heartworm medicine, and a topical medication for flea and ticks, and sent us on our way.

I was still looking for his family, but less actively. The idea of him hanging around was beginning to grow on me. He seemed to want to be wherever I was; it was unusual, if not comforting. I'd grown used to having him nearby.

"I'll be back soon, boy," I told him, scratching behind his ear before I slipped out the door, closing it behind me and locking up.

I gunned it down highway 28 to the 401. It took me twenty-five minutes to get to Cobourg. I pulled up to the curb outside of my ex-girlfriend's house, barely putting it in park before I jogged up the walkway, my eagerness to see Sawyer propelling me forward.

My knuckles rapped against the door, and it swung open a moment later. Cheryl stood in the doorway, her red hair hanging in a thick braid over her right shoulder, her green eyes boring into me with disdain. "You're late."

"By two minutes," I retorted, cocking a brow.

She rolled her eyes, turning her head. "Sawyer! Your dad's here!"

I heard my daughter's footsteps as she raced down the hall from the living room, her blonde hair up in two braids over her shoulders, her green eyes sparkling with excitement. "Daddy!" she squealed, jumping. I crouched, catching her in my arms and lifting her.

"Hey, baby," I said, hugging her. "How was your week?"

"Good!" Sawyer grinned, nuzzling into me.

"She's got dance rehearsal tomorrow morning at eight," Cheryl said, her lips thin. She held Sawyer's bag for me. I reached out, taking it from her.

"I know," I replied, setting Sawyer down so she could say her goodbyes.

"Her costume is in the bag. Please make sure you get it back to me in one piece," she added spitefully.

"I will. Have a good weekend. We'll see you on Sunday," I responded, keeping my tone amiable.

"Bye, Mommy! Bye Baby Sis!" Sawyer said, pressing a kiss to her mother's growing stomach. Cheryl smiled affectionately at her, and some of my internal irritation eased. She may be selfish and manipulative toward me, but she loved our daughter, and Sawyer was pretty stoked about getting a baby sister in four months.

I took Sawyer's hand in mine, and we walked down the driveway to the truck. Opening the rear passenger door, I helped her climb into her seat, listening while she chattered happily at me about school and dance. I buckled her in and walked around to the driver's side, stepping up into the cab.

"What do you feel like having for dinner?" I asked, turning around to look at her, my smile growing. For the first time in two weeks, I felt like I could breathe a little easier. I had my daughter back, and all was right.

"Pizza!" Sawyer exclaimed, her eyes widening with excitement. I nodded, recalling the pizzeria Gwen had suggested when she found out I was new to town.

I quickly looked up the number to the pizzeria and put in an order for pick up. Hanging up, I started the truck and shifted into gear, jumping onto the highway.

I parked against the curb outside of the pizza restaurant and walked around to help Sawyer out. She took my hand and peered up at me.

"Can we watch a movie when we get home?" she asked as I opened the pizzeria door with my free hand and held it for her.

"Sure, but first—" I said, ready to tell her about the dog. The words fell away when I looked up and saw a familiar red skirt and polka dot dress at the counter. Gwen turned her head, her eyes widening when they landed on me. She stood next to a tall guy with dark hair and brown eyes, and he touched her arm with familiarity.

Jealousy washed over me, but then I reminded myself that I had no business being jealous.

"Alaric, I see you've decided to hit up one of my recs," Gwen said, and her dark-haired friend swiveled to look at me.

He slurped from a can of Sprite through a straw, his eyes volleying back and forth from her to me.

"Yeah, I figured we'd try it out," I responded.

"We?" Gwen hadn't noticed Sawyer yet, but her friend had. He elbowed her discreetly at the same time I felt a tugging on the hem of my shirt.

"Daddy, can I get a pop?" she pleaded, looking up at me with hopeful eyes.

Gwen's gaze dropped to her, and her mouth opened with surprise. She blinked a few times, her eyes moving from Sawyer to me and back again. Clearing my throat, I looked down, smiling patiently at my daughter. "Sorry, kiddo. No pop."

"Chocolate milk then?" she bartered. Gwen smiled a little, her eyes catching mine, understanding dawning in her pewter irises.

"All right," I gave in. Satisfied, Sawyer let go of my shirt and climbed on the long wooden bench by the door. Finally, I turned to Gwen. The guy she was with was still watching us with interest.

"Oh, this is my friend, Renly. Renly this is Alaric," Gwen said quickly. I nodded, thrusting my hand out to shake his. My father used to say you could tell a lot about a man by how he shook hands. Renly's grip was feather light, and given the way he swooned at my touch, the jealousy I'd initially felt evaporated.

Renly wasn't a threat. Not that he should have been in the first place.

"I've heard *so* much about you," Renly remarked, earning a hard jab in the ribs from Gwen. She glared at him, and he grinned innocently.

"Nice to meet you," I managed, doing my best to ignore the discomfort I felt at this interaction.

Sawyer kicked her legs, regarding Gwen and Renly with green eyes. "Hi, I'm Sawyer," she said, her curious gaze landing on Gwen. "You're pretty. You look like the lady on Daddy's leg."

"Aww, thank you, that's really sweet. I think," Gwen looked at me quickly. "It's not a zombie tattoo, is it?"

"Pin-up girl," I clarified with a grin. Sawyer was referring to the tattoo of a pin-up girl holding a welding gun on the back of my left calf. She had dark hair and red lips. I'd gotten it years ago and hadn't drawn the same parallels as my quick-witted daughter. Of course, the damn thing was at the back of my leg, and I didn't often see it.

But now that Sawyer had mentioned it, I could see the resemblance. It was very befitting of Gwen, and ironic, in a sense.

"Oh, well, that's cool," she managed, biting her lip a little. She appeared to be uncomfortable too, or maybe she just didn't know what to say.

The whole situation had spiraled completely out of control. I hadn't told her about Sawyer because I only counted on one night, maybe a repeat or two if I ran into her at the bar again. But now that we worked together, seeing her was unavoidable, and repeats were completely off the table. Which was unfortunate, because Gwen looked incredible in that dress.

"Williams?" the server called, standing behind the counter with two white pizza boxes and a paper bag. Gwen stepped up to the till and paid. She glanced at me over her shoulder once, immediately turning to look at the cashier when she caught me looking at her.

I stood aside to let them pass with their takeout. Renly held the door open, and Gwen paused, looking at me with indecision. She opened her mouth to say something, thought the better of it, and smiled.

"Enjoy your pizza," she said politely—her voice an octave higher than usual—before she fluttered out the door.

"Can I help you?" the server asked, eyeing me with consideration.

"Yeah, I put in an order for pick up. Petersen."

"Oh, right, I've got that right here for you," she said, turning around to the metal warming shelves behind her. I'd ordered a cheese and pineapple pizza for Sawyer, who was the only kid I'd met who liked pineapple on her pizza, and meat lovers deluxe for myself.

"Can I get a chocolate milk, too?" Sawyer piped up, standing on her tip-toes to see over the counter.

"Of course," the server said warmly, opening the refrigerator and grabbing an individual carton.

"Thank you!" Sawyer grinned brightly as she reached for the chocolate milk.

"Let's not open it until we get home, all right?" I said, swiping my card through the reader. She nodded, eager to just hold it.

Gwen

"Holy shit, you didn't tell me he had a kid!" Renly said, scandalized.

"I didn't know," I replied, glancing back over my shoulder at the pizzeria and worrying my lip. If he had a kid, did he have a wife, too? He didn't wear rings, but that didn't mean anything these days.

"Wow, though," Renly sighed dreamily, reaching his car and looking at me over the top of it. "I don't have ovaries, but if I did, they'd implode. He's a fucking DILF, Gwen!"

"Tell me about it," I grumbled, crotchety. My libido was out of control and seeing Alaric tonight in dad mode definitely didn't help. It shouldn't have been so seductive to watch him be a father, and I felt incredibly betrayed by my lady bits.

My womb had screamed *put a baby in me* so loudly that I was surprised Alaric hadn't heard the damn thing. Of course, it didn't have a voice, so that probably helped, but still. Bad uterus, bad.

Not that there was a chance in *hell* I'd listen to it. I didn't feel like an adult myself yet and knew I wasn't anywhere near ready for a kid. The idea of having something else *that* dependent on me made me want to break out into hives.

"But kids," Renly pointed out, his nose wrinkling with disdain. "That can't be very fun."

"Definitely not," I said, looking up as the pizzeria door opened again. Alaric held it as his daughter twirled onto the sidewalk in front of him, and it was all I could do to not let out a ridiculous, dreamy sigh of my own. I was fully aware that I was reacting the exact same way I had when I saw him with Tig.

Watching in the side mirror as Alaric lifted his daughter into his massive truck, my treacherous ovaries melted like butter.

Ren put on his blinker, jarring me from my reverie. He pulled from his parking spot, heading to my apartment. It was only a ten-minute drive, and within minutes of landing on my couch, we were diving into the pizza like we'd gone months without food.

Since reaching his ideal body weight, Ren didn't usually let himself let loose like this, but even he couldn't deny a slice from the pizzeria. Every time he came home, we indulged. But Ren would make me pay for it when he woke me up to hit the gym in the morning.

He took a huge bite of pizza and chewed, staring at it

lovingly. "I will hate every part of working this off tomorrow, but damn it...it's soothing my soul."

"Tell me about it," I sighed before taking another bite. "You're a bad influence. I wasn't supposed to eat fast food again until after Kelsey's wedding."

"Dieting?"

"Poor." I laughed, sighing. "Turns out I sort of suck at managing my money. Or at least not blowing it on comfort food and impulse purchases in an attempt to make myself feel better."

"I'm sorry," Ren winced, setting down his slice.

"No, it's all good," I said to Ren. "I'm relieved I have an endless supply of cute outfits. They've been coming in handy lately."

"Dress to impress, that's what I always say," he nodded in agreement. "Seems to be working, too." His eyes twinkled.

"What are you talking about?" I laughed awkwardly.

"The man was practically undressing you with his eyes. It was hot." Renly pointed out.

I shrugged, although, inwardly, I was squealing and tap dancing with excitement, and so very thankful to not be imagining his attraction to me.

I knew the faces he made when he was taking pleasure in something. I knew what he looked like when he was coming. I'd seen the heat pool in his eyes, and I knew he still wanted me.

He was just...fighting it.

I cleared my throat. "Well, anyway. I've started writing again. This story is just flowing right from my fingertips." I shook my head, bewildered by it. I hadn't had creative bursts like this in years. "When it's done, I'm going to look into publishing it. You only live once, right?"

"Sounds like someone got a new outlook on life screwed

into them," he teased, giving me a goofy, crooked smile. He was happy for me, ecstatic even. Ren knew how much writing meant to me, and he knew that I put the pen down for months after Erik had stomped on my heart.

The night I met Alaric, I'd discovered something within the wreckage—a pulse. It was faint, but it was beating again. The numbness was gone, and I felt renewed. I poured my emotions into my manuscript, knowing that they could live there free and safe from the real world of disappointments and letdowns.

"Ha, but kind of…yes," I said excitedly. I bit my lip, thinking about the manuscript. Two lonely people getting together for a single night of passion that gives them more than they bargained for. Maybe parts of it were inspired by our night together—the feral passion and fervent intensity of the night were easy to translate into passion between my characters, but this novel was a safe manifestation of desires I wouldn't dare voice.

"I'm really happy to hear this," Ren said, squeezing my hand. "I worry about you."

"Well, you don't have to, not anymore. At least not when it comes to that." I waved my hand, mentally dismissing Erik from the narrative. "Fuck that tiny-dick asshole."

"Hear, hear!" Renly laughed, toasting me with his pizza slice.

Alaric

As we walked from the pizza shop and toward the truck, my thoughts shifted from the encounter with Gwen to what was waiting at home.

I placed the pizza on the front seat before buckling Sawyer in and walking around to climb into the driver's seat. I gave her a serious look through the rearview mirror before starting the truck. "You might notice something different about the house," I told her, still watching her reflection in the mirror.

"What?" Sawyer asked, gazing at me with curiosity.

"Well, earlier this week, I had an unexpected visitor drop by, and he's going to stay a little while," I said.

"Who?"

"A dog."

"A dog!" Sawyer repeated, her green eyes widening with excitement.

"Yep. A stray dog—a dog that lost his home. He came to me for help, so we're going to find his family," I told her, figuring honesty was the best policy.

"What's his name?"

"Tig." The name fell from my mouth before I could call it back, but I figured if the dog were sticking around, he'd need a name. If Sawyer got to name the dog herself, she could grow even more attached, and that'd make things harder for her if we found his family. Gwen's suggestion fit him, too.

"What a silly name." Sawyer giggled.

"Yeah." I smiled, loving the sound of her laughter, feeling grateful to be able to hear it again. I turned, the engine rumbling to life with a twist of my wrist.

I drove slowly through town, appreciating the historic buildings and old, hometown feel before picking up speed once I'd reached 28. We continued driving down the country road, the silence broken up every so often with Sawyer asking questions about the dog.

She was practically vibrating with excitement when I pulled into the driveway and parked in front of the garage. Once I unbuckled her, she jumped from the cab.

"Come on, Daddy!" she said impatiently while I grabbed her overnight bag and the pizzas. She skipped ahead of me, dancing on the balls of her feet while I unlocked the door.

The dog was sitting exactly where I'd left him, in the entrance to the hallway. He tilted his big, black head, his tail wagging against the hardwood floor.

"Woah! He's BIG!" Sawyer exclaimed, her eyes wide with uncertainty. She moved a little closer to my leg, intimidated by his size.

I set the pizzas down on the deacon bench and crouched, putting my hand on her tiny back. "Come here, Tig," I instructed. Tig tilted his head but stood, ambling over with gentle, slow steps. "Hold your hand out, Sawyer." I gently took her hand. Tig sniffed it, then licked her, his tail wagging the whole time.

She giggled. "It tickles!"

I let them get comfortable with each other for a few more minutes. When Sawyer was fearlessly accepting face kisses from him, I stood.

"Do you want to feed him?"

"Yes!" she shouted, clapping her hands together. Tig was unruffled by her exuberance, his gentle spirit shining.

Grabbing the pizzas from the bench, we headed into the kitchen, and I set the food down on the counter before walking into the mudroom. I picked up the scooper and showed Sawyer how to fill it with kibble from the massive bag I'd bought from the pet store.

She took over, pouring the kibble into the bowl, and again, Tig sat, gazing longingly between the food and me, waiting for permission. "Go on then," I said, nodding once. Tig stood and dug in, his tail wagged. "All right, your turn, kiddo. Let's go eat some pizza."

She skipped from the mudroom, an ecstatic grin on her face. "I like Tig, Daddy!"

"That's good." I smiled at her, removing two plates down from the cupboard. Opening the first box, I put two small slices of pineapple and cheese pizza on Sawyer's plate. I grabbed four slices from the other box and put two sticks of garlic bread on my plate and one on Sawyer's.

We shifted to the dining room table, the old oak set my mother insisted that I took when I moved into this house. It was a lot bigger than my last place, and Mom said she had no use for it anymore, as she'd be joining us during the holidays.

Guilt rose when I thought about my mom, as it often did, only this time I felt guilty for not calling her back. After the dog showed up, things got a little hectic, and it slipped my mind. "We should call Grandma after we finish eating. I know she misses you."

"Okay!" Sawyer nodded, taking a bite of her pizza.

Finished with his dinner, Tig meandered into the kitchen, his head turned toward us and his tail wagging. He curled up in front of the counter, a few feet away from the table. She watched him with fascination.

"Maybe after your dance class, we'll take Tig for a walk?" I suggested.

"Can we do that?" she asked, her eyes full of concern.

"Sure, why not?"

"He isn't ours," Sawyer said, her brows knitting together as she tried to work it out.

"I bet his family would appreciate it if we took care of him until they can again. That means feeding him and taking him for walks."

"Oh, all right." She nodded. We finished eating, and I rinsed our plates, putting them in the dishwasher while Sawyer laid on her stomach on the floor with Tig. She held my cell phone in her hands, the dial tone ringing through the speakers as she called her grandma.

"Hello?"

"Grandma! It's me!" Sawyer sang.

"My little Soy-bean! I miss you!"

"I miss you too! Guess what?"

"What?" Mom asked. It was evident how happy she was to hear her granddaughter's voice.

Cheryl claimed she wasn't comfortable keeping in touch with my mother following our breakup, so Mom went from seeing Sawyer almost every other day and being the first person we called when we needed a sitter, to getting even less time with her than I did.

It was heartbreaking, given how supportive she'd always been of both Cheryl and me.

"We got a dog!"

"Really?" Mom exclaimed, true surprise this time.

"Yep. Daddy says he's a straw."

"A stray," I corrected, giving her a bemused smile.

"Hello, Alaric," Mom said, hearing my voice.

"Hi, Mom," I said, walking around the counter.

"Grandma, say hi to Tig!" Sawyer said into the phone, not wanting him to feel left out. She held the phone near his ear.

"Hi Tig," Mom said, amused. "What kind of dog is it?"

"A Newfie," I replied. "Vet said he's just over a year old. He's very well behaved. Won't go for his food until I give him permission."

"Aren't those large dogs?"

"Massive," I chuckled. "I thought he was a bear cub when he wandered into the garage Monday night. Almost gave me a heart attack."

"So that's why I haven't heard from my darling son about his first week of work," Mom concluded, entertained.

"Grandma, can you come visit?" Sawyer interrupted.

"Unfortunately, I can't this weekend Soy-bean. But the next weekend you spend with your Daddy, I'll be there, okay?" Mom replied.

"Promise?"

"Promise. I can't wait to meet Tig. Give him a cuddle for me, okay?"

"Okay!" Sawyer said, abandoning the phone on the floor and wriggling closer to the dog. Tig was laying on his side, his tail wagging as she cuddled him. He lifted his head, licking her face gently. She giggled and buried her face into his fur.

I picked up my phone, taking my mom off speaker. "I'm sorry I didn't call you back. Things got a little crazy."

"I bet." Mom chuckled. "How was your first week at the new job?"

"Great," I responded, my thoughts automatically going to Gwen first, then the work I'd done. "My boss seems impressed. My co-workers are...all right." Again, I thought of her and inwardly cursed myself.

"Good," Mom said, sounding relieved. "About the next weekend you have with Sawyer—you wouldn't mind if I pop up for a visit, would you? It's been...well, four months since I saw her last."

"Of course, Mom. You're welcome any time," I told her, meaning it. We had space—it was why I'd gone for the house in the country with five bedrooms instead of the one downtown with two.

"Great. I don't want to take up any more of your evening, so give me a call later and enjoy your weekend,"

"Thanks, Mom. Love you."

"Love you, Grandma!" Sawyer called out, still snuggling with Tig.

"Love you, Soy-bean!" Mom said. "Talk to you later." She hung up, and I set my phone face down on the counter.

"How about that movie?" I asked, stretching. It'd be an early night with Sawyer's dance class in the morning, but we had time for a movie before bed.

CHAPTER SEVEN

AGAIN

Gwen

The smell of coffee woke me from the enticing dream I'd fallen into. Rubbing the sleep from my eyes, I sat and looked around, momentarily disoriented. It had been a long time—eight months, to be exact—since I'd woken up to the smell of coffee.

I reached for my glasses and stretched before I kicked off my blankets. Dahmer protested from the pillow beside me, resenting me for disturbing him. He'd claimed Erik's side of the bed as his, and I was content to let him have it.

"Morning beautiful!" Renly's sing-song voice called as I padded down the hall.

"Hmm," I grumbled, lifting my hand in greeting and disappearing into the bathroom. After peeing and splashing cold water on my face, I joined Ren on the couch. "What time is it?" I sank onto the couch gingerly.

"Seven o'clock," he answered, holding out the second mug, almost like some kind of peace offering.

I blinked at him, taking the mug into my hands. "You realize that I don't usually get out of bed until eleven on Saturdays, right? Especially not after a night of drinking mojitos." Remembering last night, I looked around the apartment. "Where'd Kelsey go?"

"Wow," Renly tittered, shaking his head with amusement. "She left before you crashed—don't you remember? She had Elliott pick her up because she missed him."

"Oh, right." I wrinkled my nose. Now I remembered. Kelsey had shown up about an hour after we got home with the pizza —miraculously, we managed to save her some.

Renly made another batch of mojitos, I put on some music, and the rest was kind of a blur. There was a lot of talking—I could remember bits and pieces of conversations and plenty of laughter, too.

At some point during the night, Kelsey decided she missed Elliott and drunk dialed him, begging him to join us. Only, Elliott wasn't totally into the whole mojitos and girl talk thing, so Kelsey had just ended up bailing. I didn't last much longer.

"Are you joining me at the gym this morning?" Ren asked, sipping his coffee with an air of innocence.

"You would have had better luck waiting until eleven to ask me that question," I replied, giving him a stony look over my mug.

"I've got to visit Nan before I head home," Renly said.

I winced, feeling bad for momentarily forgetting the real reason for my best friend's visit. "All right," I sighed, pausing to drain half my mug. "Let me get ready."

I couldn't afford a gym membership, which was fine by me. I had no use for one, as I only really went when Renly dragged me. I preferred marathon reading to running, and the sprinting I was into involved my laptop and a glass of wine.

In high school, Ren had been just as rigorous with his fitness goals. He'd been a little chubby throughout middle school, and he later made it his mission to get fit. He'd maintained his fitness-loving lifestyle in college and beyond, while I'd let my membership expire and was content to not haul ass to the gym every morning. Today, though, I'd make an exception, because that was what friends did.

We ended up driving to Cobourg to go to the gym chain Renly had a membership at. He signed me in as a guest, and we split up to use the locker rooms before meeting at the treadmills.

"You've got an evil soul, Ren," I sighed, pressing buttons on the treadmill to get it moving. I planned on going my own pace—blessedly slow. There was no way I'd be able to keep up with him—he spent an hour every single morning working out—but at least I was supportive.

I watched him increase the speed and incline on his treadmill, and I waited patiently for him to warm up. All it took for me to spill my guts was good pizza and a few mojitos, but Ren was more likely to talk while he worked out. It was as if he had to keep his body busy to discuss the inner workings of his mind.

His quirk always struck me as a little peculiar, but everyone was different. Kelsey was tight-lipped about her deeper feelings and emotions, but she'd sing like a canary when she was behind the wheel.

While I waited, I speed-walked, taking frequent sips of water to combat my dehydration. Hitting the gym this early on a regular day felt like torture to me but hitting the gym this early after a night of mojito drinking was *brutal*.

Ren didn't seem bothered in the slightest; he was full-on jogging and hadn't broken a sweat. Meanwhile, I'd started sweating the moment I walked up to the treadmill.

Nevertheless, I would endure, because judging by the heaviness in Ren's gaze, something was eating my friend.

"You know, you think you know someone, and they do something so out in left field that you're wondering what the fuck?" Ren randomly blurted, the corner of his lips pulled down in a frown.

"Care to fill me in?" I huffed, already out of breath from my limited efforts. Maybe I should consider reinstating my membership—I was completely out of shape, and I didn't think I could blame last night's mojitos for it. Perhaps the eight months of shitty food and minimal activity were the cause.

Renly sighed heavily. "Just drama with Brian," he replied, increasing the speed on his treadmill again. Not to be outdone, I turned mine up by two notches.

"What did he do?"

Brian was Renly's boyfriend, and the reason he stayed in Oakville, landing his fantastic job.

"He keeps dropping the *M* bomb." Ren turned his head to look at me, his brown eyes wide and a little fearful.

"So? What's wrong with marriage?"

"Everything's wrong with it," he retorted, shaking his head. "The whole institution is flawed. Not to mention, I don't want things to change. When we got together, Brian was on the same page as me—marriage and kids weren't even a thought in his pretty little head. Now, he can't stop talking about weddings *and* babies."

He shivered as if Brian longed for a murder spree not a domesticated life with him.

"Oh, gee, how terrible. You've got someone who wants to spend the rest of their life with you and raise children. How horrendous," I responded dryly, arching my brow to show him I was only teasing.

"I don't want kids." Ren frowned. "And I don't need a piece of paper to prove I'm in love with someone."

"But if Brian does?" I pointed out gently, sending him a beseeching gaze. "And if you really *are* unmovable on both those things, you should talk to him. He deserves to know."

"Ugh, I know. You're totally right. I just…I don't know what to say to him."

"The truth." I shrugged. My thoughts unwillingly went to Erik. I'd planned our entire life together before I even realized he didn't want any of the same things I did—or at least, he didn't want them with me. That had been quite the punch to the heart and the pride.

In hindsight, I was beginning to realize he had done me a favour, but it didn't make the prospect of starting over with someone new any less intimidating.

"What if the truth breaks us up?" Renly voiced, looking at me with uncertainty.

"Brian is awesome and so are you, but ultimately, you guys are at a fork in the road, and you may end up having to take different paths. It sucks, but…what else can you do?"

"How'd you get to be so smart?" He shook his head, hiding a proud little smile, although his irises were tinged with sadness.

"I got dumped?" I shrugged, pausing the treadmill to guzzle more water. I was sweating profusely, but we'd only been there for twenty minutes. Not that I was watching the clock.

Ren stopped his machine too. He lifted his water bottle and drank from it, watching me with a peculiar look on his face. "I like this new you." He stepped off the treadmill, and I followed him over to the weights, frowning a little.

"What was wrong with the old me?"

"Nothing was wrong with the old you." Renly arched a brow. "Except that tumour you had for a while."

"What tumour?" Ren gave me a pointed look. "Oh, right. Him. Yeah, many ways, things are better without him. I just kind of miss having someone around. Waking up to coffee was pretty mint."

"Well, keep your eyes on the prize, and remember: squats are your best friend," he responded, winking at me as he tossed a large exercise ball in my direction.

"What are you trying to say?" I asked, narrowing my eyes at him.

Ren let out a huff, halfway between a sigh of exasperation and a laugh. "You have a great ass, Gwen. But pizza will make it doughy, so do squats."

"I just ran on the treadmill."

"You were speed walking at best." He laughed. "Besides, you don't need to focus on cardio so much. If you do, you'll risk losing that great ass. Squats will just build it up."

"I don't think it needs any more building up," I muttered, sullenly heading to the mirror with the exercise ball.

Alaric

I held open the door, and Sawyer twirled around on her tiptoes, spinning into the foyer. We walked up the stairs to the dance studio, her little voice chattering happily about all the things I'd missed out on since the last weekend we spent together.

The room was packed with miniature ballerinas and their parents, mostly mothers, although I spotted a handful of men.

All eyes went to us as we walked in, and I was aware of the scrutiny of some of the other parents.

I didn't exactly fit the dance parent mold.

"Hi, Miss Claire!" Sawyer said, coming to a stop in front of her dance instructor, a young woman in her late twenties. I'd met her a few times before in passing, after the few dance recitals I'd managed to find out about in time to catch.

"I believe we met after the Christmas recital? Nice to see you again," she said, smiling warmly at me before her gaze dropped to Sawyer. She appraised my daughter's hair and raised her eyebrows, impressed at the tight ballerina bun I'd wrangled her long locks into ten minutes before leaving the house earlier that morning.

A lot of women instantly doubted a man's ability to dress his children and do hair. I'd never wanted to be the kind of father that added to that stereotype, so I didn't shy away from learning how to do those things. If I could weld at great heights, there was no reason why I couldn't put my own daughter's hair into a ballerina bun for her dance class.

But I had no doubt Cheryl had probably warned Claire that she'd need to fix whatever disaster of a hairstyle I attempted. Hopefully, it'd get back to Cheryl, and maybe one day she'd even lay off naysaying my abilities.

Claire smiled warmly at Sawyer. "Why don't you go line up with the other students?" she suggested, tilting her head toward the classroom.

"Okay! See you soon, Daddy!" Little arms wrapped around my leg, and she was off—joining her friends as they filed into the studio.

"Classes are an hour long. Parents can feel free to leave and come back at the end of the class, or they can hang out in the waiting room." Claire said, gesturing to the seats arranged in the waiting room. "There's a little café down the street that serves good coffee."

Chairs were filling quickly, so I grabbed one against the far wall facing the classroom door. I pulled out my cell phone, intent on keeping my head low. Technically, this was still Cheryl's territory—and it felt like it, with the way a lot of the other parents were looking at me.

No doubt she'd filled them in on her version of events. That was just the kind of person Cheryl was; she always had to come out as the saint, the innocent party, while I was always the bad guy.

"Are you Sawyer's dad?" the woman sitting in the row of plastic chairs across from me asked, staring me up and down. She had blonde hair chopped in a bob, and deep brown eyes that assessed me keenly.

"Yeah," I responded, working to keep my tone polite and friendly. Cheryl would have a field day if the other dance parents' complained about my attitude.

"Oh, that's lovely. I see where she gets her gorgeous blonde locks from." The woman giggled flirtatiously. She moved to the seat beside me and thrust her hand at me. "I'm Gabriella's mom, Cindy. Sawyer's a head taller than my Gabby, and she's in the 95 percentile!"

"Nice to meet you," I managed, shaking her hand. Cindy's thin lips stretched into a big smile.

"Sawyer's mentioned more than a few times that you moved closer. I think Cheryl said you were from Ottawa?"

"Yeah, Ottawa," I answered stiffly, uncomfortable with this complete stranger knowing facts about me.

"How are you liking Northumberland County?" Cindy inquired.

"It's nice," I said, hoping she'd pick up on my two-worded

replies and drop the interrogation. But she didn't get the hint, and for the next hour, Gabriella's mom talked at me. Not really to me, but at me, telling me about her daughter Gabby's progress with dance and any other thought that fluttered through her head.

Aside from the occasional nod of agreement or hum, Cindy didn't require me to add much more to the conversation. Which was fine by me.

Eyeing the clock, I let out a sigh of relief and stood when the hour was up, and the doors to the dance room opened.

Miss Claire stood in the doorway, watching while the students filtered out. I made a move to walk away, but Cindy's fingers gripped my bicep lightly. Pausing, I turned to look at her, trying to conceal my irritation.

"We should get the girls together for a playdate some time," she suggested hopefully, her fingers loosening and her hand dropping to toy with her hair.

I let out a tempered sigh, trying to figure out the best way to shut Cindy's hope down without coming across as a dick. "Cheryl's in charge of playdates. Unfortunately, I only get Sawyer every other weekend, so our time is…"

"Short," Cindy finished, smiling with understanding. "I totally get it. I'm a single parent, too. We could always get together during your kid-free time," she added.

"I don't think my girlfriend would like that," I said, lying through my teeth. I didn't have a girlfriend, but I had zero interest in Cindy, and I wanted to stop that thought in its tracks before she got the wrong idea.

"Oh, I hadn't realized you were seeing anybody," she said, her eyes widening with surprise. "Cheryl never mentioned… well, nevermind." Cindy's cheeks flushed, and she dipped out pretty quick after that.

Opening the front door, Sawyer bolted in, going straight for Tig, who was standing in the hallway, his tail wagging like a propeller as she flew at him and buried her face into his furry side.

"Hi, Tig!" Sawyer said, nuzzling into him.

"Go get changed, and we'll head out for that walk," I told her, smiling with warmth at the sight.

"Okay!" she practically shouted, taking off down the hall and up the stairs. She'd always been a pretty self-sufficient kid and had learned at a young age how to get dressed on her own.

Ten minutes later, I heard her running for the stairs. "Take it easy. Use the railing!" I called up, waiting for her in the mudroom.

I helped her into her pink spring jacket, and we walked out onto the back deck, Sawyer and Tig racing ahead of me. "Daddy, can we make a garden?" Sawyer asked, looking over her shoulder when she'd reached the overgrown garden beds.

"We could give it a try." I shrugged, smiling a little.

"Now?" she asked, her eyes sparkling.

"We don't have any plants or gardening supplies, so we'll have to get some." I chuckled. "But we could make it our next weekend project."

"Okay," Sawyer sighed, longingly looking at the garden beds before we continued walking through the grassy fields behind the house.

Tig kept pace with Sawyer, never letting her venture too far from his sight. We stayed out there, exploring the woods for a good two hours before we headed inside for lunch.

"Hi, Mommy! Guess what? Daddy got a dog!" Sawyer said, her words coming out in an excited rush as she raced up the sidewalk and threw her arms around her mother's legs. Cheryl's chin lifted, her brow furrowing as she looked at me.

"You got a dog?" she asked, her tone annoyed. "Without talking to me first?"

"I don't see why I have to ask your permission to get a dog," I retorted, on the defence. I could have pointed out all of the times she hadn't bothered to give me a heads up before making a life-altering change, like leaving me and then moving in with her boyfriend, but I didn't. I choked those thoughts back, trying to release the frustration I felt.

Sawyer didn't need to witness it.

"Its dander better not be on her clothes. You know I'm allergic."

"Oh, come on, Cheryl," I grumbled, shaking my head. "Do you police your friends who have dogs, too?"

Her eyes became dangerous slits. "Say goodbye to your father, Sawyer. You'll see him in two weeks."

"Bye, Daddy!" Sawyer said, looking up at me with wide eyes that were a little sad and apologetic. She likely felt responsible for getting me into trouble with Cheryl, even though she wasn't. Her mother would have found some other reason to be mad at me.

"Bye, munchkin," I told her, crouching with my arms open. She ran into them and hugged me tightly. Pressing a kiss against her temple, I wished things could be different.

Better, somehow.

"I love you!" Sawyer said, kissing the apple of my cheek.

"I love you too. I'll see you soon, okay?" I said, and she nodded. Sawyer took off running up the steps, disappearing through the front door of her mother's house. Cheryl went to follow her in. "Cheryl, wait."

She turned, placing her hand on her growing belly. She was about five months pregnant now and due sometime in September. "What?" she demanded.

"I was wondering what your plan is when the baby comes."

"It's none of your concern." She folded her arms across her chest.

I sighed. I'd expected her to be standoffish about it, but it didn't make it any less frustrating. "If you need help with Sawyer, I'm here. I can pick her up from school, take her to dance lessons, whatever you need. I'm only thirty minutes away now."

"Mason's mom is coming to stay with us. We'll be fine," Cheryl replied, tilting her chin up, her red hair catching in the setting sun.

"But I live one town over, and I don't mind taking her more to help while you recover from the delivery."

"I don't need help with Sawyer," Cheryl snapped. "I need you to back off."

I brought my hands up to my face like I was praying, and covered my nose, my eyes never leaving her face. "All I want is more time with Sawyer, and I thought I could help you out in the process. I didn't move here to intrude on your new perfect life with Mason, I just want to be closer to our daughter. Can you at least think about it?"

She shook her head back and forth like she wanted to tell me no again. I needed to walk away before we got into another argument. If I could keep my cool, I might be able to convince Cheryl to change her mind, but I knew if I lost my temper it would never happen.

As much as I hated it, I had to play by her rules—even if they sucked.

"Fine, I'll think about it." She relented, whirling around and stomping up to her door.

I walked away, my gaze focused on my truck, my heart pounding with adrenaline and frustration. I sat in the cab for a moment, my fingers gripping my key tight, and peered up at the house.

I could see movement in one of the upstairs rooms, a curtain moving away from the window and a small face peering out. I waved, smiling although it pained me, and she waved back.

Sawyer watched as I drove away for another eleven days.

CHAPTER EIGHT

LEAVE HIM WANTING

Gwen

On Monday morning, Dad walked into the office with Alaric through the shop doors. I was sitting at my desk, working a quote for a client.

Hearing the sound of the heavy door clicking shut, I glanced up, blinking once to make sure I wasn't daydreaming again. I drew in a composing breath as they approached.

Dad stopped before my desk, his fingers tapping against it distractedly. "I need you to photocopy Alaric's welding tickets. He needs clearance to go on a job site."

"You're sending him out into the field?" I asked, surprised. It was only Alaric's second week on the job. Usually, it took new employees months to earn Dad's trust, if they ever did. They'd have to do shop bitch tasks—sweeping, cleaning up, painting, things like that—before he'd let them go to job sites.

"Yes, he'll be with Mitch."

"All right," I said. Mitch Whitfield had worked for Williams

Tech for fifteen years as the onsite foreman. He was one of my dad's most trusted employees.

"Great, I'll leave you to it." Dad nodded, turning and heading back out to the shop. The heavy metal door fell shut behind him, and the room instantly felt void of oxygen.

"You seemed surprised, should I be worried?" Alaric joked, reaching into his back pocket. I tried not to watch the tendons in his forearms working as he pulled out his wallet, but it was fruitless. I was hypnotized by him.

Clearing my throat, I raised my eyes to look at him, my lips tugging up in a slight smile. "I guess I am, a little. We've had a few incidents in the past with employees not representing the company to my dad's liking, so he's really picky about who he chooses to send to job sites. It usually takes people *months* to earn his trust."

"I get it. I was a little surprised too." Alaric chuckled lightly. He opened his wallet and removed a stack of cards—his welding tickets and certifications for all of the job safety courses, and held them out to me.

I reached out to take them, the tips of my fingers brushing against his calloused palm, and tried to hide the effect he had on me; the way touching him so briefly had sent me straight back to the night we spent together. Memories of his calloused hands on my skin taunted me, and I knew my cheeks were heating up—along with some of my other parts.

I wanted more than anything to feel those hands on my body again.

Turning, I walked toward the photocopier. I scanned each card, conscious of his heavy gaze on me. I licked my lips, stealing a glance at him over my shoulder.

Alaric's eyes smoldered as he looked at me. He lingered on my bare legs and the pleated floral skirt I wore. It made me want to press my thighs together, to try and contain the ache.

I shouldn't want him. There was a lot about him I didn't know. Like what his relationship with his daughter's mother was. Maybe he was an adulterous dickhead, but still—my body craved him, and a part of me knew that wasn't true. It couldn't be.

Looking into his blue eyes, all I could see was his desire for me. Contained, but burning beneath the surface. It was...all-consuming. I'd never had someone look at me that way before, and it thrilled me while simultaneously terrifying me.

Clearing my throat, I tucked a strand of hair behind my ear. "How's Tig?" I asked, deciding to go casual instead of asking the questions that blistered on the tip of my tongue.

"Great. He really took to Sawyer," he replied, shaking his head as he leaned against my desk. He folded his muscular arms across his chest. "Slept against her door the first night, then beside her bed the second. If I'd have let him, he'd probably have slept in her bed with her. He wasn't happy last night."

"Why not?" I tilted my head, pressing the copy button. Although we were separated by two desks and ten feet, Alaric's presence smashed into me like a monsoon. Every molecule between us was charged.

"Sawyer went back to her mother's. Guess the dog missed her." Alaric responded.

I wanted to grin, pleased that I hadn't had to dig the answer out of him at all. He'd been honest, and I think it threw him off guard. He shifted, seeming a little uncomfortable with his admission.

He wasn't with his daughter's mother, and Alaric's statement about how he wasn't in a good place for a relationship made complete sense. He was just as bruised by love as I was, if not more. No wonder he hesitated.

Instead, I dialed it back a lot, giving him a slight smile.

"Sounds like someone's wagging his tail into your heart," I teased, my blood thrumming in response to the way he looked at me.

"Maybe," he responded, his gaze still fixated on me. I went back to my task, concentrating on keeping my hands from shaking.

I wanted to ask him more questions, peek inside him a little, but I bit them back, knowing they were far outside the scope of casual.

"So," I said, returning his cards to him once I'd finished scanning and photocopying them. "How was it?"

"How was what?" he asked, his deep-rooted gaze still on my lips.

"The pizza? From the pizzeria?" I clarified, giving him a tiny half smile.

"Oh, yeah. It was good," Alaric replied, his concentration on my lips never wavering. I burned beneath their intensity in the most euphoric of ways. It was baffling and enslaving.

"Just good?" I asked weakly, my thighs trembling through the suspended moment.

He leaned forward, just a little. "It was the best pizza I've ever eaten," he clarified, his blue eyes—which I'd just realized had flecks of green within them—were locked on my face, and the innuendo wasn't lost on me.

"Oh," I breathed. Alaric was looking at me like he wanted to claim me. I'd seen that look before—several times during the night we spent together, but to my great disappointment... nothing happened. He remained three feet away; close enough to reach out and touch but far enough away that it couldn't be mistaken as an accidental brush.

His lips twitched; he was fighting the sexual tension snapping between us, too. The realization made me giddy. "Mitch is probably waiting for me."

"Yeah, probably. Good luck on the job site!" I said, backing away from him.

Alaric held my gaze for one lingering moment before leaving the office, and I sank heavily into my computer chair, my breathing labored.

I was worse than a schoolgirl with a crush. I got tongue-tied whenever he was around, and I didn't know how to act or what to say around him.

He looked at me like he wanted to devour me, but he kept his distance. He had great restraint, better than me. If it were up to me, I'd have jumped his bones a hundred times by now.

But I was trying to play it cool, not frighten him off with my exuberance. I wanted to prove to him we could keep it casual, and I couldn't do that if I appeared too over-eager.

Even though I *was* eager. Very eager.

He was enticing, and I wanted to get to know him more. I wouldn't let myself go as far as to think of a relationship—I knew he was battered, just as I was, and I wasn't entirely sure *I* wanted that.

I did, however, want to have mind-blowing sex on the regular, and I'd prefer to have it with him. I felt utterly and completely safe with him, and he turned me on more than anyone ever had before. I wanted more of that feeling because it fueled me.

If he was into the idea, it could work; we could totally be casual hook-up friends.

It was better than the other option, which was living with a constant lady boner, cursed to constantly have to look at the holy grail of penises and never have it again. I shivered, distraught at the possibility.

The metal door swung open, and I sat up straighter in my seat, hoping to catch another glimpse of Alaric. My shoulders dropped a fraction, but I smiled cordially at my dad. "Forget something?"

"Yes, your mother asked me to relay a message to you," Dad scratched at his chin. "She wants you to come over for dinner tomorrow night."

"Why didn't she just call me?" I frowned, resisting the urge to roll my eyes. We were at work, after all.

"She says you never call her back," Dad replied with the corner of his lip curling up. "Dinner's at six."

"All right," I sighed. I'd actually managed to avoid dinners at my parents' house for three weeks, which was pretty impressive, but if I held out any longer, Mom would show up at my place or worse—here.

"Excellent," Dad said, turning to head back to the shop. "Oh, coordinate a meeting with George for Thursday morning, would you?"

"On it," I replied with a nod, my gaze returning to my computer screen.

Alaric

I hadn't wanted to leave that office, hadn't wanted to stop talking to her or looking at her. But there was work to be done, and I didn't want to keep Mitch waiting. I'd left, with the mountainous pile of words still sitting heavily on my tongue.

Although Mitch had seemed friendly enough when I met him earlier that morning, after hearing from Gwen how rare it was to score a position on the installation team so early on into my employment here, the pressure had doubled.

Mitch was already waiting in the work truck when I stepped outside. He seemed like a jovial guy in his mid-fifties with salt and pepper hair and a beard trimmed close to his face. His dark shred eyes seemed to miss nothing, and I'd heard whispers from other guys in the shop that he was a lot like Russell—kind of tough to impress.

We were all set to go work on a church restoration in the city, the truck loaded with supplies.

When I ran my own shop, we did a few projects for other trades companies, but nothing like what I'd be handling today, although I had my working at heights certificate.

I'd have to climb rafters and be tied off, and my stomach was tight with nerves. I didn't like heights, never had, but I'd deal. I'd get the job done, and I'd do it right.

Two men were sitting in the back, and when I climbed in, Mitch handled the introductions.

"Guys, this is Alaric Petersen. Alaric, that's Rob—" he said, pointing his thumb over his shoulder, at the red-headed guy behind him, "and that's Brandon," he nodded at the second guy.

"Hey, man," the guy behind Mitch, Rob, nodded in greeting.

"Sup?" Brandon asked, barely looking up from his phone.

"Don't let these two knuckleheads fool you, they're actually hard workers," Mitch gibed, a friendly grin on his weathered face.

"Thanks, mini-boss, that's a compliment coming from you," Rob retorted, and Mitch laughed deeply before he put the truck in gear.

"So, how do you like Williams' Tech?" Mitch asked as we left the shop parking lot.

"I'm enjoying it," I replied, meaning it. There was something new to do every day, and it was always challenging—engaging.

"What do you think of Gwen?" Rob interjected, looking between Mitch and me with a glint in his eyes. Mitch remained focused on the road, turning onto the westbound onramp.

"Seems nice." I shrugged, keeping my tone apathetic.

Disengaged.

"She's hot, huh?" Brandon added, smirking a little. I said nothing. I was busy trying to keep my hands from curling into fists.

I didn't like shop talk—didn't like participating in it or overhearing it, but when it was centered around Gwen—well, it made me want to punch the little punks straight in the teeth. She didn't deserve to be spoken about like she was some prized filly at the county fair.

"Have some respect. Gwen's a nice girl," Mitch scolded, giving Brandon and Rob a hard look through the rearview mirror.

"Oh, I'll respect her. I'll respect her *good*." Rob smirked, sitting back in his seat.

"You're too much of a chicken shit to respect her good," Brandon tossed back, laughing.

The anger and flash of possessiveness that rolled around in my stomach were unnerving, and I bit down on my tongue to prevent from imploding. But never had I wanted to deck somebody so much before.

We pulled up to the shop around six o'clock. I didn't have to look to know that Gwen was long gone, and I tried to ignore the disappointment that settled when I realized I wouldn't get to see her.

Thankfully, Gwen's name hadn't come up again that day, and I fervently hoped it wouldn't be a regular thing, or I'd have a hell of a time biting my tongue. It was boorish behaviour, and it enraged me.

It also forced me to admit that she had taken up space in my head, and it was frustrating. I did my best to tamp down thoughts of her, but it wasn't easy.

I felt possessive over her. I'd had her, she'd been mine for a night. I knew I could have her again—knew it like I knew how to create the perfect bead weld.

Mitch drove around and backed the truck into a parking space near the rear of the shop. The massive garage doors that essentially made up the rear wall were opened still, and I could see a couple of employees finishing up welding on a huge metal beam that nearly took up the entire length of the shop.

We started unloading materials, and as we were doing that, Russell came out through the massive garage doors.

"How'd it go?" he asked, coming to a pause near the tailgate of the truck. He eyed Mitch and then me, waiting for someone to fill him in.

"Went great, we're now on track to finish by Thursday," Mitch answered, slamming the tailgate shut. "Especially if you keep sending Alaric out with us; the guy's a beast. We'll probably finish the job twice as quick with him around." He chuckled, looking at me and giving me a solid nod of approval.

Russell smiled. "That's what I like to hear," he said, clapping me on the back. "Not that I'm surprised."

"Thank you, sir," I said, relieved.

"Well, I'm going to go tell the boys to wrap it up," Russell said decidedly, nodding once before he turned and headed back to the shop.

I rolled my head, trying to work the kinks from my neck. I was exhausted—my muscles were still burning from the day's exertion. Climbing the beams had been sketchy at best and terrifying at worst. But the church itself had been a thing of marvel.

Mitch had been great to work with, and when Rob and

Brandon did their job, they weren't that bad. Tolerable, even. They all knew what they were doing, which made my job a little easier.

Mitch paused before following, looking at the three of us still lingering by the tailgate. "Be here bright and early tomorrow, fellows. Five thirty on the dot."

We all nodded—message received—and watched as Mitch followed Russell into the shop.

"See you tomorrow." I nodded to Rob and Brandon, grabbing my helmet and lunch bag before walking across the parking lot to my truck. I climbed in, bone tired and weary. I made the drive home on autopilot, turning on my road like it was second nature.

Gwen

At six on Tuesday night, I knocked on my parent's front door. The intended goal was to pacify my mother, get a free and delicious meal, and slink out—preferably before anybody could grill me about my love life, or lack thereof.

The freshly painted dark navy door swung open. Mom's arms wrapped around me in a big hug, and I felt a little homesick. Although she drove me nuts ninety percent of the time, she gave the best hugs. I knew she meant well and loved me.

"Hi, Mom," I said, my voice muffled by her shoulder. She stepped away, eyeing me keenly.

"You look—nice," she said, a secretive smile gracing her painted lips as she took me in. "Come on in, everyone's just sat down to eat. You're right on time."

That had been intentional, and Mom gave me a look that suggested she knew it. I smiled apologetically. "Sorry. Dahmer managed to escape, and I had to chase him around," I said. It was partially true. He'd tried to escape, and I did have to chase him, but I caught him pretty quick.

The rest of the time, I'd dawdled. It was kind of challenging being around Kelsey and our parents at the same time. She seemed able to handle adulthood a lot better than me, and I always felt that difference more when we were all together.

My *singleness* stuck out like a sore thumb.

Kelsey sat across the table beside Mom's chair, with Elliott to her right beside dad. I took my place in one of the vacant chairs, trying not to look at the empty one beside it.

I couldn't understand why my mother wouldn't just remove the bloody chair. It wasn't like someone was randomly going to occupy it without me giving her a heads up, anyway, and frankly, the sight of it made me feel morose.

That empty chair was the perfect metaphor for my life.

In an immature act of defiance, I pulled the empty chair to the corner of the dining room before I moved my chair to the middle, ignoring Mom's lifted eyebrows and the smile Kelsey tried to hide.

"So, Gwen, how's work?" Mom asked as I settled into my chair and moved my placemat over.

She passed me the mashed potatoes, and I kept my eyes on the bowl as I scooped some onto my plate. "Work's good." I shrugged, passing the potatoes along in time to reach for the dish of green beans. I took some before giving that to my dad.

"We've got a new welder who really knows what he's doing," Dad commented. I froze for a fraction of a minute before reaching into the basket in front of me for a dinner roll.

Kelsey caught my eye, her lips curling in an enigmatic smile. My eyes narrowed at her in warning, and she lifted a brow. I knew she wasn't about to blab my dirty secret in front of our parents, but I didn't want her dangling it, either. Mom was just as sly as Kels was. My sister and my mother were cut from the same cloth, while I was more aloof.

The black sheep, because my father certainly wasn't aloof. He was commanding and intimidating at times, with a soft underbelly—for us, anyway.

"What do you think, Gwen?" Dad added, glancing at me pragmatically before taking a bite of grilled chicken. Uncomfortable, I shifted in my seat, pushing my glasses up on my nose.

"He seems to come highly recommended," I said, my tone a smidgen too high. I cleared my throat, holding up my finger as I guzzled back a long sip of water. My eyes landed on Kelsey while I drank, and she mouthed *'very'* at me with a bemused smirk. I wrinkled my nose at her, turning my attention back to Dad. "Mitch said he was impressed."

"Yup," Dad nodded, a satisfied smile on his face, his eyes distant. "He was a smart hire, for sure. He used to own a shop just outside of Ottawa."

"Dad." I frowned, shaking my head slightly. "Employee confidentiality," I added pointedly. Although my heart raced with unease, I drank up this new bit of information greedily.

I didn't want Alaric to be a conversational topic tonight. I needed to nix it before I gave myself away. Unlike Kelsey, I was not very good at concealing my emotions.

"Right." He winked at me, likely pleased that I was finally displaying some kind of workplace morals. I'd taken my job a little more seriously lately because now I had a reason to look forward to going in every day.

"Well, that's good," Mom said, her eyes going from me to Kelsey and to Dad again. She sensed something was up.

Kelsey caught on too, and she cleared her throat. "So, Mom, about Sunday…"

"Oh yes, dress shopping!" Mom smiled, her eyes

brightening as she focused her attention completely on my sister. I sagged with relief, and Elliott grinned with amusement at me.

"I'll pick you and Gwen up around eight thirty. Janice is going to meet us in Toronto, and before lunch, we'll hit up a few of the bridal stores I picked out."

"That sounds perfect." Mom nodded, her smile growing.

"I also figured we could drive to the venue and check it out. Gwen hasn't seen it yet."

"I'd love to see it again." Mom replied earnestly. She was completely in her element. I'm pretty sure she was more excited about the wedding than even Kelsey was. I knew she'd been waiting for this day since the first moment she held Kelsey in her arms. For me too, which is why she usually put pressure on me about my dating life. Mom wanted me paired off with someone, living a life of domestic bliss.

Conversation faltered for a moment while we all dived into our dinner. Everything melted on my tongue, the way only a home cooked meal made by my mom could. I closed my eyes, savouring the flavours for a moment before her voice had me crashing back to reality.

"So, Gwen. Have you decided who you'll be bringing to the wedding?"

"Renly." I shrugged, shovelling a bite of potatoes in my mouth.

Mom pursed her lips. "Don't you want a date you can actually, you know, connect with?"

"I connect just fine with Renly," I pointed out, knowing what she was referring to, but pretending to be obtuse.

"She means a more romantic selection," Kelsey supplied helpfully, her eyes twinkling with mischief. Even though we were well into our twenties, Kelsey still loved to torture me.

"Hmm, yeah...no." I took a cue from her and pursed

my lips.

Mom opened her mouth, about to say something that would nettle me, likely, but Kelsey cut her off. "Mom, there's going to be plenty of single guys at the wedding," she reminded her.

"You know, I'm perfectly content with *not* being set up," I said lifting my hands up, palms out in surrender. "This isn't the middle ages, anymore. Women don't *need* to be in committed relationships in their early twenties."

"But don't you want to, sweetie?" Mom asked, her voice kind and her words washing over me like a bucket of ice-cold water. "I just hate to think of you in that apartment all alone, that's all."

"Right, well." I looked up at the ceiling, letting a heavy sigh escape my lips as I shook my head slowly. "I'm not alone. I have Dahmer *and* friends, you know."

Mom's frown lines deepened. She hated the name I'd given my cat. She felt it was in poor taste, while I thought it was ironic.

"All I'm saying is you don't have to keep the lease, Gwen. You should come home, save your money."

"I appreciate the offer, but I'm okay. I like living alone, I like my privacy, and I like my cat—which I wouldn't be able to keep if I came home."

Mom sighed deeply, the corners of her eyes creased with exasperation.

"Marlene," Dad interjected, giving her a look that warned her to quit it. I smiled gratefully, and he nodded, his eyes twinkling before he returned to his dinner.

Somehow, I made it to Friday without spontaneously combusting. It helped that I didn't see Alaric for the rest of the week—he was busy installing products on site for the first part of the week, and Friday my dad had him cutting and assembling a platform in the shop.

For the past four days, I tried to wait as long as I could, hoping I would catch a glimpse of him—or rather, have *him* catch a glimpse of me. I was still going all out with my appearance. I was, as Kelsey put it, peacocking.

I wanted him to notice me. I wanted it to be hard for him to forget about the night we had, and I wanted him to crawl on his knees, pleading for a repeat.

Which is why I was forcing Kelsey to talk to me on the phone while I discreetly dawdled, waiting for Alaric to come by for his check. "Tell me again why I'm doing this?"

"Because you love me, and it's your fault. If it weren't for you, I wouldn't have had such incredible sex, and I wouldn't be fixing for a repeat like some kind of sex junkie."

"Please stop saying that word to me," Kelsey said dryly. "So what's the plan if he *doesn't* come for his check?"

"He will," I said confidently, my gaze landing on the clock on the wall. Ten to five. Two minutes later, the door to the shop swung open. "Okay, yeah. Nine o'clock at the Watering Hole. I'll see you there."

Alaric's gaze never wavered, and I knew he heard me. Dropping my phone into my purse, I smiled brightly at him. "Oh, hey!"

"Hey," he nodded, flipping through the stack of envelopes, his eyes returning to mine every so often. Like he was waiting.

I knew he'd asked for a rain cheque, but I hadn't wanted to bring it up again. It felt desperate, and I wanted to play a little hard to get—even if though I melted into a pool of wanton need whenever he looked at me.

Grabbing my red handbag, I turned off my computer, leaning forward a little more than necessary. I was trying to play up my assets, and my ass was one of them. I stood, adjusting the hem of my round-collared sheath dress before turning. It was a fun short sleeve dress, and the black, ivory and plaid pattern complimented my curves and my complexion.

I was totally peacocking and unashamed to admit it.

I passed by Alaric, locking the door to the shop. I didn't need to look over my shoulder to know that he was tracking my movements with hungry eyes. I waited for him to say something, but he remained silent. Brooding.

Walking by him again, I met his gaze head-on. I smiled, just a little curve of my lips, and watched his pupils dilate. I lingered by the door, waiting some more, hoping he couldn't see how fast my heart was beating.

Alaric pocketed his cheque and strolled toward the door, his arm brushing against my elbow as he moved by me. I drew in a breath, my gaze rising to find him looking down at me, his eyes flaring with hunger. He held the door while I typed in the code and then slipped past him.

In all that time, he hadn't said a word, so I continued walking.

"Have a good weekend." I smiled, looking over my shoulder before sashaying to my car. I felt his scorching scrutiny the entire time, but I didn't look back. The intention was to leave him wanting so that he'd show up at the bar tonight.

I pulled from my spot and drove home, hoping like hell my plan would work. All we needed was to get away from the work setting, and then I would be able to show him that we could easily separate play from work.

CHAPTER NINE

CASUAL

Alaric

I watched as Gwen's taillights disappeared, frowning after her. Shaking my head, I trekked out to my truck and climbed into the cab, trying not to think about the fantasy of driving straight to her place for another night of intense sex.

To my disappointment, Gwen hadn't mentioned drinks again, as she had the weekend before—at least, not to me. I knew she was still planning on going—I heard her making plans with someone else when I walked in.

The wave of jealousy that hit just about knocked me on my feet, and when it became abundantly clear that she wasn't going to extend the invite to me, that wave of jealousy became a tsunami.

I told myself it was better this way, anyway. My attraction to her was a palpable thing, a dangerous, discernible thing. When she'd passed me in the empty office to lock the shop door, her perfume had consumed my senses. It took everything I had to not push her up against the door and pull her sensual dress up over her hips.

And that was bad—real bad. I wasn't even past the probation period, and my new boss would probably annihilate me if he caught me anywhere near his daughter.

I'd only known Russell Williams for a short while, but he was an imposing force of nature. Unforgiving, demanding, and he expected a lot of his employees. He was a hard ass to work for, but I understood him. I related to him.

But I wouldn't earn any favours from him if I crossed that boundary, and I needed this job.

Driving home, the tail end of Gwen's conversation still kept circling around in my mind. I wondered who she was meeting at the Watering Hole. Turning onto my road, I pulled up the driveway.

Tig shuffled over from the mudroom, his tail wagging in greeting. I stroked his big head and let him outside, standing on the back deck while he relieved himself.

If I didn't know any better, I'd say that Tig was still searching for Sawyer. Poor thing missed the kid as much as I did. Eventually, he'd get into the routine.

I whistled, and he came back up the porch steps and walked over to the dog bed we had bought him over the weekend. Sawyer insisted he needed a few things to be more comfortable, so we took him to the pet store and picked out some toys and a dog bed for him. The kid had me wrapped around her little finger, and I dropped close to four hundred dollars on the dog by the time we left the pet store.

Tig flopped down on his pillow, chewing a water buffalo horn. It had been one of the many purchases we'd made, and he loved it. The dog acted like he'd never been given a bone before, and he wasn't the least bit aggressive about it. He was riveted by it, and several times over the past week, he would bring it up to me to show me, like he couldn't believe it was his or like he wanted to share with me.

I bent forward, rubbing behind his ear, and his tail thumped against the floor in response.

After showering, I got dressed quickly and headed back downstairs to feed the dog and myself. I grilled up some chicken and potatoes on the barbeque, skipping the vegetables. It was safe to say, I ate like shit when Sawyer wasn't around, but I couldn't be bothered to put much more of an effort into it.

I ate standing at the counter, fighting the urge I had to take a drive to the Watering Hole more and more with every minute that ticked by. Finishing my meal, I set my plate down with a heavy sigh that made the big dog lift his head and shoot a questioning stare at me.

"This is probably a bad idea," I murmured, glancing at the clock on the microwave. It was nine o'clock—and Gwen was probably sitting at the bar, waiting for…well, whoever had taken my place.

Tig huffed and laid back down, offering no help to my internal moral dilemma.

I should go to the shed and work on a project, something to distract myself from making another poor decision, but I couldn't suppress the desire I felt for her. It grew every time I saw her.

Each time I spent any length of time alone with her, for those brief moments, I forgot why it was such a terrible idea. I almost took what I wanted from her, knowing she'd give it to me—her want was as palpable as mine. It was a manifestation that I was struggling to hide.

Unable to shake her flirty gaze from my head, I grabbed my keys and shoved my phone and wallet into my pockets. I was curious—curious about who she was planning on meeting, if not me.

It was nine-thirty when I finally pulled up at the Watering Hole. I parked about a block away and walked up, pushing open the bar doors and walking in.

The Friday night crowd was thick, but my eyes still found her with ease. She sat at the bar, facing her blonde friend—the same girl that had ditched her the night we met. The relief I felt in my chest was unorthodox. She glanced up and saw me, the smile on her face deepening when our eyes locked.

I wanted to move through the crowd and make my way to her, but I didn't know what I'd say to her, so I headed to the other side of the bar and ordered a whiskey.

Sliding the tumbler to me, the bartender took the bill I passed with a flirty smile. I looked past her, watching as Gwen's friend stood. They hugged, and the blonde grabbed her purse before leaving the bar.

When the door swung shut behind her, Gwen turned her head to look at me. I held her gaze, lifting the tumbler to my lips, unable to resist undressing her in my mind's eye.

She gave me a crooked smile and stood, picking up her clutch and moving around the length of the L-shaped bar to join me on the opposite side.

She'd changed into a little black skirt, the hem falling just below the swell of her ass. Sliding into the free stool beside me, she brushed a strand of her long hair behind her ear.

"Fancy seeing you here," she said as though she'd known the whole time I'd show. She bit her lip as she stared at my mouth. She exhaled, and I felt the heat of her breath envelop me.

"Yeah. I probably shouldn't have come," I confessed. Her brow furrowed with confusion.

"And why not?" she asked, tilting her head, trying to figure me out.

"Well, you are the boss's daughter."

"So?" she arched her brows pointedly. "I don't plan on telling him, do you?"

"No," I replied, pausing to take a sip of whiskey. I was nursing it, but my throat felt impossibly dry.

"Well, then. We're on the same page there. Next issue?" she asked, almost as if delegating a legal document.

"I'm not in the place for a relationship," I repeated the words from two weeks ago, wondering if they sounded as hollow as they felt.

"I never asked for a one," she replied, blinking once.

"What do you want, then?" I asked, looking at her dead on. Reading the curve of her lips, the vulnerability in her eyes, and the hesitation in her movements.

Her white teeth sunk into her bottom lip and she shrugged. "A casual sex friend, maybe?" I chuckled, shaking my head a little, thinking she was joking. "I'm serious. I want some no-strings-attached fun, and, well, I had a lot of fun with you…if you know what I mean."

"I know what you mean," I said, my voice a little gravelly, remembering how much fun we'd had together. I glanced longingly at her lips, considering my options. "What's the likelihood of you father dropping in unannounced?"

"One percent?" She shrugged. "I mean, you're more likely to run into Kelsey, and she wouldn't blab about this to our dad. Trust me."

"Who's Kelsey?"

"She's my sister…the girl that just left? She was there the night we met? Obviously, she knew we hooked up before I knew we worked together," she replied. "Kelsey's just happy to see my interest in men is somewhat restored."

"You have an interest in me?" I cocked a brow, fighting off a smile.

"Duh." She rolled her eyes playfully, her dimples flashing. "You've got an incredible body, and you know how to use it, so I'd say I'm definitely interested. But honestly, I can't handle a relationship either. I just want...casual."

Gwen was offering me up rare liberty, one that I selfishly wanted to take advantage of. "All right, Gwen. We'll give it a try."

"Your place or mine?" she asked, tilting her head and giving me a sultry smile. I barely had to think about it.

"Your place is closer," I said, and she nodded in agreement before standing and turning for the door. Abandoning my whiskey, I followed her onto the street.

"Kelsey drove. I told her I'd find my own way back."

"Seems you did," I joked, my stomach churning with nervousness the closer we got to my truck. I wanted her, desperately, and yet my adrenaline surged, my nerves tingling with the impending storm. Instinct told me to tread carefully, but the hesitation faded when she slipped her fingers through mine.

She dragged me down a narrow alley between two stores, turning to press her hand against my chest and backing me up against the nearest brick wall, as if she sensed my internal pause and wanted to chase away my apprehension with her touch.

Her hands dropped down my torso, her fingers pressing the thin material of my shirt into my flesh. She lifted the hem, her nails raking against the space between my lower abs and hip flexors.

Encompassed in the dark, we were alone, the only sound was our bated breath. A thousand unspoken secrets lingered between us. I lowered my head, capturing her lips and kissing her. My hands tangled in her hair, and I deepened the kiss.

"It's strictly a thing of convenience," she assured me—or maybe herself—when I pulled my lips from hers to look at her, to give her another chance to rethink what we were about to do, her hands brushed against my straining erection, applying just a touch of pressure, enough to drive me beyond reason. "At work we're colleagues, and after hours...we're booty-call friends. If you're otherwise occupied, I'll find something else to do with my time."

"Such as what?" I growled, my eyes narrowing in on her face. Her words were offhand, and they should have soothed me. But I didn't like the idea of her occupying her time with another guy in the slightest.

"Does it matter?" she retorted, arching a delicate brow at me, her smile playful and chalk full of delicious sin. I swallowed my answer as her lips found mine again. She tugged at my bottom lip with her teeth, elevating my worries and fueling my urgency.

I hadn't been able to chase her from my mind in two weeks, and I was tired of fighting it. Having to see her frequently and not do a thing about the burning need I felt to bury myself in her again was exhausting, and she was propositioning a solution that could work.

It was a dangerous game, but I wanted to at least try to play it. I knew it'd be worth the risk.

My hands slipped beneath her skirt, and I gripped her ass, tugging her body against me, my denim-clad cock aching to be inside her. "Let's go," I ordered, setting her down and taking her hand, tugging her the rest of the way to my truck.

I unlocked the doors, and we climbed in, stealing glances full of anticipation the entire seven-minute drive to her apartment. I parked out front, walked around the front of my truck, and met her on the sidewalk. She took my hand, grinning, and led me up the walkway to the glass doors to her apartment.

Someone had propped the door open with a brick, and music filtered down from an apartment toward the back of the building.

"Is that safe?" I frowned, looking up the stairs to the second floor. I could see the doorway to her apartment.

"Probably not." She shrugged, opening the door and stepping over the brick. She kicked it back with a cheeky grin, and we walked upstairs, the door slamming shut and locking behind us. "Some of my neighbours lack common sense—and common decency," she added, pulling her keys from her purse.

"At least you're self-aware!" the elderly lady across the hall snipped, slamming her door abruptly.

"Does your neighbour wait by her door for you to get home or something?" I asked, recalling her from the night I met Gwen.

"It seems that way," she grinned, her eyes dancing with humour. "I think she just likes to get her jabs in." She looked at her neighbour's door thoughtfully before shaking her head and unlocking the door to her apartment.

I pressed against her from behind, laying a sucking kiss to the side of her neck. She shivered, her breath tumbling from her lips, and pushed the door open. She turned her chin to look at me as I ran my hand along her ribs.

Walking us through the open door into her apartment, I paused long enough to close the door and lock it behind me, while she moved just out of my reach and slipped her shoes off.

My eyes never left the curve of Gwen's ass displayed in a remarkable black leather skirt, the hem of it ending just below her knees. Her red halter top left her shoulders and back exposed.

If I had to take a guess on what her favourite colour was, I'd have to go with red. If it wasn't red, it was certainly my favourite colour on her.

The moment the door closed, Gwen was before me, her fingers tugging at my belt, freeing the buckle. Distracted by the hard planes of my abdomen, she raked her hands against my flesh, igniting a resounding hunger within me.

She hadn't bothered turning on the lights, and the pale-yellow glow of a streetlight out front guided me to her. I brought my hands up to frame her face, lowering mine to kiss her deeply.

As we kissed, she popped the button of my jeans and yanked the zipper down, her hand slipping into my boxer briefs. Her smooth fingers wrapped around the base of my cock, her grip steadfast. Air escaped my lungs in a whoosh as she slowly pumped me. She smiled, a dare in her eyes.

She dropped to her knees, peering up at me as she slowly pulled her shirt off and unhooked her bra. Her breasts spilled forth, the nipples tight and begging to be sucked.

She let her clothes fall to the ground and took hold of my shaft, stroking it. It was such an arousing sight, and I jumped in her hand.

Gwen's lips wrapped around the tip, and I ran fingers through her thick tresses, tugging it into a nice fist full to keep it out of her way. She started bobbing on my cock, her torturous tongue and lips working the head of me while her hands pumped my base.

I squeezed my eyelids shut, dropping my head back as I let out a carnal groan. Her mouth was heaven and hell all at once —the sweetest torture. But I wanted more.

Pulling free of her mouth, I tugged her up, my lips crashing to hers with ferocity. She responded with identical vigor, her lips and tongue stroking the fire coiling in my abdomen.

Without breaking the kiss, I picked her up. Her thighs tightened around my hips as I walked forward, toward her bedroom. My cock rubbed against her center, and I could feel how ready she was through the lace panties. I gripped her ass tighter, digging my fingers in and tugging her down against my erection.

She let out a heavy moan, her head dipping back and her pelvis arching against me. Reaching her bedroom, I dropped her down on the mattress and crawled over top of her, my hands gliding up her body to tangle in her hair. I rutted into her, brushing against the silk of her panties. I could feel her heat, feel her wetness, and it drove me delirious.

I sat up, tugging my shirt over my head before I dropped between her thighs, pushing them open. I held her gaze as I sampled her with my tongue. She let out a little whimper, her back arching off the mattress.

I groaned, her flavour bursting on my tongue and sending a jolt of desire straight to my cock. I slipped my index finger into her, and she let out a gasp of pleasure as I curled my finger and worked her sensitive bud with my lips and tongue.

"I'm going to—I'm going to come," she panted, tightening around my finger.

Gwen

My thighs shook as I came down from oral orgasmic heaven, and I let out a shuttering breath, my skin erupting into goosebumps.

Alaric stood up, reaching into his back pocket for his wallet. He grabbed a condom, ripping into the package with his eyes still on my body.

It was easy for me to throw my modesty out the window, with the lascivious way he looked at me. He kicked his jeans and boxer briefs off and rolled the condom on, his eyes slowly moving from my center—bared to him—to my navel, to my breasts, to my lips, and finally—my eyes.

The sweeping reverence I saw there made my breath hitch. There wasn't a casual thing about it, and there was nothing casual in the way my heart reacted to it. Before I could comprehend what it all meant, Alaric was back on the mattress, moving between my thighs and settling there.

His lips pressed against mine as he entered, sliding slowly into me, giving me a moment to adjust to his girth and length.

It didn't take me long; ever since the first night we'd spent together, my body had craved this. Him. The way he filled me, so completely, so deeply. He slid in and out of me with hard, sure thrusts, each one of them pushing me closer and closer to another freefall orgasm.

Alaric's lips moved to the side of my neck, and kissed me there, softly at first, before he sucked down and nipped lightly.

It pushed me over the edge, and my back arched as I exploded around him. My toes curled, and I moaned through it. Alaric didn't stop, his thrusts growing faster and harder, propelling me toward another shattering orgasm. I could feel my core tightening around him, and his brow furrowed as I clenched.

His pelvis slammed into me twice more before he buried himself inside me, as far as he could. Groaning against my neck, he came.

I took a shuttering breath, clenching around him, milking every drop. He let out a quiet laugh, drawing out and flopping beside me.

"I think we both needed that," I remarked, my voice a little shaky still. I turned to look at him, my cheeks flushed and my pulse racing.

"I think you're right," he chuckled, shaking his head. "Maybe if you hadn't tortured me all week, I might have displayed more restraint."

"I didn't torture you." I laughed. "Did I?"

He gave me a look, cocking his brows and gazing lewdly at my body. "I think you knew what you were doing."

"Not really, but I'm glad it worked," I admitted, smirking. "You aren't planning on leaving before midnight, are you, Cinderella?" I arched a brow at him.

He chuckled, shaking his head a little, his hand finding the curve of my hip. "I've got some time."

CHAPTER TEN

BOOTY CALL

Alaric

She fell asleep in my arms again, and this time, I hesitated even longer when it came time for me to leave.

I shouldn't stay, it would give the wrong impression. But I wanted to stay even more than I had the first night.

This time, Tig was waiting back home, so I had no choice but to ease from her bed. She slept on, too spent to be roused by my subtle movements. This time, I left a note with my phone number on her nightstand.

I locked her door, trudging to my truck, moments from earlier washing over me and chipping away at my armour. She was easy, friendly and engaging—and strangest yet, I enjoyed talking to her.

We didn't talk about heavy things, just safe topics—topics you'd discuss with just about anyone. We both had walls around our hearts.

But when we touched, we both spoke a different language,

one that wasn't that of walls. It was a language of unbridled passion. She awoke something that resided so deep inside of me; I'd forgotten it was there until she set it free.

It was a surreal thing, to carry this knowledge after two heated hookups, but Gwen was like a drug. She'd quietly slipped into my system, and now I was hooked.

I told myself that I could balance it all—work, Sawyer, her. Keep it all separate, keep the lines from blurring, but I knew it was a lie.

Already, I craved her.

At nine o'clock the next evening, my cell phone buzzed with a text from an unfamiliar number. I'd just hopped out of the shower after a day of clearing the weeds from the gardens out back. I wanted to get the heavy, potentially boring work out of the way for my next weekend with Sawyer.

And, I'd needed to do something to occupy my time. I hadn't heard a whisper from Gwen all day, and I felt both relieved and a little disappointed by that. Leaving my number had been a momentous thing to do, something I hadn't done since Cheryl.

But I'd asked for casual, and she'd pressed that she needed it too, and I was relieved by the silence while being simultaneously tormented by it.

I grabbed my phone off the bathroom counter a little too eagerly. Unlocking it, my eyes slid across the screen as I read the message twice.

Hey, it's Gwen. Just wanted to let you know…I had a lot of fun last night. Feel free to text me any time you want a repeat. ;)

Her message alone gave me a half-chub, and the invitation behind it only added to that. I wanted to hop on my bike and drive out to see her, but it was too soon.

Me: *Duly noted. I'll definitely take you up on that offer.* ;) I sent back as I strolled into my bedroom. I set my phone on the top of my dresser, pulling open drawers for a pair of well-worn jeans and a t-shirt. I dressed, unwilling to acknowledge how frequently my eyes darted to my phone.

Then it rang, vibrating against the counter, and I picked it up quickly.

"Hi, Mom," I said, leaving the bedroom and walking down the stairs. "Sorry I missed your call earlier. I was doing some yard work." I crossed over to the refrigerator. I opened it, grabbing a beer from the shelf, and closed it. Cracking the top, I took a deep sip, my eyes going to the clock above the microwave as I drank.

"That's all right; I figured you were busy." She said without an ounce of irritation. My mom knew me well—she knew I was a lot like my father, that I couldn't stay idle. She never took my silences personally, which made me feel guiltier for disappearing on her as often as I had. "I'm just calling to make sure it's still okay that I come out next weekend?"

"Of course, we're both looking forward to seeing you. Sawyer wanted to do the gardens, so we're going to be planting some things." Mom loved gardening; it was one of her favourite pastimes.

"That's wonderful!" Mom said, and I could hear how excited she was. "Well, I'm just about to head out with the girls. We're going to catch a movie!"

"Have fun." I smiled. "Talk to you later. Love you, Mom."

"Love you, too," she said fondly. "I'll call you later this week."

I was just about to put my boots on and head to the garage when I realized I'd received a new message.

Gwen: *Would it be casual if I told you I'm horny for you? Because I am. If you're not busy, you should come over for a bit. If you are busy… well. I'll just have to entertain myself ;)*

I opened it, my cock hardening at just her words. Before I could reply, she sent another message—a photo of the lower half of her face, below her eyes.

Her lips and her collarbone being the focal point, with that steampunk bird on her collarbone, her dark hair pushed behind her creamy shoulders. The top curves of her breast filled the bottom portion of the photo, cutting off before her nipples. It wasn't a nude picture, but it was erotic as hell, and it made my hands twitch with the urge to drive to her place.

I stood in the foyer, staring at that picture, my desire and my head warring with one another. Tig seemed to know before me —usually, he'd follow me out to the garage and lay down with his head facing the driveway while I worked on various projects. That meant he was at my heels, waiting impatiently to get to the garage, but he'd already settled down on the foyer rug.

Dumping the remainder of my beer down the bathroom sink, I paused to grab my truck keys before locking up.

Can I stop for anything? I texted her before I put the key in the ignition and turned it.

Got it covered. Just hurry. ;)

I drove ten clicks over the speed limit until I got closer to town, then I forced myself to slow down. I pulled up to the curb in front of her building and parked. Running a hand through my still damp hair, I opened the door.

Stepping out, I shut the door and hit the lock button on the key fob while walking up the short concrete pathway to the building doors.

Music pumped from somewhere within the building, same as last night. Like the night before, someone had placed a brick to keep the door from closing fully, and I shoved it aside with my boot after opening the door.

I took the steps two at a time, and before I could raise my fist to knock on her door, it was swinging open.

She was dressed in a white tank and a pair of black sleep shorts; no bra, I could easily make out the rose hue of her nipples through the thin material of her top.

"Points for providing fast service," she teased, standing aside to let me in.

"Well, it was a sexy photo," I replied, unashamed now that I was in front of her. She flushed prettily, her lashes brushing against the lens of her glasses as she dropped her gaze for a moment. I stepped toward her, my hand slipping around her waist, my thumbs brushing over her hipbone before I walked her backwards, pinning her against the door.

I ground my pelvis into hers, and she let out a moan. I caught it with a kiss, pressing my lips to hers. My tongue swept across her bottom lip, begging for entrance, and her lips parted eagerly.

Each stroke of her tongue was the kindling, and each pass of her fingers against my skin was the gasoline, the friction of our bodies the only spark required to make us both ignite.

She let out a tortured gasp, her head dropping back against the door with a dull thud as I sucked on her neck. My hand slipped beneath her tank top, and my fingers brushed against the undersides of her heavy breasts before I grabbed hold of one, squeezing and rolling her nipple between my thumb and index fingers.

"Alaric," she moaned, her hands wrestling with the button of my jeans. Finally, I felt the button give. Gwen worked the zipper down and pushed both my jeans and my boxers down enough to free my goods.

As her fist enclosed around me, my fingers slipped into her sleep shorts, finding her slick with need. My fingers sank into her, and I felt her clenching around me.

The pad of her finger swirled the pre-cum against my crown, and I let out a low growl, withdrawing my hand and picking her up. I carried her to the nearest piece of furniture—the sofa.

I set her down and sank to my knees, tugging her shorts off in one fluid movement. I kissed her pelvis, turning my head so that I could get a taste of her as my tongue slipped between her folds.

Her legs trembled, and my need was exorbitant. I reached for my jeans, pulling a strip of condoms from my back pocket. Gwen tugged her shirt off, her breasts on full display for me.

She was exceptionally gorgeous and so responsive that not being inside of her was beginning to feel painful. I had to rectify that.

I ripped open a condom, rolling it on quickly before I picked her up. My pants and boxer briefs were around my hips, but Gwen worked them down with her heels. Finally freed, I toed off my boots and turned, falling back on the couch, bringing her down with me.

The tip of my cock brushed against her wet core, and then all thoughts flew from my head as she sank down onto me, taking me to the hilt.

"Fuck, Gwen," I growled, closing my eyes as her core tightened. I gripped her hips, pulling her against me as I rocked into her. She rode me, and I met her thrust for thrust, eager to fill her, eager to get my fill *of* her.

My eyes didn't leave her face the entire time, as I hungrily watched her pupils dilate with pleasure. My fingers dug into her hips, and she let out a whimper before I felt the rush of her orgasm. "Do you like it rough?" I asked her, pulsing inside of her.

"I guess I do," she said, her voice a little shaky and her eyes bewildered like she'd been caught off guard by it.

Making sure I had a hold of her, I stood carefully, still managing to keep inside of her sweet heat. I kissed her deeply, holding her ass and moving her against me. I walked until we reached the wall, and I paused to look into her gray eyes. "Let me know if it gets to be too much."

She gave me a sly grin, arching her pelvis against me. "Bring it."

I started to drive into her, fucking her against the wall, supporting her lower back as I pounded into her. She came around me and let out the sexiest of moans. Her breasts pressed against my chest, and the whole thing was sensory overload for me, and I let out a deep groan as I came.

I'd fucked plenty of women in similar ways, but never had I been as affected by them as I was by *her*. Being inside her was sheer ecstasy.

I pulled out and lowered her to the ground, still supporting her as she regained her balance. Once she was able to stand on her own, I went to the bathroom to discard the condom and clean up a little before I rejoined her.

She'd put her tank top and shorts back on, although she had two glasses of water on the coffee table. She looked up at me from the couch, a satisfied smile on her face. "I really needed that," she admitted, somewhat dreamily. "You have a magic cock."

"Just a magic cock?" I joked, bending to pick up my boxers and jeans.

"Well, you've got magic fingers and magic lips and a magic tongue too..." she amended, frowning thoughtfully. Reaching for one of the cups, she drank from it. The flash of insecurity I saw in her eyes was gone almost as quickly as it appeared.

"You're pretty magical yourself," I told her, pulling my jeans over my hips. I buttoned them before picking up the second glass. Taking a long sip, I sat down beside her on the couch. I needed a moment to catch my breath.

My gaze slid to hers, and I exhaled deeply when I caught her checking out my chest.

"So, what'd you do today?"

"Yard work," I said. "You?"

"Nothing, really. Mentally preparing myself to go wedding dress shopping tomorrow." I tensed a little, and she glanced at me, her lips twitching with amusement. "My sister's getting married, so we're going wedding gown shopping." She explained, bemused. "It's going to be pure torture. I'd almost rather do yard work."

"I thought women liked stuff like that." I laughed.

"Most women do, but this woman? No thanks. Especially not with Kelsey's future mother-in-law present. That woman's a nightmare." She shivered. "I would have rather spent tomorrow drinking beer in my underwear and watching *Game of Thrones*."

"You like that show?" I asked, my cock stirring at the mental image of her in her underwear.

"Obviously," she said, giving me a pointed look. "If your hair was dark, you could pass as a Dothraki."

I laughed deeply, shaking my head a little, my eyes moving across the room to the bookshelves that took up the far wall. She had the complete *Game of Thrones* series on one shelf, along with various character bobbleheads and a signed, framed photograph of her with some of the cast.

"I've never seen it," I admitted, shrugging a little.

"Wow, really? I don't know if I can continue being your

friend," she teased, her smile betraying her words. "Honestly, it's a cool show. You'd probably love it. Swords and gore and tits and ass. There's something for everybody."

She set her glass down and climbed onto my lap again, straddling me. Her hands moved up my chest, around my shoulders to rest at the back of my neck.

"Maybe I'll check it out." I chuckled as she moved closer, pressing her lips to mine.

Gwen

Sunday morning, I awoke completely relaxed with high spirits. I listened to music while I showered, dressed, and did my makeup. When Kelsey texted that she was out front of my building, I was already slipping into my most comfortable pair of Vans.

After Alaric left Friday night, I had the deepest sleep of my life, sedated by all the orgasms. When I woke on Saturday morning, I felt renewed and spent the entire day writing.

Of course, by writing, I'd worked myself into a horrible state of arousal and had ended up practically begging Alaric to come back.

But he had, and we had sex twice before he left.

Whistling cheerfully, I locked my apartment and practically danced down the steps. I climbed into the front seat, flashing a dazzling smile at Kelsey. "Good morning, sister face."

"I take it your chat with Alaric went well."

"It did. We've agreed to try casual." I shrugged. "But I don't want a word of this uttered today. Mom doesn't need to know. We're just having fun, and she always makes a huge deal of this kind of thing."

"You used to, too," Kelsey noted with some concern.

"Yeah, but I've learned my lesson," I argued, lifting my chin and ignoring the whispers of my heart. It was hard not to be affected by Alaric; he was the ultimate package, but he was also completely emotionally unavailable, and I needed to remember that.

"Oh, I get it." Kelsey nodded, understanding dawning on her expression. She pulled onto the road and started to drive toward our parents' house to pick up Mom.

"Get what?"

"You're still trying to play it cool. Gwen, I saw how he looked at you. It's pretty obvious how he feels about you."

"He wants me. That's all." I shrugged, trying to dismiss her words, feeling uncertain and worse...hopeful. This was precisely why I needed to shut down this topic; I couldn't afford to have those kinds of seeds planted in my mind. "Like I said, we're just having fun. So, could you let me have that without making me overanalyze things? Because I have a hard enough time not doing that on my own. I don't need you adding to it."

"Sorry," she said, sending a concerned glance my way. "Just be careful."

I sighed. "Fine, but can we drop it now? Today is about you and finding you the perfect dress for your perfect day," I said, steering us back to safer waters as our parents' driveway came into sight.

"That's true. Today *is* about me," Kelsey said gleefully as she turned down the gravel driveway. As we pulled up to my parents four-bedroom, three-bathroom brick house, Mom walked out the front door, closing it behind her.

I surrendered the front seat to her and climbed in the back, thankful that we still had another two hours before I'd have to deal with Janice. Speaking of which, I was going to need a coffee—stat. "Hey, could we maybe stop for coffee?"

"Sure," Kelsey said, waiting until we were both buckled to

put it in reverse and back up. She turned around, driving down the gravel driveway slowly. "We'll hit up the travel centre."

Satisfied, I sat back against my seat and pulled my phone from my purse. I had no new texts. Before the disappointment could set in, I pulled up Renly's name and sent him a message.

Me: *I'm about to spend the day dress shopping with Kelsey, her future monster-in-law, and my mom. Please send wine.*

I didn't have to wait long for a response, as Ren's phone was never far from his hand.

Ren: *I think they serve champagne at bridal boutiques.*

"Oh my God, do they actually serve champagne at bridal stores?" I demanded, looking up from my phone. Mom turned around to frown at me, flabbergast by my interruption. "Sorry, I just, I didn't know they did that."

"As I was saying, Kelsey," Mom said, turning back to look at my sister. "The Dominican is a beautiful place for a honeymoon."

"I like the idea of going to Iceland." My sister shrugged. "Or Europe."

"Paris would be romantic." Mom nodded with agreement. "Although it would be cold in February."

"I don't mind, and neither does Elliott. I'm sure Paris is just as beautiful in February as it is in the summer."

"Oh, it so would be, Kels!" I said eagerly, leaning forward a little bit. "And you could take the train to Amsterdam. Actually, I think you can take the train pretty much anywhere."

"That's the plan," Kelsey admitted, grinning ruefully. "We kind of want to see as much of it as we can."

"That sounds interesting. What does Janice think?" Mom asked.

I groaned. "Who cares what Janice thinks? It's their honeymoon, not hers."

"She's paying for it," my sister pointed out, glancing at me through the rearview mirror. "She said she wanted to send us to the Dominican, but neither Elliott nor I have a burning desire to go there. We've always talked about seeing Europe."

"So tell her that you want to go to Europe, then." I frowned, not seeing the dilemma.

"We're going to, but Elliott wants to be there so please don't say anything," Kelsey replied, catching my eyes in the mirror again and giving me a pointed look.

"You know I love a good secret." I arched a brow.

CHAPTER ELEVEN

FREE FALL

Gwen

I deserved a medal of some kind for putting up with Janice. After spending the last hour with her, I had a newfound appreciation for my mother. She really wasn't all that bad. Compared to Elliott's mom, ours was a saint.

She had a complaint about everything, and I mean *everything*. Every dress that Kelsey tried on, she'd spew out some kind of ridiculous flaw in it.

The saleswoman cleared her throat, and Kelsey stepped out in a beautiful Viera lace on tulle dress with a sweetheart neckline. It was decorated with Swarovski crystals and an embroidered lace hemline. Kels' entire demeanor changed when she looked at herself in the mirror, but then Janice's displeased tone shattered the moment.

"No, that's not it either." She insisted, dismissing the dress as she had the other six before it.

"Woah. Hang on. What are you talking about, Janice?" I

demanded, pointing at the dress. "Just look at it! It fits her perfectly, and it's totally her."

"It looks dirty," Janice said, eyeing the dress with disdain. "Try on the ball gown I selected."

Kelsey looked at herself a final time in the mirror before pivoting. "It makes sense to try on all the dresses, but so far, this one is my favourite." She said with confidence, giving her future mother-in-law a polite smile before she followed the sales lady into the change room.

"I happened to like the silver undertones," I said to Mom, rolling my eyes.

"Gwen," Mom scolded me for my tone, but I could tell she agreed with me. Still, she made polite conversation with Janice while we waited.

I pulled my phone out, my finger hovering over the Facebook icon before tapping it, opening up my notifications. I nearly dropped my phone with surprise when I read that Alaric had accepted my friend request.

Wait, what friend request? I thought frantically. Admittedly, I'd pulled up his profile a few times over the last week or so, but I hadn't requested him. Or at least, I hadn't meant to.

Still, he'd accepted the request. Finger hovering over his name, I hesitated for only a moment before clicking it.

More of his profile was revealed to me, but it still didn't really give me any closer of a look at his life. The few photos he'd been tagged in were from years ago, and he didn't seem very active on it now.

I lingered on a photograph of him with his arm around the shoulders of a red-haired woman as she held a tiny pink bundle. The grin on his face as he gazed down at the baby made my heart clench.

The love and adoration in Alaric's eyes as he gazed admired

his newborn daughter took my breath away and made me ache acutely for something more.

"Gwen?" Startled at the close proximity of my mom, I dropped my phone. I leaned forward and picked it up quickly, my face flushed.

"Jesus, Mom. Do I need to get you a bell?" I demanded.

"I said your name seven times." Mom shook her head, her brow furrowing as she gazed at me with suspicion.

"Well, you have my attention now." I sighed, trying to recover from not only being startled but from the distressing realization that I was in *way* over my head.

Mom's frown deepened, and she nodded toward the little stage set up with mirrors where the sales ladies had brides-to-be model the dresses they tried on. Kelsey was wearing a strapless ball gown this time, with scattered lace embellishing the tiered layers of tulle—a lot of tulle.

My sister gently moved her hands up the lace bodice, her fingers fluttering over the material.

"See? Aren't you a vision," Janice declared, standing up for the first time and smiling with pride. "You'll steal Elliott's breath from his very lungs in that."

I stood too, taking in the soft scoop neckline. I hated to admit it, but Janice was right—the dress was beautiful, and Kelsey's expression had changed yet again with it, so she was feeling something.

"Oh Kelsey, it's stunning too," Mom said, her eyes misting as she took in the sight of my sister in the gown.

"So, which one is it going to be, Kels?" I asked, giving her my full focus and trying to make up for having zoned out on her grand entrance.

"What do you think?" she questioned, turning to look at me, her slender fingers running over the Swarovski crystal belt.

"You look amazing in both," I told her, speaking the honest truth. She turned back to the mirror, studying it with her lips pursed.

"The tulle isn't too much?" she asked, looking from Mom to me with concern.

"Kelsey, your wedding day is basically the only time you'll have an excuse to wear a super gaudy dress," I pointed out with a mischievous smile.

"I really think the ball gown looks best on you," Janice added. She'd sent me an offended look when I called the dress gaudy, but I hadn't cared. Shrugging, I faced Kelsey again, giving her a pointed look to remind her it was her wedding.

"I love them both." Mom stepped forward, her eyes watery as she gazed at Kelsey. She shook her head back and forth, overcome with emotion.

"Why don't we try some veils and tiaras?" the saleswoman suggested, coming forward with a veil and a tiara in her hands. Kelsey nodded, and the saleswoman carefully put the tiara on her, arranging the veil so that it covered the back of my sister's head and shoulders, leaving her face free.

"Oh, you look like a princess," Mom choked out, the tears flowing freely now.

I sighed dreamily, my smile growing. I'd almost wanted Kelsey to go back to the other dress, just to spite Janice. I couldn't imagine how unbearable she would get for being right about this, but she was—the second dress *was* perfect. She looked like a fairytale character in it.

Kelsey turned to face the mirror, her eyes bright with emotion as she studied herself. "I think this is the one," she said softly, tilting her head a little bit.

"Turn around," I told her, and when she did, I snapped a couple of photos of her with my phone.

"What are you doing?" Janice frowned angrily as if snapping some pictures was the equivalent of doing naked summersaults all over the pristine white furniture in the bridal boutique.

"Relax, Janice. I'm taking photos so that she'll know what to show the hairstylist and makeup artist," I said, somehow placidly, despite the overwhelming urge I had to roll my eyes at her. She backed off—with nary an apology—and I resumed my task.

Moving closer to the stage, I snapped more pictures, relieved to put some distance between Janice and myself. I could only hold my tongue for so long, and I really didn't want to inadvertently spoil Kelsey's moment by telling her future mother-in-law to shut her pie hole, permanently.

"Will you be paying by cash or credit?" the saleswoman asked, her tone jovial.

"Credit," Kelsey replied, her eyes still on her reflection. I squeezed her shoulders, jumping a little bit with excitement.

"It's really happening, Kels. You're getting married!" I said, animated with excitement for this stage of her life.

"I know," she squealed back, her eyes flashing with excitement.

I smiled. "Well, I guess we should go have that celebratory champagne now!"

I walked into my apartment, dropping my purse down on the floor in front of the shelf. Sliding the deadbolt home, I let out a tired sigh and hung my head.

The day had its highs; its truly exciting moments—like

Kelsey finding *the dress*, and celebratory champagne followed by a quick bistro lunch.

But the day also had its unbearable, painful moments. Most of those unbearably painful moments were due to Janice, but a few had been my own personal hang-ups.

On the drive home from Toronto, I'd stared out the window, thinking about the photo of Alaric, Kelsey's wedding, and of Erik.

I hated that I was thinking about Erik, but weddings brought up weird feelings for everyone. Or at least, that's what movies and books led me to believe. I'd actually never been to a wedding before, so I was new to all of this turmoil, but I couldn't deny its existence.

Kelsey and Elliott were soulmates, and this was the next chapter in their lives together. I was excited for them both, and I knew my sister had dreamed about this day for her entire life. What little girl hadn't played wedding growing up? Dressed in their mother's heels and pearls?

I would be lying to myself if I said I hadn't thought about marriage when I was with Erik. I had, a lot.

I always knew that I wanted to get married one day, so naturally, I thought I'd marry *him*. I thought I loved him—and I guess I did. Or at least, I loved the person I thought he was, the person I wrote him as in my head.

But he wasn't that person, and when Erik left me, I felt stupid for having hoped for those things with him. For having thought about meshing my life so completely to someone that hadn't even had the common decency to break up with me *before* sleeping with someone new.

I didn't know if I could ever put that kind of blind trust in someone again, and that made me a little sad. Sad that I let someone break me beyond what I recognized, and angry I'd let it happen, too.

Sensing my mood, Dahmer sashayed down the hall and weaved around my feet, rubbing his head against my legs and purring loudly. I picked him up and carried him to the couch, sitting down on it.

My thoughts went back to the night before, and I sighed heavily. *Casual sex.* By definition, I didn't do *casual*. My mother said I was too passionate and empathetic. I wore my heart on my sleeve and was over-sensitive.

I had only known Alaric for three weeks, and he was already getting to me. I craved the way he made me feel, but I was scared of it too—scared because I couldn't turn off my emotions.

But emotions had no place in this thing we were doing, and I couldn't change it now…but I also couldn't stop. I was too selfish for that, and I dreaded returning to the numb, disconnected state I'd lived in for the last several months.

The likelihood that I'd end up hurt again was very, *very* high, and a smarter girl would walk away *before* that happened, but when it came to self-preservation…I wasn't always the brightest.

Alaric

I pulled into the shop parking lot just after Gwen and parked two spaces away from her. She watched me for a moment, a sultry smile on her red painted lips before she dropped her gaze and exited her car.

Desire coursed through my bloodstream at the sight of her standing. She tugged on her black skirt. My gaze perused across her creamy legs up to the white-and-black printed bodice and the sliver of skin exposed at her neckline. Her long, dark hair was pulled back into a sleek ponytail, and I couldn't help but grin at how pretty she looked.

She smiled as if she felt my gaze on her, but didn't look at me again as she strolled up to the office and opened the door, disappearing inside.

Clearing my throat, I grabbed my gear and walked into the shop through the open metal door. I nodded at Paul and Wes as I passed them, heading to my workstation for the day.

I had a lot of mistakes to fix. Not mine, some other bonehead employee had cut the parts for the Creek project wrong. The engineers were coming by tomorrow, and Russell needed the job done right—and quick.

I'd be putting in overtime tonight. After seeing how incredibly sexy Gwen looked this morning, I was a bit irritated about that fact. I'd wanted to ask her to meet me after, but I hadn't—aware of the boundaries we'd both set in place. Work was work, play was play.

Still, it had been three days since I'd last been inside her, and I was already craving another round.

Subconsciously, I was aware of how dangerous that was—to need something from someone as badly as I yearned for the feel of her. It wasn't just about her body; I coveted her time, too. The burden of everything seemed lighter in her company, and that was highly addictive and unstoppable.

Rolling my shoulders, I set to work. Watching the way the metal would fuse seamlessly, taking pride in each perfect weld, I let the sounds of my gun sauntering drown out all of my ruminating thoughts, emptying my head of everything but the job at hand.

It was ten o'clock when I finally turned off my machine and

pulled off my helmet. My limbs were exhausted and aching, but I still took time to clean up my workspace before leaving the shop, leaving it in pristine condition for tomorrow.

Someone—Russell, I'm assuming—had lingered in the office. There always had to be someone else present in the shop if an employee was working after hours, as it was a liability to work alone.

Russell was likely catching up on some paperwork, as the shop door was propped open with a door stopper. I walked through the open door and into the office to let him know the job was completed before I headed out.

I stopped short when I saw Gwen sitting behind her desk, typing away on her laptop. She looked up, her fingers never ceasing, and gave me a tentative smile. "Hey."

"What are you doing here?" I asked, my tone a little gruff and distant. I cleared my throat, looking around for Russell. But, Russell wasn't in the office. His door was open, the room dark, as empty as the meeting room beside it.

Gwen saved whatever she was working on and shut her laptop, slipping it into her black leather satchel as she stood, her gray eyes never leaving mine. "He had dinner reservations with my mom, so I told him I'd stick around until you finished."

"Why would you do that?"

"Because I know how unbearable my mother can get when she's disappointed, and she would have been *very* disappointed," she said, blinking at me and shouldering her bag.

"Right," I said, feeling awkward. She'd done it for her parents, not for me, but the knowledge that we were completely alone in the office wasn't lost on either of us, and the air was thick.

I saw the fervor in her eyes as her gaze slid down my body,

pausing between my legs, where my dick was pushing against my zipper, proudly declaring how turned on I was.

She licked her lips slowly, her eyes darkening with need. Then she shook her head as though she wanted to shake free of the tension stiff between the two of us, and looked away. "Well, if you're done, I guess we should lock up."

"The shop's already locked up," I said thickly, more affected by her than I cared to admit. She nodded, flicking off the lamp on her desk before she made her way over to me. She passed by, flicking off the hallway light. When she walked by me again, I grabbed her hand, drawing her against me, an involuntary action.

She came willingly, her eyes igniting with the same desire I felt. The scent of her drove me delirious with need, and when she moved against my hard-on, I pushed it against her stomach. "Come back to my place."

"What?" she asked, her eyes widening with surprise.

"I've been gone since six. I have to get home to feed the dog and let him out, but I need to bury myself in you—the sooner, the better." I didn't want to have to wait until I'd driven home, dealt with the dog, showered, and returned to town. I wanted to have her spread out beneath me as soon as possible.

"But…" She frowned, working over my request.

"It doesn't have to mean anything," I assured her, fearing that's where her thoughts had gone. I'd never done this—invited someone back to my place post-Cheryl and Sawyer—but I also had never done a casual, semi-regular hookup, either.

Before Cheryl, I'd played the field a little, too focused on welding to really make a connection with anyone. My connection with Cheryl had been fleeting and had only lasted long enough to conceive a baby, but I'd attempted to build the foundation of a relationship from it, anyway. For Sawyer.

This thing with Gwen, though, it was easy. She knew where I stood, and I knew where she stood. Besides, it wasn't like I was inviting her back with my daughter there.

Right now, my house was just an empty house—with multiple surfaces I could spread her out on. The thought of her on my counter had my cock throbbing against her stomach.

Her eyes flared, and she bit her lip, considering me. "All right, fine. I wouldn't mind seeing Tig again, anyway."

"So you're coming for the dog?"

"No, I'll be coming for you," she corrected, a devious smile gracing her lips.

I chuckled lowly, my eyes narrowing slightly. "You can count on that," I said, my voice husky with meaning.

"Let's go then," she said as her fingers squeezed mine gently. I looked down with surprise at the way our bodies had entwined.

She stepped back, pulling her hand free, using it to push the loose strands of hair that had fallen from her ponytail behind her ear, leaving a smear of grime on her cheek. I grinned, the sight of it made my dick throb almost painfully. I wanted to muss her up some more. "Follow me."

Walking past her, I held the door open for her while she turned out the rest of the lights and punched in the security code.

I waited while she locked up, shamelessly checking out her ass. She turned, catching me, and grinned wickedly. "Lead the way."

Heading to my truck, I glanced at her over my shoulder, subconsciously making sure she got to her car safely. Once she was inside, I climbed into my cab and started the engine.

I left the parking lot first, with Gwen's lights in my rear view mirror. My heart pounded in my chest as I drove the familiar route home. I tried not to think too much about what we were about to do, instead focusing on how badly I wanted her.

That was easy. The need to bury myself to the hilt was still the driving force behind my actions. I could admit it; I was thinking strictly with my dick, convinced it'd be okay because we both knew this was casual.

I parked in front of the garage and Gwen pulled up, parking beside me. She stepped from her car, her eyes locked on me as I approached.

Words were unnecessary; I cupped her face in my hands and brought my lips to hers. I backed her up against her car door, pressing my pelvis to hers. When I finally pulled away a moment later, she was breathless.

"Now we both need a shower." I chuckled, taking in the grayish marks my fingers had made on her perfect skin.

"You did that on purpose," she accused, smiling slowly.

"Sure did." I grinned, releasing her. We walked up the front porch, and I unlocked the door, holding it open, letting Gwen walk through first and pulling it closed behind me.

"Oh, hello there, handsome," she purred, bending forward to scratch Tig behind the ears. His tail thumped against the ground, and her perfect ass was just begging for my attention.

I ran my hands along the apex of her thighs, running them up her smooth skin, gripping the firm mounds of her ass. I applied the slightest amount of pressure, and she pushed back on me, grinding her ass against my erection.

Straightening quickly, she pivoted, her eyes finding mine in the darkened hallway. "Don't get jealous," she teased, wrapping her arms around my neck. "I'll scratch behind your ears, too, if you'd like."

"I can think of a few other things I'd like more." Before she could reply, I kissed her, greedily running my hands all over her body, marking her. She didn't seem to care that I was messing up her outfit, and she tugged frantically at my belt.

Tig let out a deep sigh from the floor.

"Hang on," I said, pressing my lips to hers quickly. I took her hand, drawing her deeper into the house.

Gwen's head moved from side to side as she took in her surroundings. "You've got a beautiful home, Alaric." She remarked, her eyes returning to me and a small smile gracing her lips.

There was something about having her here, something that felt innate. I was struck by the depth of it.

"Thanks," I managed, releasing my hold on her and crossing over to open the back door. Tig raced outside, and I closed it, turning around just in time to see Gwen's dress slip from her body. It fell to the ground, pooling around her feet, and she stepped from it, her eyes on me the entire time she stripped, baring herself to me.

She wore a black lace push-up bra and matching thong.

My reservations went with her dress; slipping away, just out of reach, replaced by the driving force to claim her again.

Thankfully, Tig hurried back, and I rushed through feeding him to get Gwen in the shower, not even feeling guilty for it.

I hopped in before her, scrubbing the grime off me as quickly as I could. Five minutes later, the shower curtain opened just wide enough for her to slip inside. My eyes locked on her—her soft curves, her smooth skin, decorated with her hidden, feminine tattoos.

Gwen had rearranged her hair so that it sat atop her head in a messy bun. She stepped toward me, her hand wrapping around the base of my dick. She squeezed lightly, pumping her arm, jerking me as the hot water flowed down my back.

I rinsed the rest of the soap off quickly and wasted no time touching her back, my fingers seeking her sweet heat as my lips grazed against hers. Softly at first, then deepening when the pads of my fingers danced across her slick slit. I let out a heavy moan, tortured by her immediate response to me.

"I think we're clean enough," she breathed, her eyes bright with urgency.

Shutting the water off, I stepped from the tub and held my hand out for her. She took it, her breasts swaying as she stepped out onto the mat, standing before me.

Her hands roamed up my chest, leaving a fiery sensation in the wake of her touch.

I picked her up, my lips seeking out the sensitive flesh of her delicate throat. Her thighs locked around my hips, and she shifted, her core brushing against the tip of my swollen cock.

Her heat was so inviting, it took everything I had to resist the urge to jerk my hips forward and bury myself deep inside of her. It'd be so easy, and the fact that I even wanted to was a warning sign, but I selfishly ignored it, carrying her down the hall into my bedroom.

I dropped her onto the mattress, relishing in the way her breasts bounced. Reaching in the nightstand, I grabbed a condom and ripped it open, sliding it on.

Gwen's legs fell open, welcoming me as I settled between her thighs. Supporting myself on my elbows, I looked down at her. The sight of her dark hair against my white pillowcase made me hesitate, but then she wriggled impatiently beneath me.

"Alaric," she pleaded as my thick crown slid against her entrance.

Her impatient wriggles stirred me into action, and I jerked my hips forward, filling her. The pleasured moans she released made me lose all sense of everything but our gratification, and I gave myself over to the feel of her body beneath mine.

I fucked her hard, felt her walls clenching and releasing, slickening with the wetness of her orgasms my frantic, deep thrusts brought her to.

Gwen's nails raked against my back, and I felt the pressure building, a tightening in my balls as I thrust harder and deeper still, bringing her to the brink of another orgasm. Her legs trembled around me as I came with a groan on my lips that had almost been her name.

I pulled out of her, instantly missing the feeling of being inside her. Satisfied, but somehow…still ravenous. I wanted her again.

"Well, that was incredible," she said breathlessly. I nodded in agreement, letting out a contented sigh, too blissed out to think much further ahead than that moment.

"It's getting late," she said, her head turning to look at the alarm clock on my nightstand. Her silky legs slid off the mattress, and she stood. "I should go."

I nodded, although a part of me wanted to grab her hand and tug her back into my bed for another round.

"I'll walk you out." I sat up too, standing up and crossing over to my dresser. I grabbed a pair of lounge pants and put them on while Gwen disappeared into the bathroom.

I left my room the same time she left the bathroom, wearing her bra and panties and grinning ruefully at me. "My dress might be in the laundry room."

I chuckled a little, leading the way downstairs, and picked her dress up off the floor, shaking it before handing it to her. She pulled it over her head and buttoned it up.

"I'm not going to be available this weekend," I told her. "It's my weekend to have Sawyer."

She looked up, not a hint of displeasure to be found in her gray eyes. Just understanding and acceptance. "Okay."

Fighting a relieved smile, I stepped toward her, catching a loose tress of her hair and tucking it behind her ear. "I'm not available this weekend, but I'm free every night this week until Friday."

"For booty calls?" she lifted a brow, smirking a little. I grinned back, shrugging in response. "I'll keep that in mind."

CHAPTER TWELVE

THOSE WALLS

Alaric

"So, are you seeing anybody yet?" Mom asked, arching a brow and taking a sip of white wine.

"No," I said, thinking of Gwen. We'd spent the last several days hooking up after work. But hooking up was about all we did. I didn't let myself think about how good it felt to be around her, how natural it was. Instead, I focused on the primal, animalistic desires between us.

"Alaric, you need to stop putting up walls. Ever since Cheryl, you haven't let anyone in. You can't let that foolish girl scare you away from love."

"She didn't," I argued, my brow furrowing.

"She did," Mom countered, looking at me pointedly. "You're so closed off now, and I worry about you."

"There's nothing to worry about," I assured her. "My focus is on Sawyer."

"It doesn't *just* have to be on her, though. You don't need to walk through life alone," Mom said softly, imploringly. She studied me for a moment, sighing heavily when I said nothing in reply. "When I lost your father, I went through a serious grieving period. The sudden absence of him, it broke me for a while. You didn't know that, because I kept it from you. You were already shouldering so much—Sawyer, Cheryl, the business, and your own grief of his loss."

"Mom." I shook my head, emotion clogging my throat.

"I never thought I could feel so lonely. But one day, I woke up and realized that your father wouldn't want me to be alone for the remainder of my life." She said, her eyes misting, although Mom was never a weeper. She was one of the strongest women I knew.

"You're right about that," I said thickly, drawing in a deep breath. Dad wouldn't have wanted her to be alone. He would want her to be happy, however that happiness came to her.

She smiled, nodding a little—she knew him better than anyone else, after all. "Nobody will *ever* replace your father, but that doesn't mean my heart isn't capable of growing to love someone new. Yours is capable, too. Cheryl's lies and deceits are not every woman's, so don't punish every woman for her actions."

I nodded, absorbing her words to the best I could. I knew she was right, but trust had never come easily to me. Less so, now.

"Anyway, I think I've had one too many glasses of wine." She chuckled, waving away the heavy tone and smiling tiredly at me. "I'm going to call it a night, I want to get up early and make breakfast."

"You don't have to do that," I said.

"Oh, it's no bother. I want to," she replied, walking around the counter to give me a hug. "Goodnight. And get a bloody haircut," she smacked my shoulder and retreated from the kitchen. I laughed, shaking my head as she climbed the stairs.

I heard her murmuring to Tig, who'd placed himself in front of Sawyer's bedroom door again. From the moment we got home, he hadn't left her side.

Turning off the lights in the kitchen, I walked into the living room and sat down on the couch. Grabbing the remote, I turned the television on, lowering the volume so it wouldn't disturb anyone else.

Although my body was tired, my mind wouldn't shut off, and I knew I'd just end up staring at my ceiling instead of sleeping, so I turned on the Discovery Channel and stared blankly at the screen.

I kept thinking about my mother's confession, guilt and shame swirling about in the pit of my stomach. My parents had been in love until the day my father died. If he'd never had the heart attack, they would still be happily married today. But, he was gone, and instead of basking in his absence, my mother found peace.

Her ability to love hadn't been shaken, despite the gravity of her loss, and yet for the last several years, all I'd done was push people away before they had a chance to get close—especially women.

There was no doubt about it; I'd used what happened between Cheryl and me as an excuse to keep women at a distance. While it was true that I'd never been in love with Cheryl, I'd been hurt badly by her actions.

Gwen was a rarity, and even I could see that. She'd given no indication that she wanted more than our casual hookup arrangement, but it was getting harder to ignore the fact that every moment I spent just talking with her was as tantalizing as the moments I spent inside her. There was something inherently *good* and easy about her, something that could almost be described as...*right*.

Being with her felt simple. Uncomplicated. The lack of

pressure from her was refreshing, and it made me think about her more than I probably should.

I pulled my phone from my pocket, bringing up Gwen's Facebook page. I'd never been one for social media, but I had a Facebook account. I mostly used it for the buy and sell groups, where I'd sometimes sell stuff I'd made that I'd lost interest in or had no purpose for.

Unlike me, Gwen had a very apparent online presence. She didn't seem to be the kind of girl to share vague-posts about her day, but she shared funny memes and interesting articles.

A soft smile graced my lips as I paused on a recent selfie of Gwen.

Her long dark hair hung over her left shoulder in a thick fishtail braid, and her silvery eyes sparkled with mirth. The smile on her face held just a hint of sultry attitude, and she was wearing the same Batman shirt she wore after the first time we hooked up. Her hand was against her chin, her fingers curled to display her manicured nails—nails that I still had scratch marks on my back from.

It was out of character for me to like other people's posts on Facebook, but I did it anyway. Gwen's smile had me tapping the reaction button before I could fully comprehend what I was doing, and by then it was too late.

A few moments later, my phone buzzed in my hands with an incoming text.

Gwen: Creeping my Facebook profile, are you?

Me: I was hoping you'd have a bikini profile pic for my perusal.

Gwen: LOL. Sorry to disappoint.

Me: I don't think you could ever disappoint. ;)

I hit send before I could overthink what I was doing. Before I could acknowledge just how *not* casual it was to be texting her like that.

Gwen: *Butter me up some more, and I just might send you that bikini selfie. Sans bikini.*

Me: *....*

Gwen responded with a photograph, and I fumbled, nearly dropping my phone as I waited for it to open.
The snapshot was of her body from the collarbone down, her pert breasts pushed up in a silky pink bra, her milky skin on display for me. I did a double take when I realized that her left hand was slipping underneath her matching panties.
Any reservations I'd had about our flirtatious text banter was replaced with white-hot desire.

Me: *No fair.*

Gwen: *Enjoy the rest of your weekend. ;)*

I awoke to the smell of sausage and eggs and my daughter's laughter trickling up the stairwell from the kitchen. Disoriented, I rolled over and grabbed my phone from the nightstand. It was nearly eight o'clock.
I dressed quickly before taking the stairs two at a time.
One of the dining room chairs was pushed up to the counter, with Sawyer standing on it, working alongside my

mother. She carefully spread butter on the toast, her brows wrinkled with concentration at each gentle pass of the knife.

"Morning," Mom said cheerfully, looking up at me as I sauntered into the kitchen. She glanced down, turning the sausages over so they'd cook evenly through.

"Hi, Daddy! We're making you breakfast!" Sawyer said, her green eyes sparkling with pride.

"Smells delicious," I told her, pressing a kiss to her forehead, my heart tight with the knowledge that I'd be dropping her off later tonight. Our weekends always flew by, especially this weekend, with Mom in town. "What do you ladies think about taking Tig for a hike after breakfast?"

"That sounds fun," Mom said, and Sawyer nodded with enthusiasm.

I grabbed a mug and poured myself a cup of coffee before Mom chased me from the kitchen, citing that they had no space to work with me standing there.

Stepping onto the back porch with my coffee in hand, Tig followed close behind me. Before sauntering over to the hedges near the property line, he lumbered down the steps and sniffed at the freshly planted garden that we'd spent the better part of yesterday working on.

Setting my mug on the wooden railing, I pulled my pack of smokes out and placed one between my lips, lighting it up.

After a cold shower, I'd crashed and slept like crap, unable to veer my thoughts away from Gwen—or the sultry picture she'd sent me. My balls ached in the worst way every time I looked at the photo, and I'd looked at it too many times to count.

Finishing up my smoke, I put it out in the ashtray and whistled, calling Tig back while I opened the door.

Sawyer was carefully carrying a pitcher of orange juice over to the table, moving slowly. I swooped in to help, steadying her grip on it and helping her lift it to the tabletop. "Thanks, Daddy." She said with notable relief, brushing the back of her little hand across her forehead and heaving an exhausted sigh.

"Cooking breakfast is hard work, isn't it?" I teased, my lips tilting up in a smile reserved only for my daughter; my little ray of light.

"Oh, it's no bother," Sawyer said sweetly, and my smile widened with amusement, my eyes darting to Mom. It was a term she said quite often.

Mom laughed, shaking her head, her eyes shining. She carried two plates to the table, setting them down before returning for the last one and the maple syrup. We sat down at the table and dug in.

"How is it, Daddy?" Sawyer asked, sitting up straighter and watching me chew a pancake with eager eyes.

"Very good," I assured her, taking another big bite. She flashed a toothy grin at her grandma.

"You're a wonderful helper, Sawyer," Mom said, her smile warm.

Sawyer beamed, and my heart thrummed with happiness at the sight of it. I'd do anything to make my little girl happy, but I didn't have to try hard. Sawyer just was an easy going, happy kid—well-rounded and adjusted, despite the storms and changes in her life.

Cheryl was waiting on the porch when I pulled up to the curb to drop Sawyer off. I nodded at her as I walked around to help Sawyer out.

Her lips were tugged down in a scowl, and her brows were

furrowed together. This was Cheryl in full-blown pissed off mode, and I knew just by looking at her that I was in for her wrath.

"Guess what Mommy! Grandma came to visit!"

Schooling her displeasure as much as she could, Cheryl offered our daughter a warmer smile and crouched to hug her. "I can't wait to hear all about it, but first—I have to talk to your Daddy. Why don't go say hi to Mason?"

Sawyer looked at me over her shoulder, then glanced back at her mother. The excitement that had shown in her eyes waned slightly. "You're not going to yell at him, are you?"

"Of course not." Cheryl smiled sternly, straightening and holding a hand to her back.

Sawyer turned and hugged me tightly. "Bye, Daddy."

"See you soon, kiddo," I promised, ruffling her hair. Cheryl and I both watched as she walked away, looking reluctantly over her shoulder, but my ex waited until after she'd closed the door to face me, her green eyes flashing with anger. "What's this about, Cheryl?"

"You know what this is about," she said, her tone icy. "Cindy told me something interesting." I blinked, the name rang a bell, but I couldn't remember why. "She said you mentioned you had a girlfriend. I told her that couldn't be true, but she told me she saw you the following weekend at a bar with some tart."

I exhaled, working to reign in my irritation at Gwen being called a tart by *Cheryl*, of all people. Cheryl, who let Mason go balls deep while she was still warming my bed. The irony made my lips curl. "What does it matter?"

"What?" Cheryl demanded, staring at me like she didn't understand my question.

"What does it matter to you if I have a girlfriend or not?" I repeated, keeping my cool despite the anger brewing inside of me.

"It doesn't matter," she snapped, her scowl deepening. "I just don't want *her* around Sawyer."

I chuckled without humor. "You introduced her to Mason pretty early on, if I recall."

"That's different," Cheryl said, her tone as stormy as the fury in her eyes.

"That's the thing, it really isn't." I corrected, shaking my head. "I don't have a girlfriend, but whether or not I did—it still wouldn't be your business."

"I have every right to know who my daughter is spending her time with when she's not with me."

"And so do I," I reminded her, my eyes narrowing a little.

We were at a standstill, neither one of us backing down. Cheryl drew in a controlled breath. "Just tell me, before you make any introductions."

"Fine," I said amicably. Cheryl turned, about to start up the walkway, but before she could take a step, I continued. "In turn, I want you to let me be more involved."

She pivoted slowly, her eyes narrowed. "I'm happy with the schedule as is," she said.

"I'm not," I insisted. "Jesus, Cheryl. You won't even consider letting me take Sawyer to help you out after the baby comes."

"I told you, Mason's mom—"

"I don't give a shit about Mason's mom," I responded, vibrating. "I'm tired of you pushing me out of our kid's life."

"I don't push you out of her life," she argued, and the look I gave her silenced her.

"Think long and hard about that, Cheryl. In fact, take the next eleven days and do just that. I'll see you then." I turned, giving her my back and effectively silencing any response that she might have had.

Gwen

I sat on the sofa with my legs crossed, my laptop open, fingers pounding against the keys as I wrote. Music poured softly from my speakers, and I was lost—lost in a scene within my head.

After sending Alaric those flirty messages last night, I'd been restless, unable to sleep until I'd brought out my trusty vibrator to ease the ache.

Only then, I was able to fall asleep—but I woke up just as tightly wound. I dispersed some of the energy by attacking my apartment, cleaning and dusting every inch, before falling onto my sofa with my laptop and a mug of tea, transforming all that restless, wanton energy into my story.

It was satisfying in a completely different way.

While I was in the writing zone, I never bothered glancing at the clock on the far right side of my toolbar. I kept my eyes glued to the document, watching the scenes come to life before me, slightly awed by the butterflies in my own stomach.

I couldn't prevent Alaric from occasionally barging into my thoughts. I'd see, in my mind's eye, my male character doing something, and suddenly it would be an actual memory, something Alaric had said or done. The way he'd smiled or touched me and the accompanying roll of desire in my core that would follow.

Each time this happened, my fingers would freeze, and I'd huff with exasperation. He was the muse and the block, all at once.

Likely because my little masturbation session hadn't really helped ease the constant desire I'd ached with all weekend long. Especially after sending him that picture...I'd cursed myself as well as him.

But that just made the whole thing hotter, naughtier, and that—in turn—was beginning to seriously frustrate me.

I wondered if it would be crossing the line to text him, to beg him to come over again. I wanted to fill up on him, drink up that *dickspiration,* ride the high of letting go of my reservations and giving in to desire.

Give into the escape.

Give into not feeling so desperately alone, because when Alaric was here, I didn't feel alone. I didn't feel like a clock was ticking, each second booming its fleeting existence.

Sighing deeply, I set my laptop down on the coffee table and reached for my tea. I sipped it, frowning when the cold liquid touched my tongue.

Someone knocked, a fist heavy against the door. I set the cold tea down and stood, tugging down my sleep shorts and tank top, hoping despite it all. I peeked through the hole, and my heart jumped unsteadily at the sight of Alaric on the other side.

I unlocked the door quickly and opened it, forgetting that I wasn't presentable. I hadn't bothered with makeup, nor had I done much to my hair, save for tossing it up in a messy bun to keep it off my neck while I wrote. But Alaric's eyes were full of heat as they roamed my face, and at that moment, I'd never felt more beautiful.

His gaze lingered on my lips before slowly moving down the length of my body and up again, his lips curving into a suggestive smile that made the butterflies take flight. "Hey."

"Hey yourself. What brings you to my doorstep?" I asked coyly, tilting my head.

"I was on my way home. Figured I'd stop in and say hello," he admitted, his eyes still drinking me in.

"Just to stay hello, huh?"

"Maybe not *just* hello." He grinned and stepped over the threshold into my apartment.

I closed the door, and Alaric pressed against me from behind as I slid the deadbolt into place, his lips grazing across the side of my neck.

I shivered, goosebumps appearing on my flesh, each of them proclaiming just how desperately turned on I was.

"I'm glad you stopped by, to say hello," I managed, my voice sounding strange and shaky.

Alaric grunted, smiling against my neck as he tugged the front of my tank top down, freeing my breast. He continued kissing my neck while his fingers tweaked my nipple, and I sighed, pushing back on him. I ground against his erection, enjoying the feel of him through denim while wishing both our clothes would disappear completely.

He pulled his hand out, and leaned back, dragging the tank top up with him. I turned, my breasts swaying and aching for his touch. I yanked his shirt off, moistening my lips with my tongue as my gaze raked across his chest.

Words weren't necessary; I knew what he was here for, what he wanted, and I still couldn't believe *he* wanted me as much as I wanted him. Before I could get lost in that fact, Alaric's large hand cupped my chin, guiding my lips to his while his other hand slipped down my stomach, into the waistband of my shorts.

I whimpered when his fingers brushed against my sex, my thighs trembling with want. Alaric swallowed it greedily, never breaking the kiss. I felt it everywhere, and it seared. My heart pounded as he slipped two of his fingers inside.

"You're so wet," he growled, pressing his forehead to mine and dragging in a ragged breath as his fingers glided in and out.

Gasping, I broke away, trying to catch my breath. Alaric

pulled my shorts down over my hips, and I kicked them off, tugging at his belt impatiently, desperate to unwrap every inch of him. His hands moved to cover mine, and he helped me unclasp the buckle. I dragged the zipper down, but before I could push them completely off his hips, he stopped me long enough to remove his boots and pick me up.

My legs locked around his hips, and I could feel his hardness through the thin material of his boxer briefs. Shamelessly, I pressed down, grinding against his thick tip. The thin material of his boxer briefs easing the ache a little, but if he didn't get inside of me soon, I wasn't sure if I'd be able to stop myself from screaming with frustration.

Alaric grunted, sounding just as tortured as I felt. "How strong is your table?" he asked, heading in that direction.

"Not very," I said regrettably. It was a particleboard table, and I didn't trust it to support my cat's weight—let alone ours.

Alaric let out a low chuckle and turned, walking down the hallway to my bedroom, carrying me like I weighed nothing.

He set me down on the mattress and stood, grabbed his wallet from the back pocket of his jeans, and pulled out a strip of condoms before he kicked them the rest of the way off. I leaned forward, pushing his boxer briefs over his hips, eager to help him.

The tip of his cock was already glistening with precum, and I drew him into my mouth eagerly, my tongue swirling around the crown. He let out a noise caught somewhere between a moan and a growl as I worked him in and out of my mouth. It was the most erotic song, and my veins thrummed with power.

"If you don't stop that, I'm going to come."

I pulled away, keeping one hand on his throbbing cock, and using the other to cup his balls. He moaned, and I looked up at him, my lips curving into a wicked smile. "You say it like it's a bad thing."

I felt like a goddess, and it had everything to do with him. Bringing a man like him to the brink of pleasure, having that kind of power—it was intoxicating. So was the way he looked at me, the way he touched me.

Alaric chuckled, using his fingers to angle my chin up, forcing me to meet his eyes. They sparkled like an open flame, and my breath caught in my lungs. "I want to be inside you when I come."

His heady words and the look in his eyes when he said them made my heart skip a beat.

"Fair enough," I managed, leaning back and watching as he slipped a condom on. I collapsed against the mattress, my legs falling open in welcome.

He crawled over top of me, settling between my thighs. He paused for a breath, before taking me with one deep thrust, sliding into me with ease.

My walls tightened around him, and I could feel him pulsing in response. "Fuck," he hissed, drawing out the word.

Before I could form a response, he pulled out, then thrust forward again. He picked up the pace, fucking me with a steady rhythm. My nails raked against his back, urging him on, and each hard, sure thrust brought me closer to climax. My toes curled, and I let out a pleasured whimper as the first orgasm rocked through me.

CHAPTER THIRTEEN

UNSPOKEN REVELATIONS

Alaric

Gwen's eyes fluttered shut with bliss. My jaw clenched as I fought my own orgasm off as long as I could, but *Christ* she was responsive, and after three more thrusts, I couldn't hold it off any longer.

Her nails dug into my lower back, and my balls tightened almost painfully. I drew out once more, slamming into her again, thrusting as far as I could go and moaning out my release into her neck.

"So, you liked the sexy selfie I take it?" she asked a moment later, her voice somewhat muffled, and I realized then I was probably crushing her.

Chuckling a little, I pulled out and rolled over. Removing the condom, I tied it off. "Yeah, I liked it. Feel free to send more."

"Maybe I will," she said, a mischievous smile on her face. She sat up, glancing at the alarm clock on her end table while I stood and walked across the hallway to the bathroom to toss out the condom. "Are you hungry?" she asked when I returned, biting her lip.

"I could eat," I replied, my eyes dropping to her sweet pussy.

"I mean actual food." She laughed before sitting up the rest of the way. "I forgot to eat dinner."

"How do you forget to eat?"

"It's easy to do." She shrugged, not meeting my eyes. "You just get caught up in something else."

"And what were you caught up in?" I frowned when her ominous words about finding *something else to occupy her time* filled my mind. It shouldn't matter, but it did.

"Writing," she replied, her eyes sparkling with amusement. She stood, crossing over to her dresser and opening a drawer. Gwen slowly slid a pair of blue lace panties up over her thighs, and I already couldn't wait to take them off—with my teeth.

"Writing?" I repeated, the corners of my lips twitching with the urge to smile. I didn't want to reveal how relieved I was that she hadn't told me she was with some other guy.

"It's a little hobby of mine." She shrugged, her smile fading a little like she was embarrassed to admit it.

I eyed her lewdly, finally allowing my grin to break free. "What do you write?"

"Lately? A lot of sexy things," she admitted, a flush staining her dimpled cheeks.

"That's hot," I managed, my hardening cock jumping once in agreement. "I kind of want to read these sexy things."

"Why don't I show you instead?" she purred, and I grinned wider.

"Please do," I said, relaxing now that we'd steered the conversation back to a familiar, more sexual territory because I was a little too interested in her answers, and I didn't know how to feel about that.

I didn't quite know how to feel about showing up at her doorstep, either. I tried to reason with myself on the drive over, telling myself it was just the sex I craved. But... that wasn't entirely true. I came here because I felt a sense of calm when my thoughts had drifted to her, and I knew she'd relieve some of the tension.

And she did. From the moment she'd opened the door to me, I felt the tension slipping away. She was exactly the kind of distraction I needed, and I wasn't finished with her yet.

"Anyway." She smirked attractively before continuing. "I got caught up in that, and now I'm starving. I made pesto penne yesterday. It's pretty good, if you're hungry. Unless you're planning on leaving, I mean."

She spoke as if she was indifferent to whether I stayed or went, and that made me want to stay even more. It made me want to peel back her layers and see if I'd gotten under her skin the way she'd crawled under mine.

"I'm in no rush," I said thickly, my gaze slipping to the apex of her thighs.

"Down boy, food first," she scolded in jest. Grabbing a t-shirt from her drawer, she pulled it over her head and slipped from the room, blithely disappearing down the hallway. I could hear her opening the refrigerator as I dressed.

I walked down the hallway, still shirtless. I couldn't remember where I'd lost that particular article of clothing, but I wasn't overly concerned about it since I wasn't planning on either of us staying dressed.

Pausing in the kitchen entryway, I watched as Gwen pulled out a glass dish from the microwave using a dishtowel to protect her hands, while her cat weaved in and around her legs, purring.

She was captivating without even trying, and it was enslaving.

Her shirt barely covered her ass, same as the first night we met, and my cock stirred restlessly. "Smells good." My mouth watered for more than her penne.

"Thanks," she said, glancing at me over her shoulder for a moment before she set to serving it. She filled two plates and grabbed a couple of forks before walking toward me, her eyes fixated on my pectorals.

Her tongue darted to moisten her lips as she held a bowl to me, and I took it, my fingers brushing against hers purposely, as her gray eyes lifted to meet mine.

"Cheers," I said, grinning ruefully as she moved past me and set her bowl on the coffee table.

She walked back into the kitchen to open the refrigerator. "Thirsty? I've got water and 7 Up."

"Water's fine," I answered, moving to the couch.

Gwen nodded, grabbing two bottles from the door before closing it. She walked back to the living room and sat down, leaving a few feet between us. She set both bottles down and picked up her bowl, settling comfortably on the sofa with her legs crossed.

"This is the second time you've fed me," I remarked, my brows raising. "Are you trying to get to my heart through my stomach?"

"Hardly," she scoffed. "Friends can feed friends. Besides, I'm mostly feeding me. Like I said, I needed sustenance before round two." She shrugged and took a large bite.

It was oddly sensual that she wasn't afraid to eat in front of me. It made her feel more real like she wasn't concealing any part of herself like she wasn't trying to impress me. She just... was, and that disarmed me.

"Fair enough." I laughed lowly before taking a bite. The

flavor exploded on my tongue, and I moaned. "Fuck, woman. This tastes almost as good as you."

"I'll take that as a compliment." She laughed, colour staining her cheeks.

"As you should." I grinned, eating another bite, enjoying the smile my words brought to her face. The force of her beauty made my balls ache. Even without makeup, she was stunning. Flawless skin, thick lashes, and plump lips still swollen from our frenzied kisses.

Watching the way her lips wrapped around the fork sent all the blood in my system rushing south.

My cock strained against my zipper, and I set my empty bowl down, eyes still fixated on her. She smirked, taking one last bite of pasta before mirroring my action.

"Are you ready for dessert?" she asked coyly, I nodded eagerly, grinning as I watched her stand and remove her t-shirt. She tossed it aside carelessly. "Meet me in the bathroom in five and bring a condom this time." She tossed the words over her shoulder, disappearing behind the bathroom door.

She didn't have to tell me twice.

Gwen

Behind the safety of the bathroom door, I sat down on the toilet, trying to calm my racing heart.

Something had shifted. I couldn't figure out if it was him or me.

Who was I kidding, it was probably me.

Inwardly groaning, I glared at the ceiling. I needed to get myself together, and fast—the five minutes I'd given Alaric was quickly slipping away. I'd have plenty of time to sift through my emotional turbulence later when he left.

Taking a deep breath, I finished peeing and flushed the

toilet. I brushed my teeth with breakneck speed, making sure I got rid of all traces of food, and darted over to the tub to turn on the shower.

Tugging my hair free, I ran my hands through the curls to separate them. I took another fortifying breath, and my nipples hardened against the chill in the air and the anticipation.

Alaric knocked softly. "Come in," I called, looking over my shoulder to watch him. He was still wearing his jeans, although he'd unbuttoned them and was commando. His thickening erection slapped proudly against the hard planes of his stomach when he pushed them the rest of the way down.

He was so goddamn hot that looking directly at him was enough to get the juices pumping. I smirked a little, trying to play coy. "Hope you remembered the condoms."

"I did." He grinned, flashing the strip at me. I pulled back the curtain, disappearing behind it.

"There's a spare toothbrush on the counter if you want." I closed my eyes and let the hot water cascade over me.

"Is that a subtle hint to brush my teeth?"

"Yes," I admitted, poking my head out to grin at him. I laughed at the look on his face. "Relax. I have a stash of never-opened toothbrushes under the sink."

"Why?" His brow furrowed, and my heart fluttered with the possibility that he was feeling jealous. I desperately hoped he was.

"Look at the box." I arched a brow, knowing it said the name of my dental office. "They give them out every time you go, but I don't like the brand. I just take them to be polite, and they do come in handy."

"Do you do a lot of entertaining?"

"No," I said slowly. "I use them to clean the shower grout." I disappeared behind the curtain as he chuckled.

Even his *laugh* was attractive. It was like he wasn't made from the same stuff as regular people.

A couple of minutes later, Alaric joined me in the shower. He set a condom within reach on the side of the tub and moved toward me. Lowering his head, his lips brushed tenderly against mine before his hand tangled in my wet curls.

Deepening the kiss, Alaric moved forward until he'd backed me against the wall of the shower. He palmed my ass with his free hand, squeezing possessively.

He hooked my leg up and held it, moving tighter against me. I nibbled on his lip, and his cock throbbed against my thigh in response. We were slippery and wet, and when I gripped the back of his neck, he slid against my core.

We both drew in a breath, eyes fixated on the place where he'd brushed against me. The feel of his skin against my core made me whimper with want.

Alaric drew in a breath and released me, reaching for the condom. He ripped the package open, then donned the latex in one fluid motion.

Before I could question the logistics of shower sex, Alaric had already lifted me. My legs wrapped around his waist, and my back pressed against the wall of the shower. He supported me with his capable hands, sliding effortlessly into me.

I gasped at the welcomed intrusion, my head falling back against the wall. My worries about his height fell away. My hands slipped around Alaric's shoulders, along his muscular upper back. I tried to be conscious of my nails, but each time he drove his hips forward, they dug in a little more on their own accord.

I'd never been with someone so intent on my pleasure before, so capable of reading my body and what it needed. It was the strangest thing, to feel safe in his arms while feeling completely ravaged at the same time.

I shattered around him, my entire being exploding into fragments. Alaric's hips thrust forward again, harder and deeper this time, as he moaned his release in my ear.

My skin pebbled with goosebumps, and I drew a shaky breath, lifting my head to gaze at him. I was unable to contain my smile because he was looking like I'd given *him* a gift when in reality, it'd been him giving me the glorious gift of multiple orgasms.

He withdrew, setting me down carefully. Rolling the condom off, Alaric tied it and opened the curtain enough to toss it in the trash, then turned to face me. "Any sexy shower scenes in your book?"

"No." I bit my lip, shaking my head with amusement. "Usually, shower sex is rather anti-climactic."

Alaric's brow lifted, and he moved closer to me. A dangerous smile on his lips. "Did you find that anti-climactic?" he asked, his hand palming my breast. I shivered, and not just because the hot water had started to run out.

"Quite the opposite, actually. I found it very climactic," I said, my jaw trembling slightly. Noticing the cold water, Alaric switched the taps off. I threw open the shower curtain and reached for a towel. "Then again, you're strong enough to support all of my weight while still fucking like a porn star, so I'd say you're the exception, not the rule."

He chuckled lowly. "You must have been with some uncreative partners."

I snorted. "You don't know the half of it," I said ominously, stepping from the shower and wrapping the towel around me.

He followed, twisting a towel around his waist. His eyes never left mine, and tension crackled between us. His pecs flexed under my scrutiny, and he grinned dangerously. "There are many ways we can fuck in that shower, Gwen. I'd be happy to show you all of them." He capped this offer by flexing his pecs.

"Maybe when the hot water tank refills," I said, a little breathlessly.

"Yeah," Alaric agreed. He shook his head as if coming to his senses. "Besides, it's getting late. I should go."

"Oh, right," I said, my words coming out as jumbled as my thoughts. I clenched my towel closer and moved to the counter to grab my glasses. Putting them on, I could see him in the mirror from the corner of my eye, watching me, so I smiled and met his gaze. "Well, thanks for stopping by."

He leaned forward to pick up his jeans, his face right beside my thigh. I could feel his perusal, his eyes roaming my body like he wasn't quite sated yet. Straightening, Alaric moved behind me, pressing his cock against my ass. My towel fell open on its own accord, slipping between us. "It was my pleasure," he told me, grinning as he watched me in the mirror.

It seemed inconceivable that we could want each other again, but the look in his fevered eyes matched mine as he ran his free hand down the length of my body, over each curve.

No matter what, he was going to leave me wanting.

Alaric

I took a deep breath, watching as she trembled beneath my touch. Her eyelids fluttered shut, and she sighed, her lips curling into a smile. "How are you already this hard again?" she asked as my cock jumped against her ass.

I tugged her against me, my fingers falling between her legs, cupping her. The pads of my fingers stroked against her sex. Bringing my lips to her earlobe, I spoke quietly. "How are you this wet again?" I countered, smirking as we made eye contact in the mirror.

She shuddered as my finger sank inside her and turned her face to look at me. I dropped my jeans and brought my right hand to stroke along the smooth, delicate column of her neck.

Gwen turned, her breasts brushing against my chest as her lips slanted against mine. She nipped at my lower lip as I hoisted her up, plopping her down on the counter and stepping between her legs.

"I thought you said you had to go?" Gwen asked, her nose scrunching a little as she smiled.

"I can spare a few more minutes," I told her, selfishly prolonging the inevitable. I wasn't looking forward to the silence of my empty house, especially not after a weekend having both Sawyer and my mom around.

I knew the moment that I left, everything that drove me here in the first place would come back at me like a freight train.

She brought her hands up to cup my face, pressing her lips to mine, and arched against me. Her lips and tongue moved almost desperately against mine. I shifted, my crown brushing against her entrance, and shivered in response to the urge I felt to drive forward.

Gwen's eyes fluttered open, and she pulled away, her eyes searching mine again. I don't know what she saw there, but she took a shaky breath and gave me a willing smile. "Is this what you're looking for?" she asked, one of her hands dropping to reach the foil wrapper beside her.

My cock throbbed against her slick entrance in response. "Can you handle another round?"

"Can I?" She arched a brow, challenging me, and ripped the wrapper open with her teeth. She looked so incredibly sexy that I couldn't help but press against her a little.

It was closer than I'd gotten to someone in years, and that should have scared me into leaving—but I was no longer thinking with my head.

She trembled, and I backed off a little, my restraint tested enough. Gwen rolled on the condom, guiding it down my thick length.

I lifted her, entering in one fluid motion. She leaned back, her wet hair spilling over her shoulders.

She felt a little swollen, so I moved gently, taking my time, watching her face to make sure I wasn't hurting her. Her eyes were dark with desire, and she grew wetter with each thrust.

I licked my fingers and played with her clit. Gwen dropped her head back and moaned softly, and sensing that she was close, I picked up the pace a little. Her legs trembled as she came.

Spurred on by her orgasm, I fucked her harder. My hips jutted forward with powerful strokes as I sought to bury myself in her. My balls tightened, the pressure building as I slammed my hips forward once more.

The last thrust did it for her again too, and she moaned before letting out a pained yelp.

I pulled out quickly, concern etching my face. "Fuck, are you okay?"

"Yeah, I'm fine. It's just a leg cramp." She laughed, rubbing at her calf. I took over, working the muscle with my hands. A few moments later, she let out a sigh of relief, and I felt the muscle release. "Thanks," she said, appreciatively. "For the coitus and the massage."

"Any time." I winked, peeling the condom off and tossing it in the trash before offering her my hand. She took it and slid off the bathroom counter. She leaned forward to pick her towel up, wrapping it around her body. When she straightened, she gripped the counter, and it slipped forward.

"Shit," she said, her brow furrowing as she wiggled it again. We'd managed to loosen the counter from the wall.

"I'll fix it," I offered sheepishly.

"You don't have to," she said quickly. "My landlord can do it. It's his job, after all..." Lost in thought, she worried her bottom lip.

"It's not a big deal. I have all the stuff to do it at my place." I scooped my jeans off the floor and straightened. "I'll bring them next time you text me begging for my cock," I added with a smirk.

She laughed. "All right, fine. Whatever."

"Whatever?" I prodded teasingly.

"I'm tired, and my brain doesn't exactly work during this time of post-orgasmic bliss. If you want to fix my counter, who am I to stop you?" She shrugged, leaving the bathroom and heading for her room.

My socks were on the floor in front of her nightstand, so I followed her in. She was pulling on a pair of sleep shorts. I reached for the socks, jumping back when a gray paw shot out and swiped at my hand.

Gwen's cat had hidden under the bed and didn't seem impressed with my close proximity to him. He let out a low hiss. "Dahmer, don't be a dick," Gwen ordered, her lips twitching with a bemused smile.

I reached again, managing to get them without the cat trying to scratch me, but he continued his low growling until I backed away.

Gwen walked me to the door, pausing to pick up my shirt and toss it to me.

I caught it, pulling it over my head. I put my boots on and stood, watching while she opened the door. "I'll see you tomorrow, maybe." She smiled.

"Maybe," I repeated, the corner of my lip tugging into a

half-smile as I moved past her. I hesitated, my hands twitching at my sides with the urge to touch her. I resisted. I nodded, forcing my legs to move forward.

I didn't let myself look back, either. Not even when I heard the soft click of her door closing.

CHAPTER FOURTEEN

DEFINED...SORTA

Gwen

I had a difficult time getting up for work Monday morning after I'd spent half the night tossing and turning, pressing a finger to my lips every so often as I relived every kiss, every sigh. It hadn't made for a restful night.

And I hated myself for it, for already catching feelings, but really...*he* was to blame. He wasn't supposed to be this... perfect. He was everything I never knew I wanted, and he made me feel things so intensely.

As much as I tried to fool myself into thinking that there was something in his gaze, in his touch, I knew these feelings were likely one-sided. My blessing and my curse was an active imagination, and I was well aware of my tendency to get ahead of myself.

So, I'd resolved to distance myself, just a little. Until Wednesday, at least. Or maybe Tuesday. After reaching that conclusion, I finally fell asleep, but that was around two thirty in the morning, and suffice to say, I wasn't exactly wide-eyed and bushy-tailed this morning.

I was walking with my head down, looking at the stack of papers in my hands as I walked back to my desk from the copier.

"Morning, Gwen," Dad said cheerfully as he strolled through the office.

I jumped a little, startled. I hadn't heard the door open, I'd been so lost in my muddled thoughts. "Hey, Dad."

"You look tired, are you feeling okay?"

"I'm fine," I assured him, smiling. "What do you need?" Dad didn't typically make social calls, so if he was coming into the office, it was work related.

"I need you to make up a newsletter about the Canada Day barbeque and send it out to all employees. It's in two more weeks."

"Oh, right." I nodded, having completely forgotten about the annual barbeque. Normally, I'd have sent the newsletter out by now. "I'll get that done today."

"Excellent. And give Grant Hernandez a call. I need him to come in sometime this week to look over the blueprints for the ravine condo project."

"What happened to George? I thought he was the engineer for this project." I frowned, confused.

"George has fucked up on the blueprints twice now, I need Grant. Get him here, okay?"

"Of course," I said, jotting down a note on the pad of post-it notes on my desk.

"One more thing," Dad said, sending me an apologetic smile. "Your mom expects you at dinner Friday night."

"Ugh, but I came over last week," I muttered, scowling. Dad arched a brow, wounded. "Come on Dad, every time I'm around her she makes me feel like a spinster for still being single, and then she starts listing off every available bachelor that she knows."

"Your mother just wants to see you happy," Dad said sternly, walking toward my desk and coming to a stop in front of it. His pewter eyes sparkled with amusement.

"Who says I need a man to be happy?" I frowned, crossing my arms. "Erik certainly didn't make me happy."

"Erik wasn't really a man," Dad responded, his eyes darkening with a smidgen of anger. He'd been pretty pissed when Erik had left me, thus crushing my spirit and heart, and he'd never been a fan of my ex-boyfriend. I pity the fool that truly raised a hand to hurt either Kelsey or me; they'd meet Dad's wrath and then some. "Besides, you don't want her to chase you down, do you?"

"Nope, I wouldn't want that." I sighed. "I'll be there."

"Great." Dad grinned, tapping my desk once with his knuckle before turning and heading back into the shop.

Alone again, I heaved an Oscar-worthy sigh and sank into my chair. I flipped through the business card carousel for Grant's information. Finding it, I picked up the phone and dialed the number.

"Grant speaking. What can I do for you?"

"Morning Grant. It's Gwen from Williams' Tech. Russell needs you to come in sometime this week to go over the blueprints for the ravine condo project."

"I thought George was on that project?"

"Russell needs it done right, and he needs it done now," I replied. "Can you do it?"

"Of course," he said, pausing. I heard shuffling before he spoke again. "I'll be in the area between eleven and one. I'll stop by then."

"Thank you," I said. "Have a great day." I placed the phone on the cradle.

With one thing crossed off my to-do list for the day, I started on the next task; the newsletter about the barbeque. I liked to make my job as easy as possible, so I opened last year's newsletter and started changing things around to include the proper information for this year.

A few hours later, the bell above the office door chimed, and I looked up from my computer screen as Grant Hernandez strolled in.

He walked purposefully over to my desk with a charming smile on his handsome face, his dark eyes taking me in with appreciation.

Grant was an attractive guy with dark eyes and hair, and beautifully tanned skin, but he was also one of the guys who *knew* how good looking he was.

At twenty-eight, he'd begun to make a name for himself in the construction industry as one of the top architectural engineers. He was always charming when he came in, if not a little flirtatious.

"Good afternoon," I greeted him with a professional smile, ignoring the interest in his perusal as I pressed a button on the phone that connected me with the shop. Grant was a known flirt, and I'd long since grown unresponsive to his charms. Besides, I had enough man problems. "Russell, Grant is here to see you."

It had taken me a while to get used to addressing my father by his first name at work, but now it barely phased me.

"Looking as gorgeous as ever, Gwen," Grant said, taking my hand and shaking it. I arched a brow when he held on a moment longer than necessary and tugged it from his grip. He winked and leaned forward. "I heard a rumour you were single."

"Ha," I said dryly, my eyes narrowing. "What's it to you?"

"I happen to be single, too," he informed me, his eyes still on me.

"Good for you," I said dryly, my smile growing a little colder. I heard the connecting door open, but I didn't bother looking up. I knew it was probably my dad.

"Let me take you out sometime," he offered, his teeth flashing as his smile deepened. "I know a great restaurant near the lake."

Dad cleared his throat, saving me from having to reply. "Grant. I've got the blueprints in my office if you'll follow me. Gwen, why don't you take that lunch break?"

I already had my lunch break, but I didn't bother to argue with him about it. I'd take a second one. Nodding, I grabbed my purse and smiled politely at Grant before moving around my desk.

I glanced over my shoulder as I opened the door. Grant's head was turned, and he was still watching me with a smarmy grin that held none of the warmth of Alaric's smiles.

When I returned to my desk twenty minutes later, Grant's business card was on it, only he'd also added his personal number and urged me to call him.

I stared at it for a few moments before tossing it into the wastebasket beside my desk.

Despite the many well-rounded excuses that I easily

conjured in my mind, I managed to make it through the day without texting Alaric.

My self-restraint was pretty good—for someone so weak and susceptible to giving in. A slight breeze could have sent me spiraling in his direction, and I would have gone happily. Skipping, even. But thankfully, our paths didn't cross. If I had to look directly into his blue eyes, I was afraid I'd be forced to face the truth.

That I most definitely was suffering from *the feels*. I'd thrown out Grant's number without a second thought. I had no desire to hang onto his number *just in case*. I knew that nothing and nobody would compare to the welder that rolled so suddenly into my life like a summer storm.

Sighing, I kicked off my heels and let my purse fall to the ground with an audible thud. Strolling down the hall to my bedroom, I tugged down the zipper of my skirt.

Crossing the threshold into my room, I tossed my work clothes into the hamper and went to my dresser, pulling out a pair of yoga pants and a t-shirt. Casual enough that I'd be comfortable, but just dressy enough that if someone—like, say, *Alaric*—happened to stop by, I'd still look cute.

Usually, I changed within moments of arriving home—and not just because I preferred to be comfortable. Dahmer was known to wreak havoc on any material in sight with his claws, and his fur got *everywhere*.

I'd lost many of nice clothes when he'd jumped on my lap for snuggles, as he'd always end up digging his claws into the material when he finally hopped off.

While I'd gotten Dahmer fixed as soon as he was old enough, I'd opted to skip out on declawing him. I was convinced it was inhumane. Instead, I just bought a scratching post and hoped for the best. So long as I made sure to keep my closet door closed, changed when I got home and gave him the attention he craved, we were good.

Dahmer meowed from the slipper chair in the corner of my room, where he preferred to spend his days. "To be a cat," I muttered, shaking my head as I watched him stretch leisurely. He meowed again, his green eyes watching me in a way I didn't quite trust. He was full of pent-up energy, and if he didn't burn it off, he'd get mean. "Come on then," I sighed, turning and leaving my room, snatching the tiny laser beam from the top of my dresser.

It was one of Dahmer's favourite activities, and one of the easiest ways to work off some energy. I heard him jump down, his steps audible on the laminate flooring as he trailed after me.

I grabbed my phone from my purse before I sat down on the couch, just to have it nearby. Flicking the laser beam on, I pointed it on the floor in front of the furry terror. He lurched into action, chasing the little red beam of light wherever I directed it. I tried to keep my focus on him and not my phone, which sat silently beside me, with nary a message.

My stomach tightened with an emotion somewhere between dread and disappointment that I still hadn't heard from him.

A door across the hall open and closed, followed by footsteps shuffling across the carpet and three impatient taps on my door. "Girlie, are you in there? Got some package from the Amazon for you. The man wouldn't stop ringing the buzzer."

Hearing Mrs. Hewitt's voice, I stood and quickly crossed over to open the door.

She thrust the box at me, and I took it gratefully. "Thanks, Mrs. Hewitt. I'm really sorry about that."

"You should be. It was irritating and inconsiderate." Mrs. Hewitt said crossly before turning to leave.

"Well, thank you again, Mrs. Hewitt."

"You're welcome," she said, scrutinizing me for a moment before she continued across the hall.

Alaric

I was at the shop for five o'clock that morning to meet Mitch, and then we spent an additional two hours on the job site, just trying to get it done so we didn't have to come out again.

I hadn't heard from Gwen since I left her place, but that hadn't stopped me from thinking about her all day long.

Before leaving my house, I'd tossed the supplies I'd need to fix her counter into the backseat, intent on repairing it as soon as possible. I knew it was just another excuse to see her again.

It was nearly six when we finally got back to the shop, and I couldn't leave quick enough.

"Hold up a moment, son." I froze at the sound of my boss's voice and turned, keys in hand, watching as Russell approached my truck. I couldn't remember the last time I'd been intimidated by a girl's father, and it went past him being my employer. "I just spoke to Mitch, and he gave another glowing review of your performance on site. You've completed another job ahead of schedule."

"I didn't do it myself," I responded, shrugging and hoping like hell I didn't look as uneasy as I felt.

Russell let out a low chuckle and scratched the back of his head thoughtfully. "Well, I appreciate the hard work." He said, his eyes twinkling.

"It's my job, sir," I told him, my hand twitching at my side.

I gripped my keys a little tighter, not exactly trusting the calculating look in my boss's eyes as he appraised me.

Russell cleared his throat. "I'm going to toss you in the shop for the rest of the week. We fell a little behind on the Creek project after a few measurement mishaps, and I think throwing you in there will help bring us back up to speed."

"Of course." I nodded, relaxing marginally. It wasn't about Gwen.

"We need to be on track to start assembling by Wednesday next week."

"I can make it happen," I told him.

"Great. You have a good night, son. See ya tomorrow," Russell said, nodding once before turning and heading back into the office.

I hit unlock on my remote and climbed in, letting out a heavy sigh. I rolled my neck, working the tension out, and shoved the key into the ignition, turning it with a flick of my wrist, guilt churning in my gut.

I should head straight home, end this thing between the two of us. Clearly, I was having a harder time keeping things casual and compartmentalized.

Maybe I don't want to.

The thought caught me completely off guard, and it was accompanied by the mental image of Gwen's head thrown back in ecstasy as I drove into her over and over again.

Normally, it was easy to keep sex separate from feelings, but I was beginning to realize that nothing about what we had was normal.

Not the way I burned for her, not the way she crept into my thoughts at mundane moments, and certainly not from the wave of calm that washed over me the closer I got to her.

I hesitated with my hand on the gearshift. Conflicting thoughts rolled around in my head—the conversation I had with my mother over the weekend, the one-sided argument I'd had with Cheryl, and my own wants and desires, my own fears and hang-ups.

The kicker was I knew what my dad would say if he were still here. He'd tell me to stop being an idiot and get the girl. Find a way to make it all work.

Tugging the gearshift, I pressed my heavy work boot down on the gas pedal and rolled from the parking lot, steering my truck in the direction of her apartment.

I parked at the curb and hopped out, opening the rear door to grab the supplies I'd tossed in. I made my way to the entrance, slowing when I saw the brick propping the door open.

Opening it, I climbed the five steps to Gwen's apartment, pausing in front of her door. I took a breath and raised my fist, knocking hollowly against the cheap wood. A few moments later, it swung forward.

Gwen's dark hair was pulled back into a ponytail, and she was wearing pants that looked painted on. Her eyes widened with surprise. She hadn't been expecting me, but she smiled brightly like she was happy to see me.

"Hey. Figured I'd stop in and fix that counter top," I told her, trying to ignore the nervous pounding of my heart that betrayed why I was really there. To see her.

I walked in, my heart slowing its frantic pulses. "Oh, you don't have to do that," she said, turning and heading back into the living room.

"It'll take fifteen minutes," I said, removing my work boots.

"Hmm, and are you expecting sexual favours in exchange for manual labour?" she asked, smiling at me over her shoulder.

"I don't expect anything," I replied, my lips twitching into a smile as I neared her. "I broke it. I'll fix it."

"All right," she breathed. I moved past her and continued to the bathroom, to fix the counter we'd broken.

Music started playing from the living room. Some kind of pop/hip-hop band I'd never heard before. It was so vastly different from what I listened to, and so completely her that I couldn't help but smile and shake my head.

Fifteen minutes later, I cleaned up my tools and put the lid back on the concrete cement before I looked over at Gwen standing in the doorway, wearing just the t-shirt. She tugged it over her head, letting it fall to the ground behind her, smiling playfully as she moved toward me.

"You'll want to let it set overnight, but it's good to go," I said gruffly, swallowing hard as I watched her hips sway with every step.

"Thank you." She hid a smile as she tilted her head, watching me, seeming to see everything and miss nothing. She stopped before me, her fingers deftly releasing my buckle and tugging down the zipper of my work jeans.

Her hand wrapped around the base of my cock before I could respond, and I let out a grunt as she pumped me with one hand and tugged my shirt up over my abs with the other, her nails raking against my skin.

I pulled it the rest of the way off as she moved on to my pants, pushing them down over my hips. She leaned away from me then to start the shower.

"I can't stay long," I warned her as she straightened and turned to me.

"That's okay," she said, and I could tell she meant it. Her lips curled in a slow smile as I moved against her, brushing her hair from her face with my hands. Looking into her eyes, it was impossible to deny how effortlessly she'd gotten to me.

She stepped into the tub, and a moment later, I followed. I let the water pelt my back while my hands slid against her slick hips. Gwen's arms wrapped around my neck, and we kissed, the water streaming between and all around us.

"Why don't you show me another one of those ways to have amazing shower sex?" she suggested, speaking against my lips and arching a brow.

I grinned, completely up for the challenge, and turned her so that she stood with her back to me.

"Thanks again," she said, tucking a damp strand of hair behind her ear. "You saved me from having to call my landlord." Her nose wrinkled a little as if the thought of having to call her landlord troubled her.

"Don't like your landlord?" I asked, setting down my supplies against the wall so I could pull on my boots, my eyes still on her. She was gravity, and I couldn't seem to tear myself away.

The last thing I wanted to do right now was leave, but I knew I had to. Tig was waiting for me.

"I guess you could say that." She shrugged as I made my way over to her; watching her lips as they curved into an attractive smile as I approached. "He's kind of sleazy."

The smile faded from my lips, and I lifted my chin, a wave of protectiveness overcoming me. "Is he giving you trouble?"

She laughed, her smile widening. "I can handle myself."

"I'm sure you can." My lips twitched.

"I appreciate the concern, though," she remarked, eyeing me suggestively. "It's a turn on."

"Is it now?"

Gwen laughed again stood on her tip-toes to kiss me. "I'll see you later, Alaric."

"Yeah." I nodded, scooping my stuff back up as Gwen opened the door for me. "See you later." My gaze lingered as I stepped out into the hall.

CHAPTER FIFTEEN

HUMP DAY

Alaric

I rolled up to the shop around seven o'clock, and I was surprised to see only Gwen's car parked in the lot. Pulling up close to the shop door, I killed the ignition and watched her for a moment, moving around in the office, turning on lights, unaware of my eyes tracking her.

If she was the first to arrive, then the shop wasn't open yet. I'd have to go in through the office. Exhaling, I grabbed my welding helmet and opened the door. Catching movement in her peripheral, Gwen looked up.

The bell dinged when I opened it, and Gwen moved toward me with purpose. "Alaric," she said, her gaze sliding slowly from my face to my body.

"Gwen," I replied, my lips twitching into a smile. I lifted my chin, my brows furrowing. "Is the shop open yet?"

"Not yet," she replied, moving toward me purposefully. She stopped in front me and looked up, a smirk dancing on her painted lips. "You're the first to arrive."

The urge to wrap my fist around the thick braid over her shoulder, drag her to me and kiss her was staggering.

"Come over tonight," I murmured.

"And why would I do that?" she challenged, her eyes betraying her.

"Because you want to." I shrugged. "And I want you to."

She inhaled sharply and bit her lip, holding back a smile. "Fine."

"I'll text you," I said, moving closer to her. Overcome with the need to claim her mouth, I'd forgotten all the reasons why I shouldn't. Damn the consequences.

I looked over, spotting her father through the office doors as he spoke to Mitch in the parking lot. All he had to do was turn, and he'd see how close we were standing.

She nodded, and I slipped through the shop door. The last thing I heard was the sound of her heels clicking as she walked back into the office.

I headed to my workstation and set my welding helmet on the bench, taking a moment to refocus. Distractions could be dangerous on the job, and I had a lot of cutting to do.

Cracking my knuckles, I pulled my helmet over my face and got to work.

Hell-bent on finishing the support beams, I ended up staying later than I intended. I lost track of time, and when I looked at my phone after finally setting my welding gun down, my stomach lurched when I realized it was past nine.

Texting Gwen to let her know I was just finishing up, I pulled off my coveralls and hung it on the hook by my workbench. I cleaned up my workstation and locked up the shop, leaving through the office and locking the connecting door on my way through.

I could see the top of her head when I walked past the front desk. She looked up when I came through, and I slowed, everything stilling when she smiled. She set her pen down and closed the notebook she'd been writing in, and I swallowed hard.

"Where's Russell?"

She stood, turning out her lamp and sliding the notebook into her purse. "He left a couple of hours ago," she replied, turning to me and flashing a mischievous grin.

Gwen bit her lip, her gaze heating beneath my leisurely perusal of her body. I moved toward her, watching the rise and fall of her breasts.

I leaned forward, my lips meeting hers softly at first, until she pressed herself against me, running her hands along my jaw. Her fingers tangled in my hair, and my hands dropped to her ass as the kiss deepened.

Breathless, she pulled away. Shaking her head, she watched me with fascination.

"What?" I asked, breathing heavily, just as affected.

"Nothing," she said quickly, shaking her head and biting down on her bottom lip as she moved closer. Her breath fanned out against my lips, and I breathed her in, everything shifting and realigning. Around Gwen, everything meant more. I felt deeper, saw clearer, felt steadier.

She was gravity.

But before I could form a coherent follow-up thought, Gwen's lips were back on mine, her hands tugging at my belt, her warm palms slipping against my torso and sliding down until they wrapped around my cock.

My right hand tangled in her hair while I dropped my left

one to her breast, kneading it, running my calloused fingers over the sensitive bud of her nipple. The thin material of her blouse did nothing to conceal it, and I let out a tortured groan. "Gwen..."

She nipped at my bottom lip playfully, smiling as she pushed my Dakota cargo pants and boxers over my hips. "Are you scared of getting caught, Alaric?"

"A little," I admitted, my eyes closing as her hand wrapping around my base. She pumped it, her fingers sliding across the tip slowly.

"Better hurry, then." She grinned, releasing me. Biting her lip, she stepped backwards until her thighs hit her desk. She pulled her skirt up slowly, her fingers slipping into the lace waistband of her thong. She shimmied out of them and tucked them into her purse, pulling out a foil packet.

I watched as she dropped the bag onto the floor, her eyes still observing me. Daring me as she lifted herself onto her desk. I stepped toward her to stand between her legs. Looking down, I watched as she rolled the condom on and scooted forward, her legs falling open, baring herself to me.

Leaning forward, I claimed her lips and slid into her, heart pounding as her slick walls clenched against me. I wrapped my arm around her, using my other arm to gently push back her monitor and keyboard so she'd have more room.

She gripped the edge of her desk for purchase, her lips moving against mine as my hips drove forward. Her thighs tightened around my hips, and when I brought my hand around to work her bud, she let out a pleasured cry, her orgasm spurring mine.

I pumped my hips once more, driving as deep as I could go before I came.

"Told you we wouldn't get caught," she said breathlessly, her lids fluttering shut when she felt my cock throb within her.

I pulled out, chuckling lightly at the frown that marred her lips at my absence. I tied off the condom, wrapped it in tissue, and discarded it in the trash bin. I looked up to watch Gwen adjust her skirt. She leaned forward and moved the monitor and keyboard back in place while I buttoned my pants.

She picked up her purse, and straightening, her eyes went to the office doors. Gwen paled, and I turned, seeing headlights enter the lot. She shot me a nervous glance before moving toward the door. "Let's go."

I grabbed her hand, dragging her back. I licked my thumb and wiped away the lipstick smudge on the corner of her mouth before releasing her.

"Shit." She panicked.

"Relax, it's gone. You look perfect,"

"I look recently fucked, Alaric," she whispered nervously, moving toward the door. I followed, stomach churning with nerves.

Gwen typed the code and held the door open. I moved through it, and she followed, locking it quickly while Russell rolled his window down. "Just finishing up now?"

"Yes, sir. I've halfway finished the support beams."

Russell's thick brows rose with surprise, and he nodded. "That's great, that means we're on track for the Creek project." His gaze shifted from me to his daughter, who'd moved around me, giving me a wide berth.

"Hey, Dad. How'd the meeting go?" she asked, stopping at the edge of the sidewalk.

"Great," Russell replied, his tone a little distracted.

"That's good." She nodded, her smile relaxing a little.

Russell glanced back at me. "Another day like today, and we'll be ready to pack up the truck Friday morning. Think you can pull it off?"

"If you don't mind me putting in the overtime," I said, nodding slowly.

He nodded, turning his attention to his daughter. "Text me when you're home safe, okay?"

"Yes, Dad. Goodnight," Gwen replied, smiling tiredly. Russell nodded, shifting his car into drive and rolling slowly from the parking lot. Knowing he could still see us in the rearview mirror, she started to move toward her car. "I'll see you tomorrow, okay?" She glanced at me before opening the door.

I nodded, waiting until she'd pulled from her spot before I turned to my truck.

Gwen

After work on Wednesday, Kelsey showed up with a binder and a stack of pristine envelops and cards, fresh from the printer.

"I need you to help me with the wedding invitations," she said, pushing her way into my apartment and setting everything down on my hardly-ever-used kitchen table.

"Aha, I knew you'd call upon my powers of calligraphy eventually," I remarked.

Kelsey gave me an unamused look. "Speaking of which, I've only been trying to get you to come over for days. Where have you been?"

"I've been busy," I shrugged before disappearing into the kitchen to grab us both a glass of wine. On my return, I paused by the counter to text Alaric a warning, should he decide to stop in on his way home. We'd had enough close calls this week. "Besides, the wedding's not for another year. We've got plenty of time."

"Do we?" Kelsey demanded with her hand on her hip and

her eyes tight with stress. "Because the wedding keeps getting closer and my to-do list keeps getting longer. Elliott is basically useless when it comes to planning things, and his mother is beginning to drive me absolutely *insane!* God, if I didn't love Elliott so much, I'd walk away from this bloody wedding!" She snapped, yanked a chair out, and fell into it dramatically.

This was so unlike my sister, and I couldn't help but feel sorry for her. "Aw, Kels. I'm sure that's a normal reaction to having to deal with Janice. I mean, I had that reaction, and I only spent the afternoon in her company. What did she do now?"

"She called the florist to change the flower order to something more *elegant*. She's been even more unbearable since she was proven right about the dress." Tears of frustration welled up in Kelsey's eyes, and I hurried over to her, thrusting one of the glasses of wine at her. "Thanks," she sighed, taking it while wiping at her cheeks with her other hand.

"Did you pick the dress to appease her, Kels?" I asked gently, pulling the chair beside her out so I could join her at the table.

"No, I didn't," Kelsey shook her head back and forth. "But that doesn't mean that she's right about everything else."

"You're right. You need to set some boundaries," I put my hand on her shoulder and spoke softly, offering her a hesitant smile. "Well really, Elliott should set them since it's his mother who's over-stepping."

"Yeah, well. You know Elliott." Kelsey sighed again, pausing to take a sip of wine. "He hates confrontation."

"You *love* confrontation. Besides, you're practically a lawyer," I reminded her, reaching for the stack of envelopes and cards.

"Paralegal assistant is not practically a lawyer," my sister responded. "And I can't hurt her feelings. She's his mom."

"But she's hurting your feelings and overstepping. She's making what should be a really exciting time a miserable experience for you," I pointed out, pulling Kelsey's binder toward me and opening it. I removed the first page of guest addresses and set to work. "Just imagine how bad it's going to be down the road…when you're having a baby, and she's all up in your space, trying to call the shots during delivery."

Kelsey shuddered. "You're right," she sighed.

"Pardon? Could you say that again? I didn't quite hear you." I grinned.

"You're right." She rolled her eyes, shaking her head a little before she took another sip of wine.

"It's an almost unheard of occurrence, but miracles happen every day."

"Speaking of miracles…how's Thor?"

"Still a gift from the gods." I smirked, masking the teetering sensation his name evoked.

"So *casual* is still working for you?" Kelsey asked, air quoting *casual*.

"It is," I insisted, focusing my attention on the envelope.

"So…you aren't planning on admitting that you've got it bad for him, then?"

"I don't have it bad for him," I shrugged, moving on to the next address on the list, my calligraphy pen gliding across the envelope.

"I can always tell when you lie, and you're totally lying. Why do you deny it? What's the harm in liking him?"

I huffed, not looking up from my task. "There's nothing wrong with liking him, Kelsey. It's a complicated situation, and I don't even know if I'm ready for another relationship."

"Stop being a chicken shit. Erik was never supposed to be your forever love. He was a filler love, and you know that."

"This isn't even about Erik. There's more to it than that," I frowned, feeling vulnerable. "I insisted on casual, and that's what he needs right now, too. It's what we both need."

"Casual is just a prettier word for an excuse," my sister declared. "It's either an excuse to keep things open or an excuse to keep people at a distance."

"Did you want to argue about my sex life or get these invitations done?" I snipped.

"I would like to do both, actually." My sister smirked.

Heaving a sigh, I leaned against the back of my chair and crossed my arms. "You're relentless, Kels. Fine. I like him. I like him a lot. I've never felt the way he makes me feel. I mean, it's completely opened my eyes to how lacking my relationship with Erik really was."

"So, why aren't you guys together?" she asked, blinking at me.

"Because." I bit down on my bottom lip, my brow furrowing. "Alaric has a daughter."

"Ah." Kelsey nodded, understanding dawning in her eyes. She was quiet, watching me as I picked up the pen and resumed writing out the invitations. "Is that...not something you want, then? A guy with a kid?"

"Don't be ridiculous!" I spat, appalled. "I don't mind that he's a father. His daughter is really sweet. But..." I trailed off, not knowing how to voice my concerns.

"It's him."

"It's both of us," I corrected, exasperated. "We've both been hurt, and—"

"And nothing, if you've both been hurt then who better to be with? Someone who will think twice before hurting you."

I nodded, pursing my lips. Kelsey made a fair point, but my

insecurities always ended up holding me back. What if Alaric didn't have time for a relationship *with me?*

Alaric

I ran the sander along the grain, smoothing what would be the surface of the coffee table I was working on. If I could build it, I did, and creating a coffee table took minimum materials and offered a distraction.

Usually.

When the wood was polished, I stained it, Gwen's dimpled smile infiltrating my thoughts.

I wondered what she was doing, and tried to ignore the simple truth that I missed her. Having her around would make everything about today better.

I'd spent the last two days in the shop, cutting and welding the support beams that had been cut six inches short the first time around.

Russell was notably stressed, and his mood affected the other workers in the shop. I understood his frustration completely—two fuck ups on one job wasn't good for business. I took his mood with a grain of salt, as it wasn't my fuck ups that led us there.

I was the one working overtime to fix the mistakes.

Tonight, I'd wanted to stop in and see her before I headed home. I would have, but she texted me as I was climbing into my truck to tell me her sister had stopped by.

So, I'd come home, and I'd been in the garage ever since; Tig snoring on the concrete in front of the open door, working on this table, thinking about her and trying not to.

Tig let out a rumbling sigh as I walked by him to rinse the brush. The table would have to dry before I could attach it to the metal frame, which meant there wasn't much else to do on the project.

I tapped the wet brush against the side of the shop sink, setting it to the side to dry before washing my hands.

I was just shutting off the lights in the garage when the sound of gravel crunching against tires had my head swiveling to the driveway. Gwen's little red car pulled to a stop beside mine, and she climbed out, her pouty lips tugging into a slight frown as she hesitated.

The grin that spread across my face was immediate and easy. Her mere presence had loosened the tightness in my chest. "Couldn't stay away, huh?" I teased, stalking toward her. I was really glad that she hadn't.

"Must be that special vitamin D," she retorted as my hand slipped around her waist. I chuckled as she brought her hands to my neck. Tilting my head down, I captured her lips with mine.

CHAPTER SIXTEEN

ROULETTE

Gwen

I walked up to my parents' front steps like I was heading to the gallows. I *really* didn't want to be there. What I preferred was to spend another evening in Alaric's arms, purposely *not* thinking about my very un-casual feelings, but Dad was right; Mom wouldn't stand for me continuing to skip dinner.

Ringing the doorbell, I shuffled my weight from one foot to the other while I waited for someone to answer. A moment later, Mom opened the door, smiling grandly at me. I frowned, not trusting her. "Mother. Why do you have that look on your face?" I asked, instantly suspicious.

When I walked in and set my purse down on the side table in the foyer, Mom retorted as if wounded, "What look? I'm just excited to see my daughter."

"Ha," I laughed dryly. Deciding to let it go for the sake of keeping the peace, I hugged her. "It's good to see you too, Mom."

"Your hair's getting so long," she remarked airily, hands fanning around my curls before she started to soothe the non-existent wrinkles in my dress.

I'd dressed up, knowing I'd be heading to Alaric's the second dessert was through. I'd curled my hair and put on a new dress—a cute pastel pink one with tiny black polka dots, a ruffled hemline, and a gathered-and-tied waist. It wasn't wrinkled, and yet my mother fluffed at me anyway, as if pruning her precious rose bushes.

"Okay, now I know for sure—you're up to something. What is it?" I scowled, stepping away from her and appraising her with skepticism.

"Don't be silly. I was just admiring your dress. It's very pretty," Mom commented as she avoided meeting my gaze head on.

"Thanks." I pursed my lips, sensing something was amiss.

Mom turned and walked down the hall to the dining room. I arched my brows, the air escaping my lungs in a whoosh.

Yup, she was definitely up to something. I trailed after her, coming to a full stop when I realized an additional person sat at the table in the vacant chair beside mine. Grant Hernandez was filling that seat now, and he looked up at me, his lips pulling into a slow smile, his dark eyes twinkling with amusement.

"Grant, you remember Gwen, don't you?" Dad said, clearing his throat awkwardly. He avoided looking at me, likely knowing how livid I was.

And I was. I was angrier than a cat that just got tossed into a tub full of water, and I was mortified, to boot. I peered at Kelsey for help, but she seemed just as uneasy as me. I knew from looking at her that she wasn't involved in…whatever this was. Elliott sat beside her, appearing as if he'd swallowed glass.

Clearly, I had my meddlesome parents to thank for this

interjection. I scowled at my father, hurt that he'd done this after our conversation about *why* I didn't like coming to these dinners. This was abundantly worse than sitting beside a vacant chair.

"Yes, I do. Hey, Gwen," Grant said with a wink, standing and pulling the chair out for me, practically giving my mother a coronary in the process.

If she could get away with clapping her hands and squealing with excitement, she probably would. Instead, she smiled pointedly at me, her brows raising, her look alone telling me not to screw this up with my sarcastic bite.

"Grant," I managed, forcing my lips into a smile and moving my feet forward. I sat, shooting another glance at my father, who was strategically avoiding looking directly at me. "I'm a little surprised to see you here."

"Your father invited me," Grant replied easily, sitting back down in his chair. I had to give him credit; he didn't seem the least bit uncomfortable by the tension rolling off practically everyone's shoulders. Except for my mom—she was the only one buzzing with excitement. Dad at least had the common decency to look ashamed of his hand in things.

"Oh, that's nice. Dad sure loves his charity causes," I responded sweetly. My father stifled a laugh, masking it quickly with a cough.

"Gwen," Mom scolded, frowning deeply.

"I know she's teasing," Grant interjected, sending me a bemused smile. "It's kind of our thing."

"I wasn't aware we had a thing," I muttered, stabbing a piece of roast with my fork and moving it to my plate. I wasn't hungry anymore, but I knew there wasn't a chance in hell my mother would let me leave without eating, and I was determined to get this night over with as soon as humanly possible.

Kelsey sniggered, and Mom sent me another withering look. I bit down on my tongue, hard, to keep myself from verbally lashing out further and pitching an epic temper tantrum.

Grant was a guest in their house, and my parents had raised me better than that. Plus, he was one of our best engineers, and I knew Dad valued him. I wouldn't jeopardize my father's company, and it maddened me that my mother used those things to her advantage.

Painful. The whole thing was utterly and completely painful. My mother asked Grant a hundred questions—about where he grew up, what his plans for the future were, what he did for fun—information that someone he was dating might want to know.

Dad could pretend all he wanted that it was business-related, but this was a setup, and everyone in the room knew it. I was vibrating with anger. This was a new low for my mother—and my father.

It was more than likely that my poor father had been caught in the crossfire. He may have mentioned Grant hitting on me to Mom, who jumped all over it like some mid-century housewife, desperate to see all her daughters married off. Since Dad literally did *anything* to make my mother happy, I could see him bending to her will.

Knowing this didn't make my anger lessen, though.

"Well, this has been a very entertaining evening, but I need to go," I said tightly, standing as soon as I'd finished the tiny sliver of pie my mother insisted that I eat. I wasn't about to let her rope me into staying any longer than I already had.

"It's barely nine o'clock, Gwen," my mother said, frowning with disappointment.

"I know. I'm sorry. I'm just exhausted," I replied, yawning and stretching a little. I waved at Kelsey and Elliott, too pissed to offer more than that.

"I should get going, too. It's a long drive back to Toronto," Grant said as he stood, his chair scraping against the floor. "Thank you for dinner. It was delicious. I'll walk you out, Gwen."

I glanced back over my shoulder, scowling. Mom's frown instantly faded, and she smiled with notable relief.

My heels clicked against the tiled floor in the foyer, and I paused to grab my purse off the side table, my hand reaching instantly into the little pocket I kept my phone in.

I pulled it out, noticing I had several missed messages. A few were from Kelsey, sent just before I arrived, warning me about the unexpected guest and assuring me she had nothing to do with it.

The others were from Alaric, telling me to let him know when I was leaving. My fingers moved quickly across the screen as I texted my response, telling Alaric I'd be there in twenty.

By the time I hit send, Grant had joined me in the foyer with my parents. He shook both my dad's and my mom's hands before turning to me. "Shall we?"

My mother watched the scene with a self-satisfied smile, seemingly unaware of how angry I was. She honestly thought she was doing me a favour.

Sickening.

I allowed Grant to lead me out the front door with his hand on the small of my back because I knew my mother would cause a stink if I were "rude" to him, but the moment the door closed behind us, I stepped away from his touch.

"Look, Grant, I'm not interested," I told him bluntly as we walked down the stone pathway to the driveway. I hadn't noticed the additional car parked beside Kelsey's SUV when I pulled up.

"I've gathered as much," he admitted with a laugh, the corners of his eyes creasing with amusement. "Coldest reception I've gotten in a while."

"I am sorry about that." I let out a frustrated sigh. "I didn't know you'd be here, and there's something extremely infuriating about parents playing matchmaker."

"Yeah, I guess they kind of blindsided you with it." He chuckled, shaking his head. We paused when we came to my car, and he tilted his head at me. "So, is it *just* because your parents set this up?"

"No." I bit my lip, looking at my parents' house. "I'm seeing someone."

"Is it serious?" Grant asked.

"I don't see why it's any of your business," I snapped, aggravated.

"Because if it's not serious, then there's still a chance," Grant replied, smiling.

"It's serious," I replied as he opened my car door.

"We'll see," he retorted, holding the door open. He flashed me a grin that suggested he was up for the challenge. It had zero effect on me.

"If that's what you wish to delude yourself into thinking, be my guest." I sighed with exasperation, slipping inside my vehicle. Alaric was unshakable, I already knew that.

Grant chuckled and closed the door. Shoving my key in the ignition, I twisted it and backed out, my eyes focused on my rearview mirror.

Light poured from Alaric's garage when I pulled into his driveway. I could see his broad back and muscular forearm as he wiped down his workbench, cleaning it.

I stepped from my car, closing the door lightly. Tig stood up from his spot in the corner of the garage, letting out a warning bark as he ambled over.

"Hi, Tig," I said, leaning forward to pet his fluffy face. When I straightened, Alaric was standing in the doorway of the garage with his arms crossed and a panty-melting smile on his kissable lips.

"How was dinner?"

"An actual disaster," I moaned, my shoes crunching against the gravel as I walked up to him. His hand pressed against the small of my back as he dragged me toward him, causing my body to spark with awareness. Desire pooled low and hot in my belly as he kissed me.

His touch quickly made me forget about Grant, about my parents, and everything else for that matter. My hands clenched at the material of his waffle shirt, and I let out another sigh when his lips left mine a moment later.

"Come on, it couldn't have been that bad." He chuckled.

Pulling away from him, I walked over to look at the coffee table he'd just finished making. "It was," I said, running my hand along the smooth plank of wood, held in place with intricate black metal bars and studs. I was in awe of his talent; of him. It stung, this realization that I'd gone and fallen for him. I was scared and trying desperately not to act like it. I didn't want to lose him by admitting what I felt, but I couldn't do it anymore. I'd wanted *him* in that chair tonight.

I was tired of wondering, tired of replaying every touch and wondering if they meant as much as they felt like they did. I had him, but not completely, and I needed to know if there was hope.

"Grant Hernandez was there." I don't know why I brought his name up. I told myself I wasn't interested in playing games, and I wasn't, but it'd get back to him sooner or later, anyway.

"The engineer?" Alaric questioned, recognizing the name. His frown deepened. "Why?"

"I don't know. I have a feeling it was my mom's idea. My dad probably told her that Grant asked me out the other day—"

"Hold up," he interrupted, and I turned to look at him. "Grant asked you out? When?" His jaw ticked with aggravation like he was mad that I'd withheld the information from him.

"Yes..." I trailed off, my brow creasing. "He asked me Monday afternoon when he stopped in to go over some paperwork with my dad."

"Why didn't you tell me?"

"I didn't think it mattered." I shrugged, watching him.

"What did you say?" he asked, moving across the garage with sure strides, the heat in his gaze enough to warp metal.

"I turned him down," I replied, my heart rate increasing with every step he took. He stopped in front of me, cupping my chin and guiding it up.

His blue eyes darkened with desire, and he brushed his thumb across my lips. "Why did you turn him down?"

Alaric

My question hung between us, and the only answer she gave was the sharp intake of breath. Without thinking, I leaned forward, capturing her soft mouth in a kiss, and my free hand drifted to her waist. When I pulled away, her eyes shone with confliction—heat warring with indecision.

"None of this feels very casual, Alaric," she finally said, avoiding my gaze.

"No, it doesn't," I said softly, moving even closer to her. I cupped her chin, tilting it up so she had no choice but to look at me.

"It kind of terrifies me," she added, her eyes tight with concern.

"Me too," I confessed.

"What now?" she asked, her frown deepening.

Although Cheryl had waved the first white flag, that truce might vanish if she took an issue to me seeing Gwen. It could be another easy excuse for her to alienate me further.

But I'd let Cheryl control the narrative for far too long. I'd allowed her to keep me in chains, and I did it out of fear.

Fear that didn't seem to exist around Gwen.

I took a breath.

"I don't really know," I replied a moment later, speaking honestly.

"Right," she breathed, nodding once like it was the answer she'd expected, but it still pained her. She took a breath, her eyes fixed on mine. "I get it. When we started this... arrangement, it was with the understanding that things would remain casual."

Something shuttered behind her gaze like she was trying to put up walls between us. I wouldn't let her erect them; I pulled her against me, bringing my lips close to hers. Her lids fluttered shut, and she exhaled. I breathed her scent before continuing. "I want this, Gwen."

Her eyes snapped open, and she smiled but with a wisp of sadness. "And what, exactly, is this?"

"It's not casual, that's for damn sure," I responded, almost growling. The knowledge that another man had asked her out —that another man had joined her for dinner with her parents —spurred me into facing the truth; I didn't want to let her go, and I didn't want to have to.

"You sound frustrated," she remarked, looking away, shielding herself.

"I am," I admitted, swallowing. "I wasn't counting on...you. On this turning into...this," I gestured between us, meaning everything from the connection we had, to the amazing sex, to the possessive streak that slashed out every time I thought of her with someone else.

I wanted her for myself, and I was afraid to lose her.

Gwen deserved a relationship or at least the promise of a future, and if I didn't give that to her, it wouldn't be long before some other guy—like Grant—did. The knowledge sat heavily in my stomach. I couldn't let that happen.

"I wasn't either," she said quietly, her eyes locked on mine.

"I guess life doesn't give a shit about plans." I chuckled lowly.

"I don't want to get hurt again," she added, pulling away from my embrace and dropping her gaze. She put her hand up as if warding me off. "I don't handle getting cheated on very well, and my trust is shot to shit."

"We have something in common then." I kept my distance, although all I wanted to do was reassure her that she had nothing to worry about there.

"You got cheated on?" she asked, eyeing me with disbelief.

"Why is that so hard to believe?"

"Because look at you. You're the ultimate package." She shook her head like she couldn't fathom what my ex had been thinking.

"So are you," I told her, my hand twitching at my side with the urge to reach out and touch her, but she was still holding her hand between us, and there were still a lot of things left unsaid that needed to be spoken. I cleared my throat, looking over her shoulder because I dreaded her answer. "Speaking of the whole package...Sawyer."

Gwen bit her lip as if considering her thoughts. She stepped toward me, her hand pressing lightly against my chest, and peered up at me. "I know she's your first priority, and I get that. She's a part of the ultimate package."

I nodded, the pressure easing in my chest. I'd known Gwen long enough to see she was telling the truth; if she were bothered by the fact that I was a father, we wouldn't be standing there talking it out.

"So how do we do this?" she whispered, her vulnerability unmasked.

"We take things slowly, do this right," I suggested, stroking the side of her jaw with my thumb. "We'll keep it between us a little while longer. Just until I figure out a way to handle my ex that doesn't make her spiral out of control."

"Okay," she said, nodding slightly as she thought it over. "Okay." Her lips turned up in a smile when I nodded, and she pressed them to mine, tasting me, her mouth moving ardently.

My hands dropped to her hips, and I pulled her against me. My cock throbbed, aching to push the hem of her dress up and take her on the nearest surface—my workbench.

Still kissing her, I lifted her legs until the skirt rode up her thighs as they locked around my waist. I pressed into her pelvis desperately. She nipped at my bottom lip as her hands tangled in my hair.

I walked forward, setting her on the edge of the workbench. Gwen's low hiss as her hamstrings touched the cold metal morphed into a moan when I tugged her panties aside to slide my finger against her slick entrance, gliding it up and down before sinking slowly inside her.

Sucking on her bottom lip, I worked my fingers against her, pumping in and out until I felt her clench around them, her legs trembling with her release. I removed my fingers, gripping her panties and tugging them down her thighs before reaching into my back pocket. I'd long since learned that when it came to Gwen, it was better to be overly prepared. My need for her was insistent.

While I was busy grabbing the condom, Gwen unbuttoned my pants and pushed them over my hips with her black heels. I fisted my cock and rolled the condom on, watching as her tongue swept across her lips, moistening them.

Gwen

We were laying in his bed, the tangled sheets the only thing covering us. Sunlight streamed through his bedroom window, patches of light hitting the dark hardwood flooring.

I'd only left the warmth of his bed—and his arms—long enough to use the washroom and brush my teeth, owing a serious amount of gratitude to Renly for ensuring I had an emergency hygiene kit in my car.

It was a little disarming, how comfortable I felt. But Alaric had assured me with his touches and the way his eyes would linger on me. He wanted me here, and I wanted to be here.

"Tell me about him."

"About who?" I asked.

"You haven't said much about your ex, but from what you have said, I've gathered that he hurt you." Alaric ran his hand along the side of my body.

My teeth sank into my lower lip, desire coiling in my core at the feel of his hands on me. But I couldn't let myself get distracted by his magical cock again.

I took a deep breath, turning my face to him, my eyes searching his. "There's not much to tell. We met in college, started building a life together, then he cheated. I found out and threw him out, and here we are."

It was a challenge to hold his gaze, especially with my anxious mind puttering along in the over-analyzing lane.

"He sounds stupid," he responded with his lips against the side of my neck. I tilted my head, giving him complete access, powerless to his touch. It eased everything, leaving desire and something else in its place—something fluttery and light.

"He was," I shivered, goosebumps erupting in the wake of Alaric's kisses. My hands ran greedily up his abs.

"Did you love him?"

I froze, my eyes focusing on his. "I thought I did," I answered honestly.

"But now?"

I bit my lip, shaking my head. "Now I know I didn't."

"How do you know?" The corner of his lip kicked up, and his eyes were playful.

"I think you know how I know," I murmured, my eyes searching his.

His gaze grew serious, and he nodded, lowering his head to press his lips to mine. His tongue stroked along the seam of my lips, seeking entrance, and I willingly gave it to him.

The butterflies took flight, swooping in my belly as the kiss consumed me. Alaric's cock jumped beside my thigh, and he grinned against my mouth.

Hot breath fanned the side of my face, and I turned my head. Tig stood beside the bed, tall enough to hold his muzzle above the mattress. He whimpered, tilting his head questioningly.

I laughed, gently pushing on Alaric's chest. He rolled off with a soft chuckle, his cock still rigid. "I guess we've been in bed long enough," he sighed, stretching.

"We could always come back to it," I reminded him, wrapping the sheet around me as I stood, peering around for my clothes. I stilled when Alaric pressed against me from behind, my body going lax against his.

"I'll hold you to it," he murmured, his lips brushing against my earlobe. "I think your dress is in the front hall." He reached around me, retrieving a pair of sleep pants from his dresser. He pulled them over his hips and opened another drawer, grabbing a t-shirt. In two steps, he was back in front of me, holding the shirt out to me.

I dropped my arms, letting the sheet fall to the ground. His eyes thirstily roamed my body. He bit his bottom lip and exhaled deeply when I took the shirt from him and tugged it over my head.

Freeing my hair of the collar, I glanced at him, biting back a smile. "So, what now?"

"Are you hungry?" Alaric asked, and Tig barked loudly twice, wagging his tail. "I make a mean omelette." He cocked a brow.

"I'm a little hungry," I said modestly, just before my stomach audibly growled. Alaric grinned and touched the small of my back. He guided me forward, and we left his room, Tig leading the way down the stairs. "I'll meet you down there." I branched off toward the bathroom.

Closing the door, I rested against it, drawing in a sustaining breath.

CHAPTER SEVENTEEN

FAMISHED

Alaric

Opening the back door, I let Tig out for his morning pee before heading into the kitchen. I grabbed a frying pan, set it on the stovetop, then reached for the refrigerator. Pulling out the eggs, and milk, I deposited them on the counter before going back for the cheese, spinach, and green onions.

While the skillet warmed, I chopped up the green onions, spinach, and cheese, cracking the eggs off the side of the pan and dropping them in one by one before sprinkling in the rest.

I hadn't made breakfast for a woman since Cheryl, but by that point, she was already three months pregnant with Sawyer.

Everything about this situation with Gwen was different. Having her in my space should have felt constricting, it should have made me uneasy, but instead, I felt balanced, like for the first time in a while, everything was right.

For the first time in a long time, I allowed myself to see a future different than the one of just existing until my next weekend with Sawyer.

Gwen descended the stairs, heading straight for the mudroom to open the door. Tig cantered in, and a moment later, he bee-lined it for the kitchen, his tail wagging hopefully, carrying his food bowl in his mouth while Gwen's laughter followed him.

"I think he's a little hungry," she remarked, walking into the kitchen. "I can feed him if you want."

I carefully flipped the omelet. "His food is in the tote under the counter in there," I told her, lifting my chin to the mudroom and watching while she disappeared. Tig, the smartest dog I'd ever met, followed her with his bowl, his tail wagging happily. I heard the cupboards opening, and the sound of kibble pouring into Tig's tin dish.

"Uh, Alaric? He's not eating."

"You have to give him permission," I replied over my shoulder.

"Seriously? All right. Uh, Tig—I formally invite you to eat. So, eat." Half a second later, the extremely audible sounds of Tig inhaling his breakfast reached my ears. I glanced up, following Gwen's movements as she joined me in the kitchen again. "Can I help with anything?"

"Just stand there and look pretty," I joked, the corner of my lip curling up in a smirk as my gaze raked across her body. She smiled, her dimples deepening, and leaned against the island.

"You think I'm pretty?" she teased, batting her lashes at me.

I adjusted my erection, giving her a pointed look while I moved over to the coffee maker. Whenever I wasn't inside her, I was hard her for her—especially when she was standing in my kitchen in just my t-shirt.

"I think you're gorgeous," I replied, filling two mugs and

placing one in front of her. I kept my eyes on hers while I put the sugar down, unsure of how she took her coffee.

Gwen reached for the sugar bowl, her fingertips brushing lightly along the side of my hand, and pulled it toward her. Opening the lid, she took the sugar spoon and deposited three large scoops, flashing me another one of her signature smiles as she grabbed the milk.

"I think you're gorgeous, too," she said, biting down on her lip as her eyes traced the planes of my stomach.

I grinned, turning back to the stove. She leaned against the island, her hands wrapping around the mug, and watched while I cut the omelet in half and lifted the pan, sliding one half onto each plate.

"So...do you have plans today?" she questioned.

"Not really. Do you?" I asked, holding out a plate to her and arching a brow. She took it, biting down on her lip before releasing it with a pop.

"Not really, no," she confessed, staring at the omelet for a moment before shaking her head and setting it down.

"Well, if you're looking for something to do...I figured I'd take Tig for a hike. It's a little overdue," I told her. Tig lifted his head, hearing his name, his tail happily thumping against the ground.

Gwen's face lit up. "I'll have to go home for a change of clothes...and shoes. Can't wear heels on a hike."

"That's true." I laughed, stealing a glance at her while I lifted my mug to take a sip of coffee, eyes still appraising her. "We're pretty close to the trails here, but you'll still want something more comfortable."

She nodded, taking a bite of egg. "Ohmergawd," she said, still chewing, her eyes wide. "You *do* make a mean omelet."

"You sound surprised."

"By this point, I shouldn't be," she sighed, biting back a smile. "It's almost unfair how perfect you are."

"I'm far from perfect," I told her, my brows creasing. She gave me a stern look over the top of her glasses. With her dark hair piled atop her head in a messy bun, she looked like the embodiment of a naughty librarian.

She smiled slowly, picking up her mug and taking a gradual sip while studying me with a straight face. My entire body buzzed in response to her, my dick stiffening with yearning.

"Are you going to shush me?" I asked, leaning forward, my lips shaping a playful grin at her sharp intake of breath.

"I have many ways of shushing you, Mr. Petersen. You'd do well to remember them," she said demurely, setting her mug down and standing from the stool.

I watched her walk around the counter, watched her run her slender fingers along the marble countertop. Her eyes were dark and seductive, and when she stepped up to me, cupping the side of my face with her hand, I drew in a ragged breath.

She considered me, standing on her tip-toes to slide her lips across mine, her free hand brushing purposely against my erection.

Still holding my mug in one hand, I pressed my free hand against the small of her back, tugging her to me.

She smiled, breaking the kiss, and stepped away. "You sure do." I managed thickly.

Gwen

I headed home to grab a quick shower and a change of clothes before driving back to Alaric's for the remainder of the weekend. My overnight bag sat beside me in the front seat of my car, and as I looked at it, my heart pounded erratically in my chest.

Sure, I'd been screwing Alaric for weeks now—hungering for his touch, thirsting for any bit of attention he saw fit to give me—and here we were. Official-*ish*, anyway. We still had the hurdle of telling both his family and mine, but we'd mutually agreed that what we had couldn't be described as casual.

That was good, right? So why did I feel so nervous?

Chewing on my bottom lip, I opened the door and grabbed my bag, telling myself that if Alaric wanted space, he wouldn't have told me to go home, pack an overnight bag, and get my ass back as quickly as possible for that hike.

The garage door was wide open, and Tig was sitting in the middle of it, watching me climb from my car. I'd changed into a pair of shorts and a tank-top, pulling my long hair into a ponytail to keep it off my back.

Alaric's eyes drank in the sight of my pale legs, and I rolled my eyes playfully. "You're insatiable."

"Can you blame me?" He smirked, shaking his head, his gaze still unwilling to move from me. All reservations I had about him not wanting me around faded.

Alaric closed the garage door, leading the way around his house. We strolled through the untended gardens—save for a vegetable patch that looked relatively new—toward the back of his property.

"It's kind of awesome that you get to avoid people and still enjoy this," I remarked, gesturing with my chin to the trail his property backed up to.

"Tell me about it." He chuckled, his arm brushing against mine as we walked side by side. Tig ambled in front of us, his tail wagging. He came across a large stick and sniffed at it before picking it up in his mouth. "It was one of the reasons I jumped on this place."

"What are the other reasons?" I asked, my curiosity piqued.

His eyes flitted to my face, and he drew in a breath. "It was cheaper than buying a house in town." I laughed, shaking my head, and he smiled as if making me laugh had been his goal all along.

I chanced a glance at him. He looked very much like a demigod with the way the sunlight enveloped him, dancing off his blond hair and golden skin. Regarding me with warmth and affection set deep in his irises, he ran his hands through his hair, tugging it into a bun with ease I envied. How he could do a killer bun without a mirror, hairspray, and ten thousand bobby pins was beyond me. Unlike most dads, he must do a great job with his daughter's hair.

I thought about asking him if he wanted more kids, but I had the sense to call that question back before it left my lips, and I redirected my brain. "Well, my mother would be envious of the gardening potential here."

"She'd get along with my mom." Alaric huffed a laugh. "Don't have much of a green thumb myself."

"Me either," I laughed. "I tried to keep a houseplant once. It died. But hey, I'm doing an awesome job keeping my cat alive."

Alaric guffawed, the rich sound of it making my inside shiver delightfully. Biting my lip, I looked ahead, watching Tig catch the scent of a squirrel. Unwilling to part with his stick, he attempted to chase after it. The wood in his mouth made him clumsy and slow, but he wouldn't let it go.

Nodding, I stepped onto a large branch blocking the trail. Tig was on the other side, tugging on a smaller section, his stick forgotten. He snapped the branch off and dragged it, tail wagging triumphantly.

The sun was setting, its fading light casting orange and pink hues on the horizon. I leaned on the railing, watching as it slunk lower in the sky.

I didn't turn when I heard the side door open or at the sound of Alaric setting two bottles of beer on the top of the barbeque.

His hard body pressed against me from behind. He rested his arms on the railing beside mine, and his lips skimmed the place where my shoulder and neck met. I shivered, leaning back against him, and exhaled.

After hiking around his property, we came back for lunch. We spent the afternoon tangled in his sheets, only rousing to cook a light dinner when I couldn't ignore my rumbling stomach any longer.

Now, here we were. Watching the sunset. Everything about this moment—this entire day—had been perfectly harmonious.

I bit down on my lip, releasing it and letting out a soft sigh. "I should go."

It was a knee-jerk reaction. I was comfortable, I was happy, and I was afraid of how good it all felt.

"Why?" His voice was muffled, and his lips still pressed to my skin.

I looked at him, unsuccessfully trying to fight a smile. "You don't feel like I'm overstaying my welcome?"

"Do you feel like you're overstaying your welcome?" he asked, lips twitching with amusement.

"No. Yes...maybe?" I tilted my head, my eyes flitting away from him. I tried to resist the pull, but it was fruitless. My gaze slid back to him almost instantaneously, and I couldn't even be mad at myself.

When his right hand rose, his fingers gently wrapped along the side of my neck, and his thumb brushed my bottom lip attentively. "What if I don't want you to go?"

His question and the reverent look in his endless blue eyes were all the reassurance I needed. "Then I'll stay," I said, the words tumbling from my lips breathlessly.

Lowering his lips to mine, he claimed me. I felt his erection against my backside as his kisses deepened. Each scorching pass of his tongue against mine matched the burning low in my belly.

He pulled his lips away reluctantly, softly chuckling as his hand dropped away from my face.

"What's the matter? Can't finish what you started?" I goaded.

"Oh, I could finish it, all right." He tilted a brow at me, his cock jumping against my butt. "I thought you'd be sore."

I laughed. "Wow. That's egotistic. Accurate, but pompous to say out loud."

He smirked, reaching behind us. "Have you forgotten how many times we've done it in the last twenty-four hours?"

"Nope." I smiled slyly, accepting the beer he offered me. In fact, I *was* sore, but pleasantly so. "I suppose I could use the break. You've practically taken up residence in there."

His lips kicked up in a grin so dazzling, it stole my breath. "Like you didn't have a hand in things."

"I was totally the innocent party," I joked, knowing I was just as ravenous for it as he had been, if not more. His arm snaked around my waist, fingers splaying across my belly as he tugged me against him.

"That so?"

I sighed dramatically. "All right, fine. I played a small part, after all."

He grunted, his lips still pulled up in a smile that made warmth burst in the center of my heart. He took a long swig of his beer with his gaze fixed on the horizon and his other hand still resting against my belly. Tingles of awareness flooded my body as his fingers curled momentarily before relaxing. I leaned against his chest and watched the rest of the sun disappear.

"Want to watch a movie?" Alaric asked, turning his face to grin at me.

Alaric

I'd never been the kind of person to believe in fate. Life was made up of choices. Every choice had a reaction, a consequence. A course of action to take.

When Cheryl told me she was pregnant, my course of action was to give that baby a stable home. I had never faltered there, although my decision to try and make things work with Cheryl had been a disservice to us both. I saw that more clearly than ever now. It led her on and created a hole in her heart. Not that I'd treated her cruelly; I was affectionate with her, and I'd been faithful, but it hadn't been enough. I hadn't been in love with her, and she'd known it.

That spark had been missing from the start with Cheryl, but it was there with Gwen. Infused into every moment spent, every gaze, every touch, every word spoken and every word left unsaid.

So, I supposed it wasn't absurd that a single weekend with Gwen would solidify just how badly I needed her in my life. She was colour, and she was vibrant. I'd woken in the middle of the night, holding her soft, naked body against mine, and I'd felt overcome with possibility.

Placing the last of the pancakes on the tray, I slid it into the oven to keep it warm. Two mugs of coffee steamed on the countertop, and I picked them up as I passed, heading for the stairs to wake her.

Gwen's leg was over the top of the white sheet, and she

slept curled toward the space that I'd vacated forty-five minutes ago, her hand stretched out on my pillow.

I set the mugs on the end table, pausing by the bed to run my hand slowly up her bare leg, slipping beneath the sheet and along the curve of her round ass. She stirred at my touch, her back arching and toes stretching.

Gwen turned onto her back and sighed, her lids fluttering open, her gray eyes still hazy with sleep. "Morning." She smiled, her sleep-laden voice making my cock stiffen with arousal.

"Good morning," I said, voice thick with lust. She sat up, the blanket falling around her lap and her nipples hardening as she stretched, purposely teasing me. My willpower was called into question, and I fought the urge to climb into bed and slip inside her again.

She sniffed, a slow smile lifting the corner of her lips as she reached for her glasses on the nightstand. "Coffee in bed?" she said, picking up the mug gratefully. Taking a deep sip, she let out a soft moan, her lids fluttering shut.

I adjusted myself, my lounge pants doing nothing to hide how hard this woman made me. "I made pancakes and bacon, too." Her eyes popped open, and I waggled my brows at her.

She bit back a grin, tucking a strand of her dark hair behind her ears. "Do you mind if I grab a shower first?"

"Be my guest." I cleared my throat, my cock impossibly hard now. Gwen's gaze dropped to my waistband, and she arched a delicate brow.

"Care to join me?" She leaned, setting the mug down on the nightstand, her eyes raking across my bare chest with appreciation. I flexed beneath her perusal, my nostrils flaring with arousal.

I bent over the mattress, my fingers tangling in her hair as I drew her close to me. My lips pressed against hers, and I kissed her deeply for a few tantalizing moments before drawing back.

"I already showered," I admitted, running the pad of my thumb along her lips before straightening. I'd grabbed a quick one in the downstairs bathroom. My hair was still damp, pulled back into a bun. A man bun. I hated that term, but it came with the territory.

"All right, I'll join you in ten minutes or so."

"Take your time," I told her. "It'll be warm."

I left, heading back downstairs to disperse some energy. I was wiping down the counter when my cell phone rang. Swiping it up, I froze when I saw Russell's name on the display.

"Hello?" I said.

"Sorry to trouble you on the weekend, Alaric, but I'm calling to see if you're interested in a little overtime. I need someone in the shop for five tomorrow."

The taps were still running, which meant Gwen was still in the shower. I let out an inaudible breath. "I can do that."

"Great. See you then." Russell replied before the line went dead. I set my phone down, a pang of guilt smashing into me.

"Everything okay?" Gwen's voice startled me, rousing me from my ruminating.

"Yeah," I turned, catching sight of her on the other side of the counter. Her hair was piled in a topknot, the few strands that had evaded the hair tie were damp and curled around her face. Gwen's cheeks were flushed, and she watched me while distractedly stroking Tig's large head. "Hungry?"

"Famished," Gwen sighed, her dimples flashing as she grinned ruefully at me.

CHAPTER EIGHTEEN

FIREWORKS

Gwen

My father's annual Canada Day barbeque was always a massive hit, with almost every single one of his employees showing up, as well as a lot of his friends and other work contacts.

A lot of planning went into the annual barbeque, and my mother did most of it. I helped out as much as she'd allow me, but I mostly just showed up for the food, the beer, and the fireworks display my dad would spend thousands on.

Since it was a family-friendly event, Dad would rent a bouncy castle for the kids. He'd done it every year since Kelsey and I were little.

I washed my hands in the bathroom sink, preparing myself to go outside and face the music.

Alaric would be coming if he wasn't there already, and he'd be bringing his daughter. I had to be on my best behaviour, because not only would my family be in attendance, but his daughter would be too.

He was worried that Cheryl would react negatively to him having a girlfriend, so he planned on waiting until he dropped off Sawyer to tell her—and I wasn't exactly ready to tell my parents.

I wasn't one-hundred-percent sure how my dad would take the news, and the last thing I wanted was to jeopardize Alaric's place within the company. I knew my mother would be thrilled to find out I wasn't going to die a spinster, but I didn't need her meddling, either.

Eyeing my ensemble, I fussed with the gathered navy blue material of the wrap top, ensuring my cleavage was sitting in the right place. I ran my hands down the colourful floral skirt and drew in a deep breath, tossing my chin up.

Slipping out of the bathroom, I walked down the stairs and through the kitchen to the sliding doors that led to the back patio. I paused, seeing Alaric standing with my father, holding his daughter's hand as she shyly peered around his legs at the large bouncy castle.

I hesitated and then jumped half a foot in the air when someone's hands gripped my shoulders. I whirled, caught off guard. "Relax, Gwen." Kelsey laughed, shaking her head at my reaction. I rolled my eyes and turned my gaze back out the window.

Letting out a deep sigh, I pivoted to face my sister. "You need to swear on the sacred powers of sisters that you will not do *anything* to suggest there's something between Alaric and me."

"I promise, Gwen. Relax," Kelsey assured me, crossing over to the refrigerator. She grabbed two beers and carried them to me. "Our latest arrival doesn't have a drink yet. Go play hostess and bring this to him."

I narrowed my eyes at her, taking the bottles. "That sounds like a terrible idea."

Kelsey frowned a little. "It's something Mom would make you do anyway. Besides, I'm sure you can carry on a conversation with him without dropping to your knees."

"You'd be surprised," I murmured, thinking about how often I ended up doing just that—dropping to my knees instead of telling him how I felt or what I was really thinking.

I swallowed back everything and pasted on a bright smile as I stepped through the sliding doors, Kelsey trailing behind me until she branched off after spotting Elliott by the food table, where the caterers had laid out hors d'oeuvres and fruit.

Keeping my smile as steady as I could, I came to a stop just before Alaric and my dad. "Thirsty?" I said, unable to utter more than one full word as I held out the beers to Alaric and my dad.

"I've still got quite a bit left," Dad remarked, raising his bottle. Alaric's fingers brushed over mine as he took one of the bottles from me.

"Thanks," he said, the corner of his lips twitching.

"Why don't you show Alaric and Sawyer the jumping castle? I should go check in on your mother and make sure she isn't driving the wait staff nuts." Dad said, chuckling lightly and squeezing my arm gently as he passed.

"Right, well, let's go see about that bouncy castle, huh?" I said with relief, smiling down at Sawyer. We walked toward the castle, where children were jumping inside, with more running around in their bare feet on the yard beside it. "Tada! The legendary bouncy castle!"

"Why's it legendary?" Sawyer asked me, her face scrunching up with confusion.

"This bouncy castle has been at every Canada Day barbeque, for as long as I can remember," I told her, grinning a little. "There's no bouncier castle around!"

"I don't want to go in alone," Sawyer said, her voice full of apprehension as she peered up at the castle and the children inside it.

"I'll go in with you," I suggested, shrugging.

"Okay!" Sawyer grinned, releasing her hold on her dad's hand in favour of mine.

"Here. Hold my beer." I winked, passing Alaric the bottle. I slipped out of my shoes and allowed Sawyer to lead me to the flap of the tent. She pulled her shoes off and climbed in, and I crawled in after her.

I hadn't been inside the bouncy castle since I was seventeen.

"This is fun!" Sawyer giggled, jumping as high as she could and bouncing forward onto her hands and knees. She continued like that, hopping backwards into the side of the castle, her braids flying up with each leap.

My wardrobe choice wasn't really the best for a bouncy castle, and I had to hold my breasts down with my arms so that they wouldn't fall from my wrap as I bounded in the inflatable castle.

While we bounced, Sawyer's eyes kept going to the two little girls and the boy on the other side of the castle.

"Do you want to go say hi?" I asked, slowing my jumps and tilting my head toward the trio. She nodded shyly, and I took her hand as we bounced over to them. "Hey guys, this is Sawyer. Sawyer, that's Noah, Cassidy, and Britton."

"Hi," Sawyer said softly.

"Want to play with us?" Noah asked, giving her an adorably charming smile. She nodded, releasing my hand.

"All right, Sawyer, I'll see you outside," I said.

"Okay, bye." She waved at me before bouncing off with the other kids. I crawled back out through the flap, trying to fix my static-charged hair.

I straightened, brushing my skirt down and looking up,

catching the acute yearning in Alaric's eyes as he watched me. I walked back up to him and slipped into my shoes, taking the bottle from him. "What?" I asked, fighting a smile at his lingering gaze.

"That was hot," he admitted, his lips curving into a grin. I chuckled and rolled my eyes.

"All I did was introduce her to a few other kids," I replied. "She's in there with Rob's son, Noah, and Tom's girls, Cassidy and Britton."

"Rob, huh?" Alaric repeated, his eyes going to the bouncy castle again.

"Yeah, he's over by the pit," I said, gesturing to the horseshoe pits on the far side of the yard, a safe distance from the area my dad had dubbed the kid zone. Rob and Brandon were playing against Mitch and Grant.

"Well, thanks for helping her get comfortable. I appreciate it." He said, his eyes returning to me, engulfing me in the familiar ache at my centre.

"What are *friends* for?" I offered with a shrug, bringing the bottle of beer to my lips.

"Friends, huh?" he asked, arching a brow, likely thinking about the very *unfriendly* things he did to me Thursday night. I know I was.

I looked past him, spotting my mother near the patio door, watching us with hawk-like intensity. When she started over, I glanced back at him nervously.

"I'll be back soon," I told him, nodding politely before I walked away from him quickly, cutting off my mother before she could make it halfway across the lawn. I could feel his eyes on me, watching me go, and that only fueled my mom's interest.

"Gwen, dear, who were you just talking to?" she asked, peering around me to assess Alaric.

"Dad's latest hire, Alaric Petersen," I replied, trying to keep my expression impassive. Mom had a tendency of making a big deal out of things, and while I'd welcomed it with Erik, I didn't want her exuberance to scare Alaric off.

"Oh, that's right," Mom recalled, her lips curling reflectively. "Is he single?"

"Mom, seriously?" I rolled my eyes, hoping she'd think my flushed cheeks were a result of the heat. "Please don't. You'll not only embarrass me, but you'll embarrass Dad and the company. Alaric is a new employee, not a contestant on *The Bachelor*."

"I'm just saying, he's an attractive man. A little hairy, but still. You two would make a cute couple."

"Mom," I groaned with exasperation—although her comment made my heart sputter happily in my chest. "Stop with the matchmaking, please. I really can find my own dates."

Mom opened her mouth, about to defend herself, but opted to smile instead. "Of course, I'm sorry. I can't help it—I want to see both my daughters happy."

"Well, *this* daughter is content figuring out her happiness on her own terms," I muttered, sending her a pointed look and hoping like hell she'd heed me.

"Fair enough," Mom said, hesitating. "I am sorry about the dinner, Guinevere. When your father told me Grant asked you out, I figured I'd give you a gentle nudge."

"I don't need any nudges," I assured her, folding my arms across my chest. She nodded with understanding, her eyes returning to Alaric.

I couldn't help it, I glanced over my shoulder too. As if he felt my gaze, he turned, and my stupid blush deepened.

"I can see that now," she remarked, a sly smile pulling her lips gradually up.

The garden gate opened, and Renly walked through with a

case of beer in his hands, his boyfriend Brian trailing alongside him. Relief washed over as I sensed an opportunity to escape this awkward, never-ending song and dance.

"Excuse me." I said before heading off to greet them. "You didn't!" I squealed, noting the logo on the side of the twelve pack—my favourite craft beer from Niagara Falls.

"We did," Ren sang, shifting the pack so that he held it in one arm and hugged me with the other. He kissed my cheek, and when we parted, I hugged Brian.

"We went to Niagara Falls for a little romantic getaway earlier this week, and we couldn't leave without stopping at the brewery first," Brian added, sending an affectionate grin to Ren.

"You guys are seriously the best," I sighed, stepping back again. "Let's get you fellas a drink."

I pivoted and led the way through the patio doors and into the kitchen. "Do you mind if I use the bathroom? I've had to pee for the last hour of the drive," Brian laughed as Ren set the twelve pack on the counter.

"Sure, it's down the hall to your right," I told him, and he nodded with relief before following my directions.

"I noticed Mr. Tattooed Thor is here," Ren remarked once we heard the bathroom door close. Both of our gazes went out the screen door, where we could just make out Alaric's form as he stood in the same place I'd left him. "Is he here as your boyfriend or?"

"Shh," I whispered, looking around to make sure the coast was clear. I'd texted Renly to update him on the hot welder situation, and he'd seemed thrilled to hear we were giving it the good old college try. "We're not here together, so act like you don't know him. I don't want him getting all bugged out by the amount of nosy family and friends I have."

"Fair enough," Ren raised his hands in surrender. "My lips are sealed," he added, pretending to zip them shut.

"Good." I nodded, relieved. "Now if only my mom would stop meddling." Sighing, I tugged the twelve pack over and opened it, drawing three beers out and setting them on the counter.

"Meddling is what your mom does best," Ren chuckled, shaking his head.

"Tell me about it," I sighed, dragging my fingers through my hair and staring off down the hallway. "Speaking of meddling...how did *the talk* go?"

"Good," Ren said, smiling and swiftly changing the subject. "I'm parched. Could I get that drink you offered?" He cocked a brow at me and looked pointedly down the hall.

I narrowed my eyes at him before turning to open the refrigerator. Renly didn't want to talk about it right now, but I knew eventually, he would, so I let him have the win. "Is white wine okay?"

"Any kind of wine is fine in my books," Ren replied. "We'll be staying with my parents for the next few days, and I'm sure that will be fun."

Ren's dad still didn't fully accept his son's lifestyle. "I thought he had stopped with the comments after your Nan and mom laid into him last Christmas?" I asked sympathetically, pouring two glasses of wine before I put the bottle back in the refrigerator.

"He did, and he has," Ren said quickly. "But, well, I think a part of him still believes that it's a phase."

"Well if he ends up being a dick, you guys could come crash at my place. I'll sleep on the couch." I suggested, shrugging.

"No, if it's that bad, we'll just leave." Ren laughed. "Or get a hotel. But Nan wanted me to try. I think she wants us to fix things before..." he trailed off, his voice tightening with emotion.

"How's she doing?" I leaned against the counter, nodding at Brian as he rejoined us in the kitchen. I handed him a drink and slid the other one to Renly, my gaze returning to him.

"She's good, but she talks an awful lot about death." He shook his head sadly. "I mean, she always has, but this time it feels different. Like she's actually preparing for it."

Brian put his arm around Ren's shoulders, hugging him from behind. "She's going to be okay. She's a tough lady."

"Yeah, she will," Ren said, his voice distant, as his hand absently went to Brian's arm. He patted it twice before shaking his head, jolting himself. "But enough with this gloomy topic. Let's get back out to the party! I hope your mom made her deviled eggs," Ren said, pasting on a smile.

"Of course she did, it wouldn't be an annual Williams' barbeque without Mom's deviled eggs," I replied dryly, grabbing two more beers.

The three of us made our way through the sliding door to the patio, and my eyes instantly went to Alaric, who was still keeping half an eye on the bouncy castle where Sawyer was still playing with the other kids.

He was dressed in a pair of beige cargo pants and a white t-shirt that clung to his muscular chest in a way that I—nor the rest of my little group—could ignore.

Alaric was single-handedly the hottest man in attendance, and I still couldn't believe that less than forty-eight hours ago, his beautiful face was between *my* thighs.

Suddenly parched, I tipped the bottle back and took a heady sip.

"He looks lonely. Let's go keep him company," Ren suggested, tilting his head toward Alaric. He didn't wait for me to reply before he and Brian were making their way over to him. I adjusted my hold on the two unopened beers in my other hand and sighed, trailing after them.

"Hey, I hope you're not too bored," I teased once we reached him, offering him a fresh beer. His head turned at the sound of my voice, and he gave me a small smile as took the bottle from me. His fingers brushed across mine again, and I drew in a breath, unsettled by how unnerving a simple, delicate touch from him was.

Noticing Ren and Brian, Alaric cleared his throat. "I'm not bored at all."

"Sawyer's still enjoying the bouncy castle?" I asked, hiding a grin.

"Remember that time we smoked a joint in there?" Ren cackled, and I shot him a withering look, hoping it would silence him, and glanced at Alaric with embarrassment. I expected to find him irritated, but the bemused smile on his face threw me off.

"We were seventeen," I retorted defensively, bringing my gaze back to Ren to scowl at him. I didn't need him sharing any high school horror stories with Alaric.

"Yes we were," Ren teased, and I rolled my eyes, looking forward—at the bouncy castle in question. "You greened out so badly, you threw up all over the grass."

"Yeah, well. In hindsight, it probably wasn't a good idea to smoke a joint, eat a bag of cookies, and jump around like an imbecile." I responded dryly. I'd learned since then, thankfully. Alaric laughed, his eyes warming as they slipped over me. I gave him a hint of a smile before turning my attention back to Renly. "Watch it, Brewster. I've got stories to spare about you, too."

"Touché." Renly bowed, yielding. "How do you like dear old Port of Hope?" he asked, looking at Alaric expectantly.

"I like it," Alaric responded, lifting his beer to his lips as his blue eyes slid to me. I averted my gaze, looking out toward the horseshoe pit. My brow furrowed when I noticed Grant standing beside my dad.

Catching sight of me too, Grant said something and my dad nodded, walking off to speak to some of the other associates while Grant started over. He came to a stop to my left, and I turned, forcing my smile in place.

"Gwen," he said, by way of greeting. "I've been sent over here by Russell."

"Ah, yes. He did mention he wanted you to meet Alaric," I recovered. "Alaric, this is Grant Hernandez, one of our contracted engineering architects."

"I've heard a lot about you," Grant said, smiling with ease.

Alaric huffed in response as they shook hands.

"Modest and hardworking," I muttered, ignoring the curious look Grant sent me. I looked away abruptly, touching Ren's arm. "Grant, you remember my friend Renly, right? This is his boyfriend, Brian."

"Nice to meet you," Grant said, shaking Brian's hand and giving Ren one of those weird clap hand-shake things. "I've seen you on TV a couple of times now. Must be a pretty cool job."

"It pays the bills," Ren replied with an illustrious smile.

Catching Alaric's questioning gaze, I explained, "Renly is an interior designer on the Home Renovation Channel's *Brightwood Interior*."

He nodded, the corner of his lip kicking up. I resisted the urge to fan myself like some shameless floozy.

"Is the drama real?" Grant added, leaning back with his hands in his pockets.

Ren tucked his chin in, smirking scandalously. "Every bit of it."

I caught my lip between my teeth, trying to rein in my

desire to take another peek at Alaric. I could sense his gaze on me, and it was making me feel all floaty.

Alaric

It was harder than I thought it would be to not reach out and touch her, the way I'd done a hundred times over the past week. Seeing her in the jumping castle with Sawyer had broken the last of the chains I'd wrapped around myself.

Witnessing Gwen and my daughter bonding opened my eyes to the truth; I'd lost control of keeping work, Gwen, and Sawyer separate in my head.I knew I was looking at her too much, but it couldn't be helped.

The flash of jealousy that surged through me when Grant had joined us, his eyes targeting Gwen, only served to remind me how deep I'd fallen. I'd wanted to drag her to my side, make it known that she was mine.

But before I could do that, I needed to have a conversation with both Cheryl and Sawyer.

"Who's up for a round of horseshoes?" Grant asked.

"We'll play," Renly volunteered, squeezing Brian's hand and winking at him.

Grant turned to Gwen, gently touching the point of her elbow. "What about you?"

"Trust me, everybody here has learned not to give Gwen a horseshoe," Ren deadpanned.

"It's true," she confirmed, nodding solemnly, her eyes landing on me.

"Alaric?" Grant challenged, watching me deliberately.

"Daddy! I'm hungry!" my daughter's little voice proclaimed as her small body pushed between Grant and Gwen, who took the opportunity to step further away from him and a little closer to me.

Her perfume caught the breeze and dragged in the layers of lilies and magnolias with my next breath.

"I can get her a plate," Gwen offered, her eyes flashing to mine, holding my gaze a little too long.

"All right." I nodded, exhaling.

"It's settled then. Game on," Renly said, strolling toward the horseshoe pit.

I looked down at my daughter, giving her a stern look. "You listen, okay? Mind your manners."

"Yes, Daddy!" Sawyer said, slipping her hand through Gwen's and peering up at her. "Where's the food?"

Gwen's dimples flashed as she grinned down at her. "I'll show you," she laughed lightly, and the two of them started toward the patio. I watched them go for a moment before turning, unsurprised to see Grant was still there.

He offered me an amicable smile. "Cute kid. How old is she?"

"Five," I replied curtly, heading toward the pit with Grant keeping up pace beside me.

"Alaric, you'll be on my team," Ren said when we approached.

"We decided we each got a beefcake, to even the odds," Brian supplied, winking at Grant. I snorted and shook my head a little, moving to join Renly on the other side of the pit.

My gaze drifted to the patio, where Gwen was helping Sawyer fill up a plate. Her sister approached, smiling warmly at Sawyer while Gwen gestured to her, introducing her.

Sawyer had fallen asleep with her head on my shoulder,

nestled in the crook of my arm. Her soft snores were muffled by my shoulder, her arms dangling limply over my back.

"That doesn't look very comfortable," Gwen remarked softly, her amusement evident. She paused beside me, turning her head to glance at us. "They'll be setting off the fireworks soon."

"She'll wake for them," I replied, knowing she would. Sawyer loved fireworks, and as soon as the first one took to the sky, she'd open her eyes. Which meant we didn't have long to talk. "Thanks for hanging out with her."

"You don't have to thank me for that," she told me, her eyes pinning me. She smiled, glancing at my sleeping daughter. "She's a great kid. Better company than most adults in attendance."

"I have to agree with you there." I cocked a brow, lifting my chin, scanning the guests for Grant.

All night, he'd competed for Gwen's attention, and I'd resented how he'd sauntered around, making his interest in her perfectly clear. But she brushed off his advances, slipping away discretely the first chance she got, her eyes always finding mine—even if she had to flutter about to draw her mother's keen eye away.

"Are you jealous?" she asked, her lips twitching.

I tilted my head, my eyes smoldering. "What do you think?" I challenged.

"I think you are," she smiled, like this pleased her.

My eyes locked on hers, the connection a perfect fusion. Before I had a chance to respond, the first firecracker went off, wheezing through the air. Sawyer's head popped up, her eyes wide and very much awake as she took in the colourful explosions happening above us.

Gwen smiled, her eyes moving from Sawyer to me before she turned to watch the fireworks, too. The smooth column of her neck strained elegantly as she looked up, and I couldn't swallow back the impulse to reach for her.

I purposely dropped the arm that wasn't holding my daughter so that the back of my hand would brush against the back of Gwen's. Surprised, she looked up at me. The fireworks looked more exquisite when reflected in her eyes.

"Ohh! Look, Daddy!" Sawyer said with awe, pointing to the sky, where a series of three fireworks were exploding.

"It's pretty isn't it?" Gwen's dimples popped as she watched my daughter take in the show. Sawyer nodded in agreement. This time, I didn't hesitate to curl my thumb around hers.

By the end of the twenty-minute show, Sawyer's head was bobbing. Unable to fight it any longer, she rested her head against my shoulder and let out an exhausted yawn.

"Time to go, munchkin," I said, shifting her to give my arm a rest.

"Okay," she sighed.

We started back toward the house, Gwen strolling beside me until we reached the patio. "I hope you guys had fun today," she said, smiling softly.

I nodded, resisting the inclination to invite her over. She smiled again—one that held so much understanding and patience in it—and headed to the sliding door, gliding through it. Casting one last look at me over her shoulder, she offered a parting smile before she disappeared deeper into the house.

Making my way through the backyard, I nodded at Grant as I passed him. Russell was standing by the gate, talking to the guests who were making their way to their cars. I paused long enough to thank him for the day.

"Thanks for coming," Russell told me, smiling at my sleeping daughter. "Looks like she had a fun day."

"She did. If she were conscious right now, she'd tell you." I chuckled, knowing it to be true. Sawyer would chat the ears off a statue.

"See you Monday morning."

"Bright and early," I replied.

He nodded, clapping me gently on the shoulder. "Enjoy the rest of your weekend, son."

"You too," I said solidly, moving past him and slipping through the gate. I walked down the driveway, reaching into my pocket for my keys, hitting unlock and pocketing them before opening the passenger door. Sawyer was still gently snoring, exhausted from all the running around. She didn't wake when I eased her into her car seat, buckled her in, or closed the door.

I looked up, catching Grant's eye as he walked down the driveway.

"Hey, wait up a minute!" he called, changing direction and moving toward me. He slid his hands into his pockets, narrowing his eyes at me with consideration. "You're the guy she's seeing, aren't you?"

I lifted my chin. "I am."

He nodded with understanding. "Well, I know when to admit defeat," he remarked, laughing lightly and shaking his head. I snorted, opening my door.

"Smart of you."

"Does Russell know?"

I scowled. "What's it to you?"

"I'm just saying," Grant said sincerely, lifting his hands in surrender. "Russell is protective of his daughters. If he thinks you're jerking her around, it'll end your career."

"Is that a threat?" I gritted my teeth, my fingers curling into a fist.

"Consider it advice from a friend," Grant said earnestly. "Relax. Your secret is safe with me, but sooner or later he'll figure it out on his own. Have a nice weekend!" He said, backing away a few steps before he turned and continued to his own vehicle.

Gwen

I peered out my old bedroom window, watching Alaric's truck pull away from the curb and disappear down my parents' street.

"There you are." Mom's voice caught me by surprise, and I jolted, turning around as she walked fully into my bedroom and sat down on the edge of the bed. She smiled hopefully at me and patted the space beside her. "I've been looking for you."

"Why?" I asked, suspicious, but sitting beside her anyway. My mother wrapped her arm around my shoulders and hugged me.

"I just miss my daughters, that's all. Can't I miss you? You were under my feet for over nineteen years. It's still a little weird without you two here, and you never tell me anything. I have no clue what's going on in your life anymore. Remember the days when you used to tell me things?"

She was fishing, and the knowing look in her eyes gave her away.

"Who told you?" I sighed, leaning away and side-eyeing her.

"Aha!" she clapped her hands together gleefully. "Nobody told me anything, I just sensed it. Does your father know?"

"Nope, and I'm not planning on telling him just yet," I replied, biting my bottom lip. "We're still figuring things out."

Mom was quiet for a moment, reflective. "It's a little different dating a man with a child, isn't it?"

"Yeah," I exhaled. "We're just taking things slowly right now. He has to tell his ex and Sawyer first."

"That makes sense."

"Do you think Dad will be mad?"

"No," Mom shook her head, smiling lovingly at me. "He just wants to see you happy."

"I'm kind of worried he'll fire Alaric," I laughed nervously, tugging at the hem of my dress.

"I don't think that will happen. He talks all the time about what a wonderful worker he is," Mom replied.

"I hope your right. But either way…could you keep it from Dad until I'm ready to tell him?"

"Of course," Mom said, squeezing my shoulder.

CHAPTER NINETEEN

OLIVE BRANCH

Alaric

"Mommy! Guess what? I saw the fireworks on Canada's birthday! And we had cake!" Sawyer exclaimed, her words escaping in a rush the moment Cheryl opened her front door to us.

"Oh that sounds so exciting," Cheryl replied, smiling.

"And Daddy's friend jumped with me in the castle too! She looks like the lady on Daddy's leg." Sawyer added, unintentionally causing her mother to glower at me.

"Is that so?" she replied stiffly, somehow keeping her smile in place.

I crouched, and Sawyer turned to me expectantly—unaware of the storm she'd unintentionally caused. If she caught on, she'd feel terrible—and I didn't want her to feel bad. She'd done nothing wrong.

"I'll see you in a couple weeks, munchkin," I said, pressing a kiss to her cheek. Placing her small hands on either side of my face, she gave me a big kiss back. "Be a good girl."

"I will! I'm always good. Bye, Daddy!" she said, twirling and bouncing past Cheryl into the house.

"Can we talk for a moment?" I asked, straightening to my full height.

Cheryl closed the front door and turned stiffly, her eyes piercing. "What, Alaric? I'm not in the mood to have it out with you right now."

"I don't want to fight. I want to talk."

"So talk."

I drew in a breath, preparing myself, and scratched at the back of my neck. "You said you wanted me to let you know when I started seeing someone, so. This is me letting you know—I've started seeing someone."

Cheryl's jaw ticked, and she nodded, her arms folding slowly across her chest. "And has this *person* been around Sawyer?" I hesitated, and Cheryl's shrewd eyes picked up on it. "Seriously Alaric, the *one thing* I asked you to do was tell me before making introductions!"

"It's not like that," I responded, my brow furrowing. "She hasn't met Sawyer as my girlfriend. We work together, so—"

"She was at the work thing you took Sawyer to this weekend," Cheryl interrupted, finishing my sentence with a cruel edge to her words. She shook her head with disdain. "Convenient of you to wait until *after* to tell me."

I clamped my mouth shut, opting for silence instead of the retort that sat on the tip of my tongue. "I don't know why you're so angry about this. You had to know that, one day, I'd meet someone else."

Cheryl gaped at me, floundering for something to say. "That's not the point; I wanted to be informed before you made any introductions."

"I haven't made introductions—at least not that one," I

replied stonily, crossing my own arms. "I planned on telling Sawyer during our next weekend."

"You can't!"

I arched a brow, challenging her. "And why not?"

"It's a bad time," Cheryl said, scowling at me. "Sawyer already has enough changes happening. She doesn't need this one. Besides, who knows how long *this one* will keep your interest?" she added spitefully.

I clenched my jaw with aggravation. "You might be right about the changes, Cheryl, which is why I wanted to talk to you about this...but you're wrong about my interest in her."

Cheryl gaped at me, her eyes widening and permeating with hurt like it pained her to hear me say that. She schooled her features quickly, masking the blow with a bitter smile. "We'll see."

Turning on my heel, I spoke without looking back. "See you in eleven days."

Cheryl's door slammed shut before I made it off the porch. I pushed air through my nostrils in aggravation, rolling my neck.

Sliding into the cab of my truck, I closed the door and glanced at the cup holder, picking up the cat I'd sculpted last night.

After carrying Sawyer up to bed, I'd been too restless to sleep. I kept thinking about how natural it had been to see Gwen and my daughter together, about how I'd wanted the whole thing. Her, Sawyer, Tig—even her demonic cat.

So I plugged the old baby monitor in, taking the receiver out with me to my shop. I needed to tinker on something, to keep my hands busy.

The result was pretty cool—a nuts and bolt cat that I hoped she would like. Setting it back down in the cup holder, I headed back to town. Parking against the curb, I jumped out and strolled into the pizza shop.

The cashier was the same woman who'd served me last time. I approached the counter and smiled. "Can you look up past customer orders on the computer?"

She peered at me with confusion. "Yes…"

"I wanted to surprise a friend with pizza, could you pull up her last order?"

"I suppose I could…I'd need the phone number." I gave it, and the cashier typed it into the computer. "A large Tempest pizza and garlic bread."

"I'll have that," I smiled, reaching for my wallet. "To go, please."

Gwen

Sitting cross-legged on my couch, I shifted my shoulders, working out the kinks. My fingers returned to and hovered over my laptop keys, and I let out an aggravated huff. The words were just…stuck.

My stomach rumbled, alerting me to the fact that it had been seven hours since I last ate something.

Setting my laptop on the coffee table, I stood up and stretched. Dahmer let out a noise halfway between a purr and a meow, his head flying up at the disturbance, his claws digging into the material. He'd been asleep on the cushion beside me for the last forty-five minutes, and his pissy eyes followed me when I started walking to the kitchen.

I paused, hearing heavy footfall on the stairs. A few moments later, knuckles rapped against the door.

Heart pattering in my chest, I forced myself to saunter to the door. Opening it, I was greeted to the delicious sight of Alaric, holding two boxes from my favourite pizzeria balanced in one hand, while his other rested against the doorway, flashing a smile that melted my racing heart.

He stepped toward me, his free hand moving to my hip as he leaned down to kiss me softly.

"He comes bearing gifts." I laughed against his lips.

"A few," he admitted, chuckling ruefully as I closed the door. He set the pizzeria boxes down on the table, keeping his eyes on me as I moved toward him. "I told Cheryl."

His tone gave nothing away. I sucked my bottom lip in, releasing it with a pop. "How'd that go?"

"It went," he said, offering me a small smile.

"I hate that I'm causing issues for you with her," I frowned, worrying my lip.

"Hey, it's not your fault." He shook his head, stepping toward me. "I'd have issues with Cheryl either way. Trust me." His hands went to my hips, encompassing me.

"Comforting," I arched a brow, tilting my head and biting back a smile as I looped my arms around his neck. I pressed my body against him, grinning coyly. "Is that something in your pocket, or are you just super happy to see me?"

"Well, I was going to wait until later, but I should have known you'd try and get into my pants the moment I showed up," Alaric teased, smiling as he reached into his pocket and pulled something out. He held his hand between us and opened his fingers, revealing in his palm a miniature cat made of nuts and bolts welded together.

"Oh my God! It's adorable!" I laughed, taking it from him and inspecting it. "I love it!" I threw my arms around him again, standing on my tippy toes to reach his lips. I kissed him, my mouth moving against his slowly, reveling in the taste of him.

"I'm glad." He grinned against my lips, his arms encompassing me. I nipped at his lip, urging him on, guided by an aching pulse in my centre.

Alaric's fingers went to the waistband of my shorts, and I

snapped back to my sad reality. "You might want to avoid doing that this week."

"Gotcha." He winked, moving his hand to cup my face. He continued kissing me for a moment longer, his tongue moving ardently against mine before he pulled away. My eyes dropped down to his jeans, noticing how turned on he was. I licked my lips, about to drop to my knees on the floor in front of him. "You don't need to do that, Gwen."

"I want to," I assured him, tugging his zipper down.

He laughed, gently lifting my hand away from its quest. He held it, rubbing his thumb over my palm in slow, tiny circles. "But I brought you pizza…"

"Damn it, you did," I sighed, ravenous for it.

"You can finally put on that *Game of Thrones* show," he added, picking up the pizza and garlic bread with his free hand and in two steps, he'd cleared the short distance to the couch.

"All right, you've talked me into it," I laughed, shaking my head while he set the pizza down on the coffee table. I went to my bookshelf, arranging the little nuts and bolts cat down on one of the square shelves before I went into the kitchen.

I grabbed us something to drink and some plates. Walking back into the living room, I stilled when I saw him lounging in the corner of the sectional. He patted the space beside him, flashing me a light-hearted smile.

Continuing, I dropped down beside him, my bare thigh rubbing against his denim-clad one. He smiled at me, his eyes bright. "You gonna put it on?"

"Right, yes." I leaned forward, grabbing the remotes. I worked on setting up the show, while Alaric loaded up our plates with pizza and garlic bread. "Okay but, for the sake of my sister's upcoming wedding—you cannot be bringing pizza over regularly."

He laughed, his eyes roving me suggestively. "I don't think you have anything to worry about."

"You haven't seen the bridesmaid dresses yet." I deadpanned, taking a bite of pizza anyway. It was my cheat week, the only bonus to this dark and grisly time. Cheese and chocolate healed all PMS woes.

"That's true." He laughed lightly. We fell quiet for a moment. It wasn't an unpleasant quiet, but a contented one. "When's the wedding?"

"June," I replied, stealing a glance at him. He nodded, taking a bite of his slice. I stifled the urge to ask him if he'd come. June was a little under a year away—a lot could happen in a year. He could lose interest, move on. He could decide all the trouble my being in his life caused with his ex and Sawyer wasn't worth it.

But the way he looked at me made those insecure, negative-Nancy thoughts fly straight out of my head.

"You could always start joining Tig and me for weekend hikes," he said, sending me a smile that made me *really* resent Aunt Flo.

Alaric

I lifted the bookshelf and set it down on the ground, inspecting it. Much like the coffee table and the two end tables I'd made before it, it had the same black metal and wood look to it.

It just needed to be stained, then I could bring it in and set it along the wall in the living room.

Tires crunched over gravel and Tig started barking. "Quiet," I instructed, and Tig fell silent, resting his head on his paws with a heavy sigh, like he felt unappreciated.

I made my way to the door, watching as a black minivan

pulled up beside my truck. Cheryl stepped out, her eyes red like she'd been crying.

My defenses fell, concern replacing the usual aggravation I felt when I had to deal with my ex.

"Cheryl? What's wrong?" I moved toward her, concerned. She subconsciously placed her hand on her stomach, her lip trembling as she stared at me.

"I can't sleep."

I cocked my head, my feet halting. "I'm sorry?" I questioned.

She wiped at her cheeks, looking away before her eyes darted back to me. "I haven't been able to sleep. Every time I close my eyes, I think about what you said…and I'm not trying to push you out, I swear."

"Sure feels like it," I retorted.

She bit her lip, releasing it to speak again, her voice trembling. "I'm sorry if I made you feel that way. I guess I…I wanted to punish you."

"Where are you going with this?"

"At first, when you told me you were moving, I thought you were coming after me." She admitted, shaking her head.

"You cheated, Cheryl. I didn't."

"Yeah, but I never really had you, did I?" she asked, smiling sorrowfully. I said nothing—she already knew the answer to that. She nodded, lowering her gaze before drawing it back up to my eyes.

"I know. I'm sorry," I told her, meaning it. She nodded again, dragging her eyes back up to me. The broken look in her eyes made my heart ache. I got the sense that there was more coming, so I kept my mouth shut.

"I didn't want to include you because you never loved me the way I needed you to, and having you show up was—is— just painful. I know it shouldn't be. Mason looks at me the way you never did, and I love him, but it still stings. So, I'm sorry for punishing you."

"It doesn't just punish me, it punishes Sawyer, too. She should get us both, Cheryl, regardless of how we feel about each other."

"I know that," she said, sorrow in place of her usual spite. Maybe she finally saw reason. Hope bloomed, and I wondered if we'd finally be able to move past the bullshit. "Mason tells me I'm irrational when it comes to you. He thinks I need to let you in more."

"What do you think?"

She nodded, her eyes welling over with tears. "I think he's right," she managed. She heaved a breath, wiping at her cheek before she continued. "I'm sorry I freaked out when I heard you were seeing someone. I just didn't like the idea of being replaced."

"Feels shitty, doesn't it?" More tears slipped down her cheeks, and I sighed. "You won't be replaced, Cheryl. I won't do that to Sawyer."

"But I did that to her and to you. I made it hard for you to be there. I was just...I was so angry, Alaric. You let me walk away without even fighting for me. You fought for Sawyer, but not me. I guess I just wanted you to feel a little bit of the anger and hurt I felt."

Hearing it from the source didn't make it hurt any less. I inclined my head, absorbing her words. "Mission accomplished."

She shook her head, more tears spilling over. It was crazy that I felt any amount of sympathy at all for her, after everything she'd put me through over the last six years.

She dried her eyes on her sleeve and drew a breath. "When I have the baby, Sawyer can stay with you. If you're still up for it."

"What about Mason's mom?"

"She can still help us out, but…Sawyer should be with you if she can't be with me."

I smiled, nodding. "Okay."

Gravel crunched beneath tires and headlights flooded the garage. We both watched as a red Mazda pulled up, parking behind my truck. Gwen killed the ignition, and the lights went out.

She stepped out of her car, her smile fading a little when she noticed Cheryl standing in front of me. Her eyes shot back to me, wide with unease, her grip tightening on the door like she wanted to bolt.

"Who's this?" Cheryl's voice was tight, and I tilted my head, encouraging Gwen forward with my eyes. She backed up, closing the door, and approached warily. "Cheryl, this is Gwen. Gwen, this is Cheryl."

"Hi, Cheryl, it's nice to meet you," Gwen said smoothly, reaching out to shake Cheryl's hand.

"It's nice to meet you too," Cheryl replied, her eyes going from Gwen to me. She drew in a pained breath, pulling her hand abruptly from Gwen's and reaching around to press both of her palms on her back.

I stepped toward her, my brow creasing. "Are you okay?"

"There're just Braxton hicks, Alaric," Cheryl replied, her breathing still labored. She glanced at Gwen again, her brow still furrowed as if she was in pain. "I just need to go home and rest. I'll be fine. I'll see you Friday."

She straightened, smiling tightly at Gwen before she passed and walked to her van.

While she backed from my driveway, Gwen turned to look at me, her brow crinkled with uncertainty. "Alaric, if I'd known she was here—"

"Don't worry about it," I told her as Cheryl's taillights

disappeared down the lane. "Now she's met you." I shrugged, not bothering to contain my smile as my hands slipped around Gwen's waist.

"She didn't look too happy about it." Her brow furrowed, and she worried her lip.

"She'll adjust," I said.

Tig finally gave up waiting for me to release him and ambled over, knocking his nose against Gwen's hip. She pulled away, looking down at him, and stroked the top of his head.

"What are you working on?" she asked, peering into the garage and catching sight of the bookshelf. "Oh, it's beautiful!"

"Yeah, someone mentioned that my house lacks bookshelves," I teased.

"Someone must be very smart," Gwen retorted, turning and slipping her hands around my waist.

I wrapped my arm around the small of her back and reached over to flick out the garage light. Opening the connecting door, I whistled, calling Tig in. He ran in ahead of us, and once he'd cleared the foyer, I swept Gwen up in my arms, carrying her inside.

She laughed until I pressed my lips to hers, my tongue sweeping across her bottom lip. Looping her arms around my neck, her lips parted, and she sighed.

CHAPTER TWENTY

PRE-TERM

Gwen

"Look, Kelsey, you don't need to figure this all out right now," I said gently, pausing to look over an email that I needed to send out before noon. My sister's meltdown was a little unprecedented, but as her maid of honor, it was my duty to reassure her.

My head was pulsing, and I could *feel* a stress headache coming on.

"That's the thing, Gwen. I *do* need to figure this all out right now," Kelsey snipped, affronted.

"You have to figure out exactly what table your guests need to sit at right now? It can't wait until we're done at work?"

"You'll probably be banging the welder," she sniffled.

"Kels," I sighed, closing my eyes. She wasn't wrong; Alaric and I had been spending every spare moment with one another. The only thing we hadn't done was to tell my parents. I planned on broaching the subject soon—just not yet.

"I need help," she pleaded.

I opened my mouth, about to speak when the phone on my desk rang shrilly. "Come over tonight, and we'll make the guest list. Bring the binder. I have to get back to work," I said, speaking over the ringing.

"Fine," Kelsey exhaled audibly. "Call me later." She hung up, and I lifted the telephone receiver on my desk.

"Good afternoon. This is Gwen from Williams Tech. How can I help you?" I recited, massaging my temples.

"I need to get a hold of Alaric Petersen." A woman said, her voice familiar. She let out a pained grunt before continuing. "It's Cheryl Evans."

Instantly recognizing her name, my spine stiffened with alarm, and I straightened. "Alaric is out on a job site right now. I can try and reach him through the on-site foreman. Can I relay a message?"

"Yes, please—" She gasped, and I could hear the hysteria in her voice. She took a few deep breaths, trying to calm herself. "I need him—" She trailed off again, letting out a groan that made the hairs on the nape of my neck stand up. "I'm on my way to Mount Sinai. Tell him that I'm—I'm in labour, and I need him to pick Sawyer up from my neighbours. I need him to pick her up and take her to his house," she added urgently.

"Okay. Of course. I'll get the message to him."

"Thank you," she exhaled, the relief palpable, and relayed her neighbour's phone number to me. I wrote it down quickly, with trembling hands. She let out a pained cry, and the phone clanged to the ground.

Shuffling ensued as someone picked it up, then the call was disconnected. I started dialing Mitch's number on repeat, knowing the on-site foreman would have his cell phone on him. I had to call three times before he answered.

"Hello?" he barked, clearly irritated.

"Mitch—it's Gwen. Is Alaric nearby?"

"He's working. Why?"

"Put him on the phone, please. It's an emergency." My voice shook, and I was certain he could hear it.

Mitch's tone changed immediately. "Of course. Alaric, come here!"

I waited a couple of minutes, worrying my lip. "Hello?"

"Alaric," I said, pausing at his intake of breath. "Cheryl just called—"

"What? Why?"

"She needs you to pick Sawyer up from her neighbour's," I began, looking down at the phone number on the post-it note.

"What's going on?" he sounded worried.

"She's in labour and on her way to Mount Sinai." He exhaled harshly, the sound of it slicing through me. "I'm sure everything's going to be okay, Alaric," I added, my tone soft.

I could hear him walking away, likely putting some distance between the other guys and him so that he could talk in private. "She's not due for another three months."

"Oh," I breathed, nibbling on my lip.

"What's the neighbour's number?" Alaric asked.

I relayed it, my fingers absently twirling the cord as I read it to him. He thanked me and hung up.

Leaning back in my chair, I stared blankly at the computer screen, trying to process the last twenty minutes, and how I felt, all while my heart pulsed painfully in my chest.

A few seconds later, my cell phone rang. I snatched it up quickly, answering when I saw Alaric's name flash across the screen.

"We're loading up now, but I'm still going to be another three hours getting back."

I glanced at the clock, noting that it was four o'clock already. "You know, I used to pride myself on my babysitting skills. I could go get her and bring her back to my place for a bit."

He was quiet, save for the sound of his breath when he exhaled. "I'll call you back in a minute."

"Okay."

I placed my cell phone on my desk and went back to staring blankly at the screen, my mind unable to focus. Ten minutes later, my phone rang again.

"Hello?"

"Hey," he breathed, sounding a little less strained. "If you're sure you want to..."

"I'm sure," I assured him. "I mean if you're sure."

"I am," he replied, the relief he felt easily detectable. "I called Cheryl's neighbour back, and she's expecting you. I'll pick her up as soon as we get back."

"Okay. Text me the address?"

"I will. Thanks again, Gwen. I...really appreciate it," he said, clearing his throat.

"I'll see you later." I smiled, hanging up.

"Who was that?" My dad's sudden appearance at my desk caught me by surprise—I hadn't heard him come in.

I straightened in my seat, trying to exude professional confidence. "That was Alaric. He had a family emergency come up and needs to go pick up his daughter. They're still on site in Barrie, so I offered to babysit."

My explanation didn't seem to ease his suspicion. Avoiding his analytical gaze, I shut down the computer and gathered my things. "That was helpful of you."

I shrugged, not looking up. "It's not a big deal, Dad." In the corner of my eye, I saw him nodding. Finally lifting my head, I gave him a reassuring smile. "Can you lock up?"

"Of course I can lock up." Dad scowled.

"Thanks, Dad." I kissed him on the cheek. "See you tomorrow morning, okay?"

Alaric

"Gwen mentioned something about a family emergency. Is everything okay?" Russell asked, intercepting me on my dash to the truck. I paused, turning to address him.

"Yes, sir. My ex went into labour. She's a few months early, and needs me to take care of our daughter." I explained.

"Let me know if there's anything I can do," Russell said after a moment.

I hesitated, clearing my throat. "I might need to take tomorrow off. I'll be setting up temporary daycare, but I'll need the day to do that. I hate to ask, but—"

"I understand," he replied, clapping me on the shoulder. He opened his mouth, about to say something further. Then he thought the better of it and nodded instead. "Just keep me informed."

"Will do," I told him, turning and opening the door. I drove as quickly as I legally could, unsure of what state I'd find Sawyer in. I hadn't been able to reach Cheryl or Mason, and I had no idea how much Sawyer knew about what was happening.

Jogging up the walkway to Gwen's building entrance, I opened the glass door and climbed the steps. I paused in the hallway, listening to the voices coming from inside her apartment. Hers and Sawyer's. It felt natural, and my ears craved more of it.

Raising my fist, I knocked lightly, and a few moments later the door opened. Gwen grinned at me, standing aside to let me in. "You got here quicker than we thought! We're just finishing up a game of Go Fish. Sawyer's kicking my behind, of course."

Walking through her door, I spotted Sawyer sitting on the couch, holding cards in her hands. "Hi, Daddy!"

Although she was smiling, the slight indentation between her brows hinted that she was concerned. "Hey, munchkin. Ready to go home?"

"Yes." Sawyer nodded, setting her stack of cards down carefully on the coffee table. "Can we call Mommy?"

"We can try." My eyes flitted to Gwen's. "Thank you," I told her while Sawyer put on her shoes.

She nodded, smilingly lightly at me. When Sawyer's head was turned, I stole a kiss, a fleeting brush of my lips against hers. "Text me later?" she whispered.

I nodded, stealing another lingering glance at her before taking Sawyer's hand.

The drive home was silent with Sawyer staring almost blankly out the window. My eyes kept going to her reflection in the rearview mirror. "Everything will be fine, Soy-bean."

"My sister's not supposed to come until October," Sawyer said hollowly, sniffling.

"Maybe she's just so excited to see you that she couldn't wait," I replied, my lips tugging up a little. This brought a small smile to Sawyer's face. She was too young to worry about all the challenges preterm babies faced, and that realization made my throat tighten.

Tig was waiting by the front door when we got home, and when Sawyer saw him, she wrapped her arms around him and snuggled into his fur.

We tried calling Cheryl a couple of times—once when we got home, and once before bed. Both times, we got her voicemail, and Sawyer left messages about how much she loved her and missed her.

She was so worried about her baby sister and her mom that it took her hours to fall asleep. I had to lay in her bed and rub her back until she finally drifted off, assuring her repeatedly that everything would be okay, and hoping like hell it would.

When she was finally asleep, I walked downstairs to sit in the dark of the living room with my head in my hands.

My phone buzzed in my pocket, and I drew it out. I had a missed text message from Gwen, checking in. I replied to it, telling her I hadn't heard anything lately, and that I wouldn't be at work tomorrow.

Gwen: *Let me know how I can help, Alaric. I'm here for you both. Xo*

Before I could reply to her, my phone started to ring, the display showing an unknown number. Since it was after eleven, I took the call.

"Hello?"

"Alaric? It's Mason." I tensed. I had limited contact with Mason—always had. Cheryl made sure we wouldn't cross paths too much, likely knowing I had a deep-set resentment toward the man. When it came to Sawyer, I did; I wanted to be the one tucking her in at night. He had her all the times I didn't, and that was hard to stomach.

"How's the baby?"

"Stable," Mason said on exhale, the exhaustion he must have felt evident in his voice. "When we got to the hospital, they couldn't stop the labour. The baby was breech and in distress, and Cheryl was losing amniotic fluid. She was born via caesarean section at eight o'clock this evening. She's got fluid in the lungs, so she's in an incubator in NICU on CPAP until that clears up. The doctor says anywhere from one to six weeks for that. They're still running tests, but everything else seems good—her heart is strong."

"I'm glad to hear," I said, relaxing back against the chair. "How's Cheryl holding up?"

"Good. She's still numb and a little out of it from the

surgery. She's sleeping now, but she wants Sawyer to come to the hospital tomorrow." Mason replied. I'm sure this conversation wasn't easy for him, either.

"What time works best?"

"Any time," Mason said. "Visiting hours go from eight to eight."

"We'll be there at nine," I told him.

"All right, thanks."

"Congratulations, Mason. I'm glad they're both okay."

"Me too," he choked out, emotion clogging his throat. "See you guys tomorrow."

We stopped at the hospital gift store so that Sawyer could get a present for her new baby sister. She picked out a soft pink giraffe baby rattle with a Harley Davidson patch and hugged it to her chest. "My sister will like this one."

I smiled. "Okay. Let's go pick out some flowers too, for your mom." We moved toward the refrigerator wall. "What about that? It has a balloon." I pointed at a white basket with assorted pink and white flowers, with a balloon that read *'It's a Girl!'*

"Yes! Mommy will love that!" Sawyer nodded eagerly, and I lifted it down. We made our way to the counter to pay before we took the elevator to the neonatal intensive care unit.

"Remember, be gentle with your mom. She's just had surgery, so she's going to be a little sore."

"Okay," Sawyer nodded seriously, her brow creased with worry. I squeezed her hand gently, and she looked up.

"It'll be all right. Everybody's going to be fine," I told her, smiling.

Knocking lightly against Cheryl's door, I waited until they'd granted us permission to come in.

"Hi, baby," Cheryl said to our daughter. She looked pale and exhausted, but she was sitting up with a tray of food nearby.

I lingered by the door, watching while Sawyer went to the side of Cheryl's bed and gave her a gentle hug and kiss. "Hi, Mommy. Where's my sister? I got her a present." Sawyer said, showing her the rattle.

"Oh, that's so sweet. She's going to love it." Cheryl smiled, taking it from her and patting the bed beside her. "I'm going to go and visit her in a little bit. Did you want to come with me?"

"Yes!" Sawyer nodded eagerly. "Can Daddy come too?"

"Only direct family can visit the baby right now," Cheryl replied, looking to me with an apology.

"Daddy's direct family," Sawyer pointed out.

"I know sweetie, but direct family to the baby. The doctors and nurses have to limit the number of people allowed in the NICU ward because some of the other babies are very sick." Cheryl explained.

"Is my sister very sick?" She frowned, her brow pinching together.

Cheryl smiled softly. "No, she's just having some trouble breathing right now. The doctor says she has fluid in her lungs. She'll be okay in a couple of weeks."

Sawyer turned to me, frowning a little. "But I wanted Daddy to meet my baby sister."

"I'll meet her when she's home," I promised, smiling at her. "Today is your day."

Sawyer's frown lines smoothed out, and she nodded. "Okay."

I moved closer to the bed, setting the flower arrangement down on the bedside table. "Where's Mason?"

"He went down to grab a coffee," Cheryl replied. "He should be back—oh, speak of the devil. There he is."

Mason strolled into the room carrying a tray from Tim Hortons and a brown paper bag. He lifted his chin at me in greeting as he passed by, setting his purchases down on the hospital tray.

His jeans and t-shirt were rumpled, and he looked exhausted. Running a hand through his short dark hair, he cast a grateful look at me. "Thanks for yesterday, man. We were so unprepared for this, it isn't funny." He chuckled, shaking his head

"Well, you both thought you still had three months," I replied, surprised to find all the old resentment and anger I'd harbored for him had dissipated overnight.

"Daddy said my sister was excited to see me!" Sawyer piped up, her eyes sparkling with infinite happiness.

Cheryl laughed a little, her green eyes misting.

"I'll be down in the cafeteria," I said, deciding that I'd intruded on their moment long enough. Mason nodded, and I strolled down the hall to the elevators.

I took the elevator to the cafeteria, stood in line for a stale coffee, and found a relatively private spot and sat down, bringing out my phone, thoughts rolling through my head.

I hadn't been to a hospital since Sawyer's birth, and it brought back a lot of memories, like the first time I held her in my arms. While overcome with nostalgia, my thoughts drifted to Gwen, to how she'd stepped up to help me the night before.

She flowed into everything, filling every dark corner of my once hardened heart. There were so many things about her I didn't know yet, but so many things I'd picked up on, not realizing how thirsty I was to absorb every detail of her.

For years, I thought there was something wrong with me. I hadn't fallen in love with Cheryl. I'd loved her for giving me Sawyer, I loved her for being the mother of my daughter, but I'd never felt for her what I felt for Gwen.

Here I was, sitting in the hospital thinking about how I believed a future was possible, that we could fill the house with so much more.

I dialed, bringing the phone to my ear while it rang.

"Hello?" Mom said.

"Hey, Mom. I'm at the hospital. Cheryl had her baby."

"Three months early? Is she okay? Is the baby okay?" I could hear the concern in her voice as clearly as her pacing.

"They're both okay. The baby has fluid in the lungs, but is otherwise healthy. Cheryl had a c-section, so she's going to need a few weeks of recovery. I'll have Sawyer during that time."

I could hear rustling on the other end of the line. "Of course. I can be there Friday." Mom worked, and I knew she had to give her boss notice.

"I can't ask you to do that. I'm just going to call around and see if any daycares have spots."

"Alaric, it's July," Mom deadpanned. "Spots will be full, and unless you have a friend out there that could help you…"

She had me there. If Mom were right about the daycares, I'd have to hope Russell could give me the next several weeks off. If I did that, I likely wouldn't have a job to return to, and I couldn't ask Gwen to take time off.

"All right," I sighed, running a hand through my hair and leaning back in the chair. "Thanks, Mom."

"It's no bother." She said warmly. "I'll see you Friday afternoon."

CHAPTER TWENTY ONE

SURPRISE!

Gwen

I lifted my hand, rapping my knuckles against Alaric's front door. Light spilled from the house, and I could see him as he made his way down the hall. I bit my lip, feeling suddenly nervous about the impulsive decision I'd made to show up.

Alaric opened the door, his eyes dropping to the large gift bag and boxes of pizza.

"I might have copied your crafty idea." I laughed, feeling a little uneasy. He was just—looking at me. His blue eyes drinking in everything. It was heavy and profound and a little disorienting, like I'd just gotten off a tilt-a-whirl.

He cracked a smile, his hands reaching out to take the pizza boxes from me. "She's quick."

"Very," I breathed, lifting the bag. "I come bearing gifts, for Sawyer. They're big sister gifts."

"Big sister gifts?"

"Yeah, it's a thing. Don't side-eye me. The big sister gets to celebrate, too." I scolded good-naturedly, stepping into the foyer. Tig and Sawyer both flew towards the door, Tig barking and Sawyer giggling because she'd somehow managed to attach a stuffed Elsa onto Tig's back by tucking Elsa's hands beneath Tig's collar. It did look pretty ridiculous.

"Hi! Oh! What are those?" Sawyer skidded to a stop, her eyes widening at the sight of the gift bag I held.

"They're big sister presents since you've joined the big sister club." I passed the bag to her.

"The big sister club?" she echoed, taking it from me with a bright smile and sinking onto the floor to open it.

Alaric's hand reached for mine, our fingers tangling. I glanced at him, and he smiled a smile that said a hundred words. He wanted me here, was happy to see me, and my nervousness about showing up uninvited evaporated.

"Oh! Pretty!" Sawyer exclaimed, drawing out a tote that had two little giraffes on it, one slightly bigger than the other, with the words BIG SISTER embroidered on it. She reached into the bag again, pulling out a pink bracelet that said sister, followed by a pink cheer ribbon that said the same thing.

"See? Big sister gifts. Get it?" I whispered to Alaric when she produced a frame. He grinned at me, turning his chin to look back at his daughter.

"What do you say, Sawyer?"

"Thank you!" she chirped happily, standing and wrapping her arms around my waist tightly. I dropped Alaric's hand, my arms going around her too. A moment later she backed away, moving to her father have him put the bracelet around her wrist.

"Very pretty," I said when she wiggled her arm to show it off.

Sawyer paused and sniffed the air. "I'm hungry," she added,

her eyes on the boxes in Alaric's hand. He chuckled, ruffling the top of her head, and I internally melted.

"Let's go eat," Alaric said, his hand moving to the small of my back. Sawyer grabbed the rest of her presents, filling the tote with her gifts. She picked up the ribbon, and I stepped forward, helping her put it on.

Shouldering her tote, she fluttered off down the hallway, the sight of her swallowed up by Tig at her heels. The dog looked monstrous beside such a tiny human.

In the privacy of the hall, Alaric's hand dropped to my ass, and he squeezed it, leaning forward to capture my lips in a brief searing kiss that made my toes curl delightfully.

"Stay a while," he murmured, and I nodded, too choked up on the swoons to reply.

Sawyer had disappeared, but slight sounds from the mudroom gave away her location. She was feeding Tig, the tinging of kibble against his tin bowl, and her command to eat followed by Tig doing just that.

"Wash up, unless you want your pizza to taste like dog food," Alaric instructed, and Sawyer skipped off to the bathroom.

"She's like, scarily independent for five," I teased.

"Tell me about it." He laughed, shaking his head as he sat the boxes down on the counter. He went to the cupboard to grab plates, his eyes flitting to mine.

"Are all kids that easy?"

"Dunno. Only have the one." He smirked, and I laughed at his factious tone.

The taps turned off, and Sawyer left the bathroom, the door clanging against the stopper. "Oops, sorry!"

"It's all right; that's what the door stoppers for." Alaric grinned, looking down to start dishing out the pizza. Cheese and pineapple for Sawyer, and meat lovers for him. "Which one do you want?" he asked, cocking a brow at me.

"I'll take a big slice of meat, lover." I winked.

He chuckled, piling it onto a plate and handing it to me. "You can have my meat later if you stay." He murmured, his voice audible to only me.

"That can be arranged," I said, smiling as I took the plate from him and motioned for Sawyer's. He passed it to me, his smile growing even warmer, and his eyes followed me while I crossed over to the dining room. Sawyer was perched in a chair, waiting impatiently for her pizza.

I set the plates down on the table as someone knocked on the door. Tig started barking, and I looked at Alaric with confusion. He frowned, equally perplexed. Setting his plate down, he left to answer it.

The door opened, and I froze, hearing my father's voice. "Where is she?"

Moving down the hallway, I glanced from Alaric to my dad. "Dad, hey. What um, what brings you here?"

My father's expression was anything but amused. His stormy eyes shifted from me to Alaric and back again, a slight tick in his jaw and his immediate smile tell-tale signs that he wasn't thrilled with me. "I could ask you the same thing."

"Well," I said, drawing out the word and looking at Alaric for assurance. He nodded, doing that ridiculous eye-smile thing that made butterflies swoop low in my belly every time, without fail. "We're together, so. Um. I'm here for moral support and pizza?"

Dad's eyes moved from me to Alaric, assessing him without warmth. "This is the first time I've heard about it."

Sawyer's voice called from the dining room. "Hello! I'm all alone in here!"

"Why don't you come in for a bit, Russell? No sense in

talking this out on the porch." My father was thrown off by Alaric's invitation, and the astonishment meant I had a slight advantage. He stepped inside, Alaric closing the door behind him.

"Daddy! I'm thirsty!" Sawyer called again.

Alaric sent an apologetic look to my father and went to tend to his daughter, leaving Dad and me alone in the hallway.

The expression my father gave me was full of disappointment. He hadn't looked at me that way since he caught me trying to sneak back into my bedroom, drunk as a skunk at seventeen.

"Dad, we planned on telling you soon, but the current situation…" I trailed off, looking over my shoulder. I could hear the refrigerator opening and closing and Alaric's deep, gentle voice as he spoke to his daughter.

Dad exhaled, nodding slowly, trying to reign in his reaction. My father was prone to act first and think later, so I appreciated the attempt. He scratched at the back of his head, mulling it over.

I pressed my lips together, tilting my head, detesting the silent route he was going for. "Well, why are *you* here?"

"To check on my employee," Dad responded gruffly, following me down the hallway. He glanced darkly at Alaric, who was placing a glass of milk on the table in front of Sawyer.

Alaric looked up when we entered the kitchen, and I was thankful that he didn't appear intimidated or bothered at all by my father's presence. He set the glass of milk down in front of Sawyer.

"Hi, Boss Man!" She waved, recognizing my father from the barbeque. His gruff expression softened some, and he smiled lightly at her. I let out an inaudible sigh of relief.

"Hello, Sawyer, how are you?" my dad said.

"I'm good! I meted my sister!"

"Met," Alaric corrected distractedly, grinning down ruefully at her before shifting his attention to my father.

Dad cleared his throat, lifted his chin a little, and leveled Alaric with a look that would have made most men tuck tail and run. "So." The single-syllable word held so much power.

"Sawyer will be staying with me until her mom recovers from her surgery," Alaric responded, keeping his gaze respectfully on my father while absently tweaking the tip of Sawyer's nose, making her giggle, before she moved away from the table. "I wasn't able to find a daycare position for her this late into the summer, but my mom is coming Friday to help out."

I hesitated, knowing how much my dad needed him in the shop this week. I could see him warring with it, with what to do. My father was a family man through and through, but he was also a businessman.

"Take the rest of the week off," Dad said after a loaded minute. His eyes went from me to Alaric, and he smiled tightly. "Be in the office Monday at seven, ready to work harder than you've ever worked before."

Alaric nodded, and Dad turned to leave. But he inclined his head when Alaric spoke, his voice low enough for only the three of us to hear.

"Just so you know, Sir…I care about your daughter. A lot. And I think she feels the same way about me. I'm sorry we didn't tell you sooner." His hand slipped through mine, and he gave it a little squeeze.

My father nodded. "This better be the last time you fuck up, son," he said, his eyes twinkling, but his voice holding a subtle threat.

Alaric nodded once, showing that he'd heard him, and that his threat didn't scare him.

Alaric

Gwen let out a sigh of relief and leaned against the door. "I am so, *so* incredibly sorry about that," she said, shaking her head and looking at me apologetically. She was mortified, and it was kind of cute.

"Don't worry about it. I get it. I'd have skinned me alive if I were him." I grinned, shrugging a little. "I should have called him sooner to let him know what was happening, but I got sidetracked."

She nodded, her long hair spilling over her shoulders with the movement. "Well, I'm sorry he got all up in your grill."

"We were going to tell him sooner or later, right?" I chuckled lightly, slipping my hand around her waist and dragging her against me for a kiss.

"Daaad!" Sawyer called. Her voice grew closer. "I'm bored! Can we play a game?"

I tilted my head. "We've got a lot of board games if you're up for it."

"Oh, I'm up for it," Gwen said, her eyes sparkling. "Prepare to lose. I am the *queen* of board games."

"We'll see about that," I said, slapping her ass before we headed back to the kitchen.

We grabbed our plates of untouched pizza before heading to the great room, where our collection of board games was stored.

Slowly, I'd unpacked this place with a fantasy similar to this in mind. I stole a glance at Gwen. My smile grew as I watched her reach for the game Sawyer pointed to. Gwen had to stand on her tippy toes, but she tugged down Candyland and brought it to the coffee table. Sitting on one of the leather couches, she made herself comfortable.

Sawyer was every bit as enthralled with her as I was, and

she sat beside her, quickly selecting her favourite piece, Princess Lolly.

While Tig settled in front of the stone fireplace, heaving a sigh of contentment that I related to, I sat beside Sawyer on the other end of the couch. Stealing a glance in Gwen's direction, I was struck by how integral this moment and all the moments that led up to it really were.

Gwen decided on Jolly, which made Sawyer giggle. "Daddy! You be King Kandy!" she said, thrusting the piece at me.

"Daddy, is Gwen your girlfriend?"

The brush in my hand halted mid-stroke, and Sawyer turned to look at me. "Would it be okay if she was?" I asked her.

Sawyer thought about it—her little nose scrunching up and her head tilting. "Yes. I like her. She can be your girlfriend," she answered after a moment of consideration.

Chuckling, I resumed brushing the tangles out of Sawyer's fine hair. I braided it, and once I finished, I tossed it over her shoulder and tweaked her nose. "Bedtime."

Sawyer yawned and crawled up to her pillow, flopping dramatically. I stood and pulled her covers up, pressing a kiss to her forehead. "Good night, Daddy," she said, another yawn following.

"Good night, munchkin," I replied, turning out the lamp on her bedside table. I flicked on her star night light, walking lightly from her room. I lingered at the door for a moment, watching the gentle rise and fall of her chest while she drifted off.

Tig was snoring softly on the floor at the foot of her bed. I left the door cracked open an inch so that he could nose his way through if he wanted to go, but knowing he wouldn't.

Downstairs, I found Gwen tidying the kitchen. She looked up as she rinsed a plate, watching me stalk over to her with purpose.

Pressing against her from behind, I moved her hair over her shoulder, kissing the skin on the nape of her neck. "Thanks for coming over tonight."

She smiled, turning off the tap and twisting so that she was facing me. Her arms slipped around my neck, and she grinned, dimples popping. "I had a lot of fun…minus my dad's interruption."

"Don't even worry about that." I shrugged it off. "In fact, before he showed up, I was going to ask you something."

"What?"

"If you'll come over for dinner Friday night?" I said, never breaking eye contact. Gwen smiled slowly.

"Are we at that stage already?" she teased.

"Woman, it's been eight weeks."

"But we haven't been serious for eight weeks," she retorted haughtily, but I caught the lie in her eyes. It made me grin, made my cock harden against her thigh. "Well, we were seriously casual, and then casually serious…" she trailed off the moment I laid a hot, sucking kiss to the secretive place along the side of her throat, just beneath her jaw—the place I knew would drive her crazy.

She writhed against me, her hands dropping to my chest, gripping the material of my shirt. I lifted my head to give her a serious look, and she laughed. "I'd be happy to meet your mom," she said, her eyes warming.

"Good. Now, for the second order of business…" I said, lifting her and setting her down on the counter. She was at the perfect height, and I settled between her thighs, eliciting sighs from her as I kissed along her collarbone and neck.

A soft moan spilled from her lips when my mouth covered her nipple over her lace bra. "Alaric," she breathed.

The sound of my name on her lips, the way she felt, all of it so deliriously arousing that I couldn't help but push my thickening erection against the place between her thighs where I desperately wanted to be.

She bit down on her bottom lip, pulling away to look at me as my fingers deftly unhooked her bra. It fell, sliding off her legs to the floor, and she moved to unbutton her jeans. Gripping the edge of the counter, she lifted her ass so I could pull them the rest of the way off her.

They hit the floor noisily, the brass button clicking on the tile. I pulled my shirt off and unbuttoned my jeans, the descending zipper punctuating the silence.

Gwen cast a worried look over her shoulder toward the stairs. I gently cupped her chin, turning her head back in my direction. "We won't wake her," I promised, my lips flitting over hers as my hand slid into my back pocket for a condom.

Pushing my pants over my hips, I rolled the condom on in one fluid motion. "You know, I am on birth control," she pointed out, smirking a little.

"I know," I gritted. I didn't need the reminder; it just made shedding the condom all that more appealing. God, I wanted to —*so badly*—but I was afraid to do it, even once. Fearful that if I truly knew what it felt like to sink completely bare into her, I'd never be satisfied using a condom again.

I wasn't deterred by the prospect of knocking her up, not in the slightest. But with her, I wanted to do things the *right* way.

I pushed into her, burying myself to the hilt. Gwen's legs wrapped tightly around my hips as I pumped in and out of her, each thrust bringing us both closer to release.

My balls tightened, pleasure surging through my veins, and I came at the same time she let out a breathless moan against my lips.

Gwen

After work on Friday, I tore through my wardrobe, looking for something to wear to Alaric's for dinner. I'd be meeting his mom, and that sat heavily on the forefront of my mind.

Every outfit I chose was too…something. Too tight, too revealing, too patterned, too plain.

"Relax, Gwen." Kelsey rolled her eyes, turning so that she laid on her stomach on my bed, watching me with a bored expression while I rooted through my closet like a maniac. "You're overthinking this."

"Of course I'm overthinking this, I'm about to meet his mom!"

"Yes, you're about to meet his mom, who probably loves him and just wants to see him happy. Since you're the one making him *very happy*, I'm sure she'll like you."

I pursed my lips and folded my arms, not overly confident. Things were going too smoothly for me to truly believe I couldn't mess up this particular step.

Kelsey sighed, standing up and crossing over to my dresser. She rooted through a few drawers and pulled out a pair of torn jean capris. Tossing them at my face and knocking my glasses askew. Then she moved to my closet and found a loose-fitting plum t-shirt, throwing that at me too. This time, I caught it.

"Casual is always in style." She arched a brow. "Wear your brown ankle boots, and you'll be all set."

"Fine," I sighed, resolved to go along with what my sister recommended. At least it took away the pressure of *actually* having to think. I changed quickly, pulling the denim over my hips. My stomach was rolling with nervousness.

"It's going to be fine," Kelsey assured me, putting her hands on my shoulders and squeezing.

"I do *not* remember being this nervous to meet Erik's parents," I muttered, scowling at my reflection critically, wondering exactly what Alaric's mom would see when she looked at me.

"Filler love," Kelsey reminded me, bumping her hip against mine. "It's like when you're in high school, and they make you take that careers course and do those fake interviews? You always nail them, because you don't care. It's just school, right?"

"Ugh, you're so right. Remember that group interview at the video store?" I shuddered, the memory of it still enough to make me break out into a cold, mortifying sweat.

"Yeah, I still can't believe you used the iconic *Snakes on a Plane* line for your movie quote." She chortled. My sister had been at that interview too, so she'd witnessed the whole thing.

She'd quoted *Bring It On* and got the job. I'd quoted Sammy boy and got slack jaws of astonishment from all—myself included.

"Great, now I'm even more nervous." I scowled. My mouth tended to get me into *a lot* of trouble when I felt jittery, and right now, I felt every bit as jittery as that day I did my best Samuel L Jackson impression—f-bombs and all—in front of two managers and ten other interviewees.

I didn't even *like* that movie, but I blurted the line out anyway.

Good times.

"Look at it this way, you can't do much worse than that interview." She grinned, picking up her purse from my bed.

"Text me and let me know how it goes. I need to go home and sit on Elliot's face or something."

"Ew." I laughed. Shaking my head, I headed to my closet, my eyes quickly landing on the brown ankle boots. I snatched them, following Kelsey into the living room, tugging them on as I went. "Well, you have fun with that."

"Leave the Sammy quotes at home, okay?" Kelsey joked as she waited beside me in the hallway while I locked up.

CHAPTER TWENTY TWO

END PIECE

Alaric

"So, tell me a little about her. What's she like?" Mom asked, turning on the tap to wash the lettuce. She glanced up at me, flashing me a knowing smile.

My mother was naturally intuitive, and I was never able to hide things from her. Before I even had a chance to tell her about Gwen myself, she sensed something was different in me.

Then Sawyer flew down the porch steps, loudly declaring that I had a girlfriend and she was coming for dinner before Mom had even gotten out of her vehicle.

"She'll be here soon," I pointed out, arching a brow. Mom gave me a look, one that I knew meant I wouldn't be getting out of it so easily. I smiled, shook my head, and continued rubbing the dry herb on the steaks. "She's funny, beautiful, smart, and talented. She's writing a book."

"Really?" Mom smiled, her eyes softening while I spoke about her. "How did you meet?"

"At a bar. I was watching my realtor's band play a gig, and she was there." I told her, washing my hands.

Tig let out a rumbling bark to let us know someone had pulled into the driveway. I dried my hands on a towel and tossed it onto the counter.

"She's here!" Sawyer shouted with excitement, racing past me down the hall with her braids flapping behind her. She opened the door and flew onto the front porch. I followed behind her, shaking my head and chuckling at my daughter's exuberance.

Gwen stepped out of the car, tucking a bottle of wine beneath her arm. Her brown boots crunched against the gravel, and she wore her dark hair in long waves down her back. She looked refreshing and gorgeous, and I couldn't help but press a tender kiss to her lips when Sawyer's back was turned.

"Come meet Grandma!" Sawyer exclaimed, grabbing Gwen's free hand and tugging on it, leading her the rest of the way inside.

Tig was occupying a lot of space in front of the door, his tail wagging happily. He licked at Sawyer's face when she passed, and she let out a giggle, dropping Gwen's hand to push Tig's face away.

"Hi. You must be Gwen. I've heard a lot about you," Mom said, smiling warmly and extending her hand. Gwen took it, shaking it with a shy smile.

"Hi. It's nice to meet you, Mrs. Petersen."

"Please, call me Barb." Mom laughed. "Oh, is that wine?"

"Sure is." Gwen nodded, holding the bottle out to her. After grilling me needlessly, I'd told Gwen what her favourite wine was.

"You'll have to have a glass with me," Mom said as four of us—and Tig—headed back to the kitchen.

I took Gwen's hand and tugged her back to me. She caught

herself, hands splaying against my chest. "You look beautiful," I told her, loving the colour that stained her cheeks.

"Thanks," she murmured, her eyes dropping to my chest and lower before she stepped back, giving herself distance we both seemed to need. If she continued looking at me that way, I'd have a hard time keeping my hands to myself. Already, I was struggling.

"Big glass or a little glass?" my mom called out, effectively dousing the moment.

"A little glass is fine," Gwen replied as we moved into the kitchen. My hand brushed against hers as I passed, rounding the counter. "Can I help with anything?" She watched as I picked up the plate of steak and the tray of tin foil wrapped potatoes.

"Everything's done except for the stuff that needs to go on the barbeque grill," I told her as I paused beside her on my trek to the back door.

"Let's go sit down and get to know one another," Mom suggested.

Gwen looked from Mom to me and relaxed when I gave her a reassuring smile. Balancing the plate on my arm, I opened the door and stepped onto the deck.

Gwen

Alaric's mom—*Barb*—smiled brightly at me as she carried the salad bowl to the dining room table.

I took a fortifying breath, hanging on to the heartened feeling Alaric's smile had brought.

"Gwen! Look! I put a picture in my frame!" Sawyer said, jumping off the bottom step and flying into the kitchen to show me.

I took it from her and looked at the photo inside the frame.

Sawyer was holding her tiny newborn sister in her arms. The breathing apparatus over the baby's small features made it kind of difficult to see the baby's face, but the look of pure love on Sawyer's face was too much.

"Aw, what a beautiful picture," I said, gently passing the frame back to her. Sawyer nodded proudly.

"Her name is Olivia," Sawyer told me. "Daddy says she looks just like me!"

"Let's have a look," Barb bent forward and peeked over Sawyer's shoulder. "Aw, she sure does! I can see it. You make sure you give your mama a hug from me, okay?"

"I will." Sawyer nodded.

"Now, go put the frame back in your room and wash up for dinner, okay?" Barb added, ruffling her head. Sawyer nodded again, pivoting and racing for the stairs. "Slowly!"

"Okay!" Sawyer called back, slowing her movements a fraction.

Barb smiled after her, then turned to look at me. "My son tells me you guys met at a bar," she said, with an amused twinkle in her hazel eyes.

"Oh, yeah." I laughed awkwardly, swishing the wine around in my glass carefully before taking a long sip. "I, uh, don't usually do the whole bar thing. But my sister dragged me out for a girl's night, and then she ditched me there...and Alaric, being the gentleman that he is, offered me a lift home."

I bit my tongue to stop the onslaught of words from spilling out. I always talked too much when I was nervous. My eyes frantically went to the mudroom, where I could see Alaric through the window of the door, still grilling. With no hope of rescue there, I turned back to Barb and forced a nervous smile.

She topped up my wine, her eyes twinkling with amusement. "I remember the first time I met Alaric's dad's parents. I was so nervous! Parents can be downright intimidating, but you don't have to worry about me."

I laughed a little, relaxing.

She winked, topping up her own glass. She eyed me reflectively, her smile never losing its warmth. "Alaric told me that you're writing a book."

"Ha, yeah." I flushed crimson, deeply embarrassed. I felt foolish admitting my little side-project out loud, let alone to a near stranger that just so happened to mean a lot to the guy I'd gone and fallen head over heels for.

"What's it about? I love reading—I'm in a book club with some girlfriends back home," she told me, strategically revealing bits about herself, likely to ease my anxiety. I smiled, appreciating her effort.

"It's a sci-fi dystopian romance novel," I replied, taking another large sip of wine.

"That sounds intriguing." Barb's eyebrows rose, and she grinned.

"Okay! My hands are clean!" Sawyer called out, taking the steps slower this time and holding on to the railing.

The back door opened, and Alaric walked through, balancing the plate of cooked steaks in one hand and the tray of potatoes in the other. He closed the door with his foot and brought the food to the counter, sending me a beholden glance as he passed by.

"How hungry are you?" he asked Sawyer, who stood on her tippy-toes beside him, trying to see onto the counter.

"Super hungry!" she declared. Alaric sent her a smile that made my internal organs—especially the baby-making ones—melt.

He grabbed one of the smaller steaks and put it on a plate, cutting it into tiny, manageable pieces.

"Need another top up?"

"Hmm?" I asked, tearing my eyes away from the tendons working in Alaric's forearms.

Barb sent me an insightful smile, nodding to my now empty glass. "Do you need another top up?"

"No, thank you. I think I'm going to switch to water now." I flushed, setting the glass on the counter. I was already feeling a buzz. Alaric opened the refrigerator and handed me a bottle of water, the pads of his fingers connecting with mine.

By the end of the night, I'd completely relaxed around Alaric's mom and had even let her talk me into another glass of wine when Alaric went upstairs to tuck Sawyer in.

We'd moved our little party to the living room, and Barb was happily regaling me with stories of Alaric's childhood.

"He's been welding since he was old enough to hold a stinger." She grinned, pausing to take a sip of wine. "He used to hang out in his dad's shop all the time."

"I can see that." I laughed, setting my glass on the end table beside me, one that I knew Alaric had made himself. "He even welds in his spare time."

"He's a lot like his father was, in that respect," Barb remarked, her eyes a little wistful. "Idle hands drove that man crazy. He could never sit still, always had to be doing something."

"I've noticed that about him." I nodded solemnly. There was a certain way people spoke when they talked about a loved one who had passed on, and I heard that in Barb's voice. The love was still there, the sadness, but also…a fondness, as if the memory brought comfort instead of pain.

"I'm delighted you came into my son's life. You've awakened him, breathed essence back into his existence." She smiled at me with warmth.

"I'm not sure what you mean," I said, feeling a little wobbly.

"Since Sawyer's birth, Alaric has lived for her. She's his light, and when Cheryl left him, the thing that wounded him most was losing time with his little girl. His light dimmed, save for those precious weekends with her. For the last several years, he's thrown himself into work and projects and kept everyone else *but* that little girl at a distance. You've opened him up again, given him a reason to take a chance. Thank you for that."

I swallowed, my eyes misting from Barb's poignant words. "Well, he woke me up, too," I admitted, biting down on my bottom lip.

Barb's hand reached over to take mine, her fingers squeezing gently before she released. "Love wakes us all up," she said wisely, capping her words with a wink.

"It does," I laughed lightly, turning when Alaric walked into the room.

"Is Sawyer asleep?" Barb asked. He nodded, and she smiled. "Why don't you two head out for a bit. I'll hold down the fort."

"I should really get going," I replied, standing. I felt emotional following the raw conversation with his mom, and I knew from experience he'd want to stay close to Sawyer.

"How many glasses of wine have you had?" Alaric asked, tilting his head with a subtle smile.

I glanced down at my empty glass. "Oh, um. Probably more than the legal limit, but you can thank your mom for that. She's really good at topping up the glass without drawing attention to the fact that she's topping up the glass."

Alaric chuckled, shaking his head. "Don't I know it. All right, I'll give you a lift home."

"On your motorcycle?" I asked, perking right up. I was tipsier than I originally thought.

"Sure." Alaric smiled, and I grinned in response.

"It was really nice meeting you," I said, turning to Barb and shaking her hand. "Thank you for all the wine—and for not being terrifyingly mean."

Barb laughed with delight. "I'm sure we'll be seeing each other again soon. Take your time, Alaric. Sawyer's safe with me."

"I know. Thanks, Mom," Alaric said, pausing to kiss her briefly on the cheek. "See you in the morning."

He took my hand and led me out of the living room. I waved at Barb over my shoulder before following him to the garage. He released my hand long enough to open the garage door and grab a helmet, tugging it onto my head.

Brushing my hair out of my face, he gave me a look loaded with significance before he reached around to slap my ass playfully. "Ready?"

"Ready!" I couldn't help feeling giddy. It was due to the mixture of wine, good feelings, *and* the prospect of a motorcycle ride.

Alaric's grin widened, and he crossed over to his bike. He swung his leg over it, straddling the bike between his powerful thighs, and beckoned with his hand for me to join him.

Gleefully, I climbed on behind him, my hands settling against his abs. The bike roared to life, the headlight coming on and pointing down his driveway.

He maneuvered it out of the garage, down the driveway and to the road.

I rested my head against his back, appreciating it all—the security I felt with him, even on the rear of a two-wheeled vehicle, speeding down an empty country road, was something I *never* had before, not even with Erik.

Comfort, companionship, contentment—maybe. But not this all-consuming love that lit me up from the inside out.

We were pulling up to the curb in front of my building all too soon, and I let out a little mewl of protest when he shut the bike off. Alaric chuckled, helping me climb off the back before swinging his leg over and joining me on the sidewalk.

He took my hand, and we walked up to the building, trading glances. He didn't seem able to pry his eyes off me, either.

We walked silently up the stairs, pausing in front of my door so I could unlock it before dragging him in behind me.

Once inside, he pulled me against him, kissing me deeply, and letting go of all the restraint he held on to during our G-rated dinner at his place. The pent-up sexual energy was off the charts, and I moaned, my pelvis grating against him.

Alaric picked me up, cupping my ass in his large hands, and carried me down the hall to my bedroom. Dahmer let out an angry hiss, flying off the bed and out of the room.

I paused to laugh—and to draw in a revitalizing breath, my eyes finding his in the dark.

He cupped my chin, gently guiding it so I'd look directly into his bright blue eyes, illuminated by the light from the streetlamp outside my bedroom window.

"It took me eight weeks to realize I'm irrevocably in love with you, Gwen, and have been since the moment I laid eyes on you."

My throat closed, emotion clogging it; my heart bursting. "I've fallen in love with you too," I admitted, my eyes misting a little.

Alaric smiled, lifting his hand to cup the side of my face. He leaned forward, pressing his lips to mine, kissing me slowly while his hands moved over my body reverently.

Finding the hem of my shirt, he pulled it over my head and tossed it aside. He cupped me through my bra, rolling my nipple through the lacy material while his other hand reached around to unclasp it. I let it fall off my shoulders, working Alaric's belt at the same time.

We made short work of his clothes before he dropped me onto my mattress. His eyes moving over my body fervently before he lowered his face to the apex of my thighs, pressing a kiss there.

His breath was hot and tantalizing against my skin. His mouth moved closer to my core, and I let out a sharp exhale, every nerve in my body pulsing. I was incredibly turned on, so completely and utterly in love with him.

"Do you want this?" he asked lowly, his eyes serious as they bore into mine.

"Yes," I said with absolute certainty, even knowing he was referring to a lot more than just his dick. His magical, beautiful dick—I sighed with anticipation, squirming against the mattress.

Alaric crawled on top of me, parting my legs with his knee, settling between them. His tip brushed against my core, and I let out a low, murmuring plea.

His arms on either side of my face, he looked down into my eyes, drawing in a breath. My heart skipped, tripping over its beat.

He slid into me with a deep thrust, filling me to the hilt. I felt the difference immediately—his skin against mine was utterly euphoric, so sinfully gratifying, so unabridged. "Alaric," I gasped, my nails biting into his back.

He pulled out, sliding back in again at a torturously slow pace as he lifted his head, his eyes locked on mine, watching the pleasure filter across my face with every thrust. I bit down on my bottom lip, trying desperately to keep my pleasured mews to a minimum.

Alaric grinned, his lips lowering to cover mine, his hands tangling in my hair as he moved within me.

"You're still on birth control, right?" he said, speaking against the side of my neck.

"Obviously," I breathed, rolling my eyes—partly in exasperation, but mostly from the delirious pleasure I felt every time he sank into me. Alaric let out a guttural grunt against my neck in response, keeping up a lethargic pace that made my toes curl.

I pushed my leg against his waist, urging him to roll over. He took me with him, his thick cock sliding out of me when he hitched my leg over him.

"God, you're beautiful," he rasped, watching as I sank down on his length. His hands went to my waist, the pads of his fingers pressing in as I arched my back, moving against him.

Loving the way he was gazing at me, I rocked my hips forward. My lids fluttered closed as I rolled them again, feeling Alaric's thighs tense beneath me as he emitted a low moan.

I opened my eyes, taking in the sight of pleasure on his face as he gazed up at me with perplexed awe that stole my breath.

I fell on his chest, my nipples brushing against his hard pecs, and pressed my lips to his. Reveling in the taste of him, the feel of him.

The friction alone of my breasts against his chest was sensory overload, especially when paired with the way he met me, thrust for thrust, pounding me throughout an orgasm so shattering, I had to bite his shoulder to keep from screaming out.

His hips jutted forward once more, and he grunted, emptying his release into me. I tightened, and he swore, chuckling a little. "Jesus, woman," he scolded, breathing heavily. He moved my hair over, pressing a kiss to my sweaty temple.

Laughing, I rolled off him, feeling a mixture of him and me spilling out between my thighs. My heart pounded, trying to regulate its beat. "Jesus, man," I mimicked breathlessly, trading a secretive smile with him.

He pulled me against him, and I settled with my head on his shoulder and my hand splayed across his chest. I could feel his heartbeat steadying beneath my palm, and I let out a contented sigh.

EPILOGUE

Two Years Later
July 2019

Gwen

I saved the document, staring at the italic words signaling the end of another story. I pushed my chair back, standing and stretching to work the kinks out of my back.

The baby kicked, making his irritation at my movement known, and my hand flew to my rounded stomach. The sensation of him moving around was something that always took my breath away.

A lot can change in a year, I thought, massaging my stomach and glancing around.

I moved in with Alaric two years ago in November, after my lease was up. Dahmer came with me, of course, and he loved our new home as much as I did. Here, my cat had ample space to roam freely, and he tolerated the dog so long as Tig left him alone.

Not long after I moved in, Alaric had renovated the bedroom off the dining room, creating a space of my own for me to write. After almost a year of living together, we got married in the backyard in October. The ceremony was small, with only our close friends and family present.

Kelsey was my maid of honor and Sawyer was the flower girl. Tig carried the rings in a basket and wore a festive bow tie like the incredibly awesome dog he was. Dahmer didn't participate in the wedding shenanigans, despite my attempts at trying to make him wear a bow tie that matched Tig's.

Cheryl, Mason, and their daughter, Olivia Rain, were even at our wedding. The birth of Olivia seemed to bring peace to Cheryl, and she started working with Alaric instead of against him.

She even begrudgingly grew to like me, after a time. When she learned that I was pregnant, she reached out to congratulate me and offered some helpful tips and reassuring words about the whole experience.

With Alaric by my side, I was only marginally freaking out about everything. The beauty about falling in love with a single dad is that you already know what kind of father he is. He would be wonderful with our son, just as he was wonderful with his daughter.

I just hoped *I* would be as good with the whole baby stage as I was the preschooler age.

Eight months after the wedding, and we were only one month away from meeting our baby boy.

Picking up my empty tea mug, I walked through the dining room and into the kitchen to put it in the sink. The house was quiet—Sawyer was at her mom's this weekend, and Alaric was in the garage puttering on a project.

I moved through the house with my hand on my back, slipping into my flip-flops—the only shoes that fit me these days—and opened the connecting door.

Catching the door opening in his peripheral, Alaric looked up. Seeing me, he turned off his welder and set his gun down, a smile gracing his lips. His muscular arms were tanned and glistening with sweat; his black beater stretched across his broad, damp chest.

He gave me such a lady boner that I forgot why I came out in the first place.

"All done?"

"Yup, finished," I said with relief, my gaze still feasting on him as he dried his forehead with a towel.

"Your second book in two years." Alaric shook his head like he couldn't believe it. He tossed the towel down on the bench, watching me with adoration. "I'm proud of you."

"Well, it's because of you. You're my *dickspiration*," I replied.

"You're the talent," he corrected, crossing over to where I was standing.

He held my belly, his large hands splaying out, feeling as much of it as he could. Our son kicked, and his eyes sparkled when lifted his head to look at me. "God, I love seeing you pregnant with my baby," he said.

"Well, I love being pregnant with your baby," I teased, standing on my tip-toes to kiss him.

His kisses still made me weak in the knees. So much so, that I swooned in his arms and felt his grip tightening. Alaric smiled against my lips, letting out a low chuckle.

"Don't laugh at me." I sulked, half-kidding. "It's not *my* fault my hormones are out of control. Plus, I'm so horny right now," I whined.

His blue eyes darkened, and he cocked a brow. "Are you now?" he asked, his cock stiffening against me eagerly. "I think I can help with that."

ACKNOWLEDGMENTS

Matt; there's nothing more attractive than a hardworking family man. Thank you for being all that and so much more, and thank you for helping me create that in Alaric. Your support and your love keep me striving.

Emerald O'Brien, Elizabeth Barone, Kendra and Lyndsay; thank you all for letting me blow up your messenger rambling incoherently about this story and these characters.

To my betas: I appreciate you all so much, and thank you for your early input in this story. You helped me make it what it is, and that's an essential part of telling a story.

Patti and Kendra; thank you for all your hard work with editing!

Shari Ryan; thank you so much for creating the most perfect cover for Alaric and Gwen!

Jade Eby; thank you for the stunning interior and formatting!

To the bloggers—I love you! Thank you for loving books, and for spreading that love far and wide.

And lastly, dear reader—*thank you for reading!*

ALSO BY J.C.

THE COLLIDE SERIES:
Collide (Book 1)

Consumed (Book 2)

Collateral (Book 3)

THE DAMAGED SERIES:
Damaged Goods (Book 1)

Reckless Abandon (Book 2)

THE REBEL SERIES:
Rebel Soul (Book 1)

Rebel Heart (Book 2)

Rebel Song (Book 3)

Rebel Christmas (Novella)

THE WELDER ROMANCE SERIES:
Coalescence (Book 1)

STANDALONES:
The Key to 19B (Novella)

ABOUT THE AUTHOR

J.C. Hannigan lives in Ontario, Canada with her husband, their two sons, and their dog.

She writes contemporary new adult romance and suspense. Her novels focus on relationships, mental health, social issues, and other life challenges.

Facebook:
www.facebook.com/jcahannigan

Twitter:
www.twitter.com/jcahannigan

Website:
www.jchannigan.com

Goodreads:
http://bit.ly/jchannigangr

Amazon:
https://www.amazon.com/J.C.-Hannigan/e/B00RPUTES2

If you enjoyed this story (or if you didn't), please take a

moment to **post a review** on Amazon, Goodreads, your blog, or whichever platform you use. Reviews help other readers find books, and I appreciate any and all reviews!

Sign up for my newsletter to receive exclusive stories, sneak peeks, and updates: http://bit.ly/jchannigannews

J.C. HANNIGAN'S
FANnigans

And if you like shenanigans, join my readers group FANnigans! There's exclusive giveaways, monthly *#WineWithJC* events, and tons of other perks of becoming a FANnigan! https://www.facebook.com/groups/FANnigans/

Made in the USA
Columbia, SC
03 September 2018